PRISONER OF DRACULA

With a start, J. Adrian Fillmore sat bolt upright on the bed, remembering everything. The crazy land of Gilbert and Sullivan songs and characters . . . the dizzy plunge into Sherlock Holmes' London . . . the wild encounters with the villainous cronies of Moriarty . . .

And now . . . Good Lord, now . . . ! Trapped in Dracula's castle!

The fantastic umbrella that had whisked him willy-nilly through these Victorian adventures was, to his surprise, still beside him. Fillmore winced at the punctures on his neck, still sticky with blood. According to Bram Stoker, vampires rarely finished off a victim in one night. But Fillmore felt so enervated that he doubted he could survive a second attack.

And the sun was going down!

"An ingenious romp that leaves one smiling and hoping for a sequel."

—*Publishers Weekly*

*denotes an illustrated book

THE
INCREDIBLE
UNBRELLA

MARVIN KAYE

A DELL BOOK

Published by
Dell Publishing Co., Inc.
1 Dag Hammarskjold Plaza
New York, New York 10017

A shorter version of Part I, entitled "The Incredible Umbrella,"
appeared in the February issue of *Fantastic Sword & Sorcery
and Fantasy Stories* magazine. A slightly revised version of
Part II, entitled "The Flight of the Umbrella," appeared in
the June 1977 issue of the same publication, and Part III,
entitled "The Pursuit of the Umbrella," was printed in the
February 1979 issue of *Fantastic*.

The author wishes to acknowledge and thank André Milos
for permission to use names and characters from the
Sherlock Holmes stories of Arthur Conan Doyle.

Dell ® TM 681510, Dell Publishing Co., Inc.

ISBN: 0-440-13390-4

Reprinted by arrangement with Doubleday & Company, Inc.
Printed in the United States of America
First Dell printing—April 1980

TO DICK WEXELBLAT
WITH LOVE FOR A LIFELONG FRIENDSHIP
AND FOR INTRODUCING ME
TO MOST OF THESE CHARACTERS;

TO WILLIAM B. R. REISS
FOR CONCEIVING THE ORIGINAL IDEA
AND THEN REPRESENTING IT;

AND THANKS TO TED WHITE,
SOL COHEN, AND PAT LO BRUTTO
FOR HAVING SUCH DEVILISHLY INTELLIGENT
SENSES OF HUMOR.

Ye Adventures of J. Adrian Fillmore

PART I

EPILOGUE

"We've a first-rate assortment of magic," said the dapper little merchant. He swept his manicured hand in a vague gesture, indicating the cabalistic paraphernalia cluttering the room's niches and nooks. "Some of my stock, in fact, is so odd that even *I* haven't begun to explore its possibilities. You have no idea, therefore, how happy I am to make your acquaintance, Mr. . . . ?" He twirled his finger in an embarrassed gesture. "Forgive my absentmindedness. When you've got one foot in this world and the other in the next, it's difficult to remember where one's head is!"

"Perhaps," said his companion, "I'd better give you my card."

"Ah, quite," said the merchant, "and I must let you have one of mine. Bit of a commercial puff, you know, but you'll find all the necessaries thereon . . ."

The two rummaged in their pockets, withdrew billfolds, extracted and proffered to one another neat white identificatory pasteboards.

The little merchant examined his visitor's calling-card with unexpressed disapproval. It *was* so dry, so lacking in showmanship . . .

> **J. ADRIAN FILLMORE**
> 38 C Pugh Street
> College Hills, Penna.
> 377-0725

"I presume this is the seat of some institution of higher learning?" he asked.

Fillmore nodded. "My alma mater, as well as my current . . . or, rather, recent locus of employment is Parker College. I teach—taught?—English literature, American drama, Shakespeare. You've heard of him?"

"Yes, yes," the other said. "He is often quoted, or at least paraphrased. In fact, we have a court of Elsinore, don't you know?"

The pedagogue puzzled for a moment, leaning his stocky frame back in the overstuffed morris-chair that occupied a corner of the magician's back-room. Then his brows unknitted. "Of course," he ventured, "there was a one-act play, was there not? *Rosencrantz—*"

"Don't tell me!" the magician interrupted. "I had rather not inquire too deeply into the literature of your time; I might grow curious as to my own fate, and you, no doubt, would be rash enough to tell me! However, if I may venture to alter the topic—?"

Fillmore nodded.

"I am rather curious to hear your tale."

"But I thought—" began the other, pointing in the direction of the fireplace.

The magician rose, walked to the side of the grate where he had propped the umbrella. He picked it up and examined it. It was a curiously large instrument and had evidently seen much usage: the handle was tarnished and the grip was frayed; the once-vibrant colors, though still startling, had faded and the material itself was worn. Holding it, he twirled it in his hands.

"Yes, yes," he said to Fillmore, "I know perfectly well your mode of passage. This instrument is one of mine, without doubt—one of my earliest models, in fact. It also happens to be the very first to make its way back to me, and the circumstance fills me with delight! I've wondered how effective some of my spells are. This makes me so happy I'm rather inclined to sing about it—"

"No, no!" his guest protested. "I've had quite enough of that sort of thing for some time, thank you. I should prefer my arias confined within the context of a recital or operatic production."

"As you will," the magician replied, somewhat vexed. "However, if you insist on prose, let me prevail on you to supply it. For I really cannot restrain myself in these climes . . ." With that, he began clearing his throat in a sort of intoned warning which might have become a full-fledged *arpeggio* if Fillmore hadn't hastened to speak.

"Very well, then. I suppose you would like the details of my trip?"

"Oh, quite," said the magician. "Begin if you will with the finding of this trinket. And, for heaven's sake, catch me up to date on your adventures here: the mixture of customs must be most amusing."

Fillmore frowned. "*That* is certainly relative to one's vantage-point. However—"

Holding up his hand, the magician kept the resultant silence long enough to replace the umbrella by the fireside. Then he scurried back to his seat. But on the way, he passed the piano; pausing briefly there, he struck up a pompous fanfare, then plumped himself back down on the sofa.

"I couldn't resist," he giggled, wiggling into a comfortable listening posture.

Fillmore cleared his throat.

CHAPTER ONE

The first semester following a seventh-year sabbatical is bound to be a let-down, but in Fillmore's case, it was disastrous. To begin with, the research grant had not come through, so he'd been forced to venture to London on his own meager nest-egg. Once there, he learned, to his dismay, that no amount of pleading, cajoling or upbraiding would enable him to study the original promptscript for *The Yeomen of the Guard*. Thus, the entire excursion had no point at all; even the opportunity to see, in person, the locality of the Boar's-Head Tavern and the monetary establishment that occupied the portion of Baker Street once tenanted by more illustrious men could not assuage the young man's bitter disappointment.

There was so little time left, and he had postponed the dissertation so long that he stood in danger of losing his position. To make matters infinitely worse, Dover had been promoted, in his absence, to dean of the arts and letters college, and that meant Fillmore would have to work with a new thesis adviser: either Cable, a total incompetent, or Quintana, with whom he simply could not get along.

The worst of it was that Fillmore couldn't care less. The planning of his sabbatical research had been so long in the formulation, and the initial correspondence had been so encouraging that the ultimate result was all the more crushing. If the trustees hadn't been sick or on vacation, he might have been successful; but the only one he'd gotten to see was a business manager who'd dismissed the quest—and his letters of introduction—with the sort of offhand rudeness that one might seek in vain to find a twin to in any other business but the theatre.

So he really didn't care if this meant the loss of his teaching position or not. He was in one of those moods in which nothing suited him—neither his name, which he'd always more or less detested; his too-stocky frame, too short to impress anyone but a Welshman; his native reticence, which consigned him to dateless nights and losing debates. He hated his job, his insufficient salary, his cramped apartment and his equally unspacious VW, which stood in its usual disrepair in the back of the apartment building . . . unwashed, untuned, uncomfortable.

It was an autumn afternoon when he walked across the leafy mall past the administration building and into the cheerless concrete shell that housed the literature college. The sun slanted obliquely through shedding treetops and flickered off the glassy particles embedded in the walkway that branched out of the mall. A girl in slacks, hair tied in a ponytail, brushed past Fillmore, teasing his nose with the overdose of perfume she'd doused upon her wrists. Somewhere a bell chimed the hour of three. As he mounted the steps to the side-door of Mallin Hall, he could just catch the reflection of his unsmiling face in the glass of the door: his penetrating eyes looked past his too-familiar features and studied the departing contours of the scented coed on the path behind him.

Sighing, Fillmore opened the door and entered the gloom of the stairwell.

"Well, well, young man, it looks like we'll be working together," rumbled Quintana without the least hint of pleasure at the idea. "We'll have to shape up, now won't we? *Won't we?*"

Standing by the triple bank of windows giving on the flank of classroom seats, Fillmore allowed his attention to wander. The autumn sun was shedding a cozy glow over the rolling landscape, and he would give much to be anywhere else than in the predictable world of the Parker department of English literature, listening to the predictable admonitions of the gross department head, Quintana.

"You know, of course, that you have one scant semester to polish off that dissertation, do you not? And that means beginning all over again, choosing an entirely new topic . . . which *I* must approve. If not—well, you certainly must be aware that I will have no recourse—Damn it, Fillmore, *are* you listening?"

Turning abruptly around, Fillmore had to waste a second refocusing his eyes to the unlighted interior of the classroom. Quintana was sitting up straight in the wooden seat behind the nicked old desk, his jowly face hard to discern in the gloom. Behind him, the green slateboard helped further weary the eyes; it was a mass of notes and diagrams pertaining to the birthdates of various Victorian writers.

"When," Quintana rasped, "will you stop woolgathering? *When?*"

"Can't say," Fillmore yawned, with no attempt to cover his mouth. "Perhaps never."

And he walked out, paying no attention to the other's raving.

* * *

Of course, it was an immature action; he was well aware how childish it must appear, how strongly it must reinforce Quintana's prejudices against him. But the oppressive midday demon of apathy had taken possession of Fillmore, buffering him from any consideration of his action's probable aftermath. At worst, he would be let go, and what matter whether that transpired now or thirteen weeks hence?

Outside, Fillmore drew in a revitalizing breath of September air. It was the kind of day when, if he were still an undergraduate, he would have gone wandering in the russet-and-green hills, writing sonnets to dark ladies he had yet to meet. Undergraduates sat about upon the campus lawns, some with books cracked, others merely enjoying one another's company. The steps of the library beckoned upward to the selfless pleasures within, but Fillmore resisted, preferring the expansiveness of the unbounded afternoon.

Walking towards the town's main street (some hundred yards down the sloping mall), he loitered here and there, watching birds pecking residues of bread from sidewalk-cracks, gazing at squirrels seeking acorns in the autumn grass. Out on the front lawn facing Old Main a company of ROTC students waited out the cadences of a military march performed by a student band. An airplane droned above; had Fillmore cared to look up and risk scorching his corneas, he would have seen the ship's silhouette partially blotting out the sun's shining round.

On such an afternoon, Fillmore decided, there was only one thing he could possibly enjoy doing. So he passed through the vaulting gate that arched the lower end of the mall and walked down Allen Avenue to the spot where he'd parked the VW. Climbing in, he nosed into the sparse traffic, made a U-turn and drove off to Interstate 15A-S.

Like a ghost keeping a vigil, Fillmore haunted all the book-and-curio shops in every burg and village within a fifty-mile radius of College Heights. Almost any Saturday, after eating a modest breakfast, he would hop into the VW and pick some likely direction: for the next several hours, he would lose himself in myriads of junk shops, antique stores, Salvation Army rescue mission centers—anywhere he could snuffle around like a foraging animal rummaging for tidbits.

Old books, antiques, 78rpm recordings, side-tables, stereopticons, Edison thick-discs, comic books and calendars: all were interesting to him; it was Fillmore's principal amusement and (fortunately for his reduced post-sabbatical budget) still remained within the reach of his pocketbook.

His favorite browsing spot was a converted garage halfway up an unpaved driveway in Bellavista Falls, ten miles south of Parker College. Nameless, it was a linoleumed place run by a woman named Rose. A perimeter of bookshelves (unfinished pine nailed together in random fashion) around the shop walls enclosed a few tables of oddities.

The selection, though limited, was frequently renewed, and the white-haired proprietress kept her prices modest . . . not that she was unaware of the value of every treasure in her stock, far from it. But Rose plain refused to profiteer, as she put it, from a pastime of her "dotage."

"Besides," she once told Fillmore, "the prices I charge keeps *my* suppliers from getting suspicious.

And sometimes that means I can get my hands on a goodie that *I* want!"

He had never been able to figure out what the specializations of the skinny little shopkeeper were, but neither did he care, since they never seemed to conflict with his greatest interests.

A third reason for being partial to Rose's place was the fact that few fellow-collectors knew of it. It was just out of the way enough to prevent hordes of knowledgeable antiquarians and scholars from stripping it bare of its treasures . . . which would have equally displeased Rose and J. Adrian Fillmore. (Gad, how he hated that name!)

That afternoon he made a delightful haul—as he was wont to call the results of any particularly weighty collectorial trip. First, there was the Benziger edition of Benson's *A Mirror of Shallot*—only the second copy he had ever seen and the first he could afford. (Rose, in her paradoxical fashion, had penciled "weird tales—very scarce" in the flyleaf, then charged him $4.00 for it.) Then, he also found a hardback edition of Carr's *The Nine Wrong Answers:* though less illustrious than the Benson unearthing, it was a scarce title nonetheless, especially since the paperback editions were all abridged; at any rate, it was a bargain at 19¢. (Where did she come up with her figures?)

From the record rack, he actually plucked a mint condition of "Dipper Mouth Blues," which he'd long decided was apocryphal, and—though he rarely bought second-hand LPs—took a chance on the venerable "Mikado" which had Robert Rounseville in the role of Nanki-Poo; it was the last remaining album of that brilliant but woefully under-recorded tenor that Fillmore lacked to make his Rounseville collection complete . . .

"Is that all, young man?" Rose asked, as she tallied up the tab.

"I think so, Rose. I seem to have gotten something—uh—interesting from most of the tables and racks to-day."

"Curios," she sniffed, resettling the rimless glasses on her thin-bridged nose. "You hardly look at them."

"Yes," said Fillmore, "but I can scarcely afford everything in the shop and—"

"Now," she interrupted, taking him by the sleeve and pulling him back to the centre of the shop, where the antique table stood, "if you don't like what's here, you don't have to buy. But I'd think, if I were going to drive all the way in from College Heights, I'd take a bare minute to inspect every last little goodie."

With a resigned shrug—but with a perfectly good will—Fillmore examined with greater care the table of odds and ends he'd casually noted earlier on his path to the books.

As he browsed, Rose stood looking off into space, no particular expression—or, at least, no interpretable one—on her puckered face. Leaning against a book-case, she kept her hands dug deep in the large pocket of her rose-print cotton dress. ("Don't care how cold it is," she would say. "I don't change to wool until the calendar tells me it's winter!")

The only sound disturbing the late autumn after-noon was the muted ticking of the ship's-clock upon the reinforced soapbox where Rose kept her cigarbox of change and bills. Several minutes passed by, but—save for Fillmore's gently sentient inspection—nothing stirred in the garage-shop.

But at last, the collector looked up from the table and sought the businesswoman's attention. He had an odd object in his hand: a long, heavy pole that ended in a large flounce of some silky material emblazoned with orange-and-yellow stripes on which various cabalistic symbols seemed to dance in pastel figurations.

It was clearly an umbrella, but its size was rather impractical: too large for everyday use, too small for beach-basking. The grip, made of blackest leather, was somewhat worn away; it seemed to turn slightly. The cloth shade was frayed, and the colors, though startling enough, were yet faded from what must have been their initial brilliance.

Fillmore couldn't place the period or design: it seemed too ludicrous for serious commercial distribution. And yet, if it were a toy, it could not possibly be lifted by even the most sinewy urchin. Perhaps it was a theatrical prop of some sort?

"Oh, that," sneered Rose. "Pretty, ain't it? It's no good—don't work worth a damn."

"How doesn't it work?"

"Won't open."

"Oh." Fillmore, disappointed, started to lay the instrument back down. As he did, he spied some inscription on the inside; pushing up the cloth a little ways, he peered to make out the words half-obliterated by frequent handling.

Along the length of the pole were three letters: NGT. Opposite them, halfway around the circumference was another line, but time also had worn it down to near-illegibility. The only thing discernible was a number and the beginnings of another word: 70 SIM—

Fillmore replaced the umbrella on the table.

"Oh, I really thought you might be interested in that one," Rose sighed.

"Well," said Fillmore, "I *might* fancy it, if I only knew a little more about it. Where it comes from, for instance. But not only is it nondescript . . . according to you, it doesn't even function. How much did you want for it, anyway?"

"It's cluttering up perfectly good table space," the woman grumbled, then waved her hand in disgust. "Give me a quarter and take it away."

"A pittance for my masterpiece?" raged the magician. "And my latest models fetch seven-and-six! And that's without those tatty astrologic symbols runed all over the cloth!" Popping a pill in his mouth, he held his pulse and waited until it slowed. "Well, never mind, lad," he said, "I pray you please resume." He delivered the latter request in recitative.

CHAPTER TWO

It was raining the following morning, and Fillmore watched the streaks of water trace interminable tears down the cold faces of his bedroom windows. He had no classes to teach that day, and he was so lethargic that he might have been content to stay in bed and stare at the patterns upon the panes.

But at length he forced himself to rise, wash his face and teeth, and shave. His attention wandered during the latter process, but the tiny wounds he kept inflicting on himself called him back repeatedly. When he'd finished with the ritual, Fillmore ruefully surveyed his face: the skin, once he'd daubed it with styptic, was clear and it showed few wrinkles; of course there was the merest trace of crow's-feet about the eyes, but that was not entirely due to age. There was once a time when Fillmore toyed with the notion of becoming an actor: daily he would emote before mirrors, working with grimace and greasepaint to cultivate a pair of Byronic eyes . . . like a "demon's that is dreaming"; brooding; introspective. The result, now that Fillmore had abandoned histrionic presumptions and now that he was a staid teacher-cum-doctoral candidate, was that his eyes always felt strained and pained: tired mirrors of a weary spirit.

He dressed slowly, choosing one of the lusterless

gray wool suits that served as unofficial uniforms for
Parker College pedants. His only flight of personal
taste was reserved for the neckwear he looped about
his throat: a loud silk ascot. Many were the stuffy after-
noons when he'd throttled his 16½ neck with a
sober Windsor-knot tie. At last, he protested the fitless
shirts at his clothier's—only to find that there was no
way short of customizing to fit his broad-shouldered
frame and thick throat into the same garment. Having
no choice but to buy medium shirts with collars too
small for him, he elected to breathe freely: leaving the
top shirt-button always open, he affected the ascot,
much to the tacit horror of the hidebound Quintana.

Fillmore supposed he ought to do his best to avoid
offending the department head on this of all days, yet
he could not bring himself to choke off his windpipe
with a tie, even under the present desperate circumstances.

He had already decided he would have to kowtow
to Quintana. Upon waking that morning with the
damp chill of autumn thunderstorm penetrating the
bedroom, Fillmore immediately recalled his rude exit
from the previous day's session. There would be no
alternative, he realized: he must humble himself, beg
forgiveness on the grounds, perhaps, that his sour sabbatical had left him temporarily witless.

Yet he took plenty of time getting ready for the distasteful ceremony. After dressing, he spent the better
part of an hour idling through the morning papers
while dawdling over a glass of reconstituted orange
juice, a half-burned piece of toast with margarine, and
instant coffee with powdered cream substitute—none
of which, fortunately, he bothered to taste. The post-
man shoved a few letters under the door; he perused
them without interest . . . a subscription renewal

form for the *Journal of Aesthetics*, an envelope full of discount coupons for popular-brand cereals and detergents, and the telephone bill.

After washing the dishes, and after he'd doused them with boiling water, Fillmore entered the livingroom, where he began to fleck the dust from the tops of the furniture. But, as usual when there were books about, his attention wandered within five minutes.

At first he leafed through his new acquisitions of the day before. Then, noting one of the stories in the Benson volume, he rooted about among his anthologies trying to find where he'd first come across the tale. Successful in that quest, he went to something else; so, by further tangencies too convoluted to record, Fillmore lost himself for the better part of an hour in the solacing solitude of his library.

Just before he remembered his obligatory ordeal-to-come, he was browsing through *Studies of Literature* when he came across an article on Gilbert and Sullivan by Arthur Quiller-Couch. One passage in particular caught Fillmore's eye:

> What disgusts one in Gilbert from the beginning to the end, is his insistence on the physical odiousness of any woman growing old. As though, Great Heaven! they themselves did not find it tragic enough—the very and necessary tragedy of their lives! Gilbert shouts it, mocks it, apes with it, spits upon it. He opens with this dirty trump card in *Trial by Jury* . . .

"What in all good hell is he talking about?" Fillmore asked aloud. "There aren't any old ladies in *Trial by Jury*. Except for the elderly, ugly daughter of the rich attorney in the judge's song. How does that go? . . .

'. . . But I soon got tired of third-class journeys,
    And dinners of bread and water;
So I fell in love with a rich attorney's
    Elderly ugly daughter.'

"And the judge becomes rich because of all the
business the grateful attorney sends his way and—

'At length I became as rich as Gurneys—
    An incubus then I thought her,
So I threw over that rich attorney's
    Elderly ugly daughter . . .'"

"Good Gad, is that what Quiller-Couch was com-
plaining about? The only person the song mocks is the
cad of a judge himself. Hmmm! I'll have to nickname
him Quiller-Grouch from now on. . . ."

Just then Fillmore spied the kitchen clock through
the living-room portal. It was just after eleven; he simply couldn't postpone the distasteful appointment
with Quintana any longer. He must seek him out and,
if needs be, grovel.

As he wrapped his scarf about his throat and struggled with the heavy rubber rain-slicker, Fillmore continued to wrestle with the problem of W. S. Gilbert's
old ladies.

It was a cliché of Gilbertian scholarship that the
librettist-dramatist treated his old women cavalierly.
Yet, thought Fillmore, I can hardly call any cogent ex-
amples to mind: Katisha, I suppose, in *The Mikado*,
and Ruth in *The Pirates of Penzance*. . . .

The thought was abruptly cut off as he opened the
apartment-house door and was nearly drenched. In his
preoccupation with the scholastic problem, he'd neg-

lected to don overshoes or take an umbrella out of the coat-closet.

Like Shelley's Frankenstein, Fillmore loved to slosh through a wild thundershower, untrammeled natural forces singeing his gray-tinged locks; but there were limits to transcendental pleasures, and this downpour, he told himself, was one of them. If it meant his hair-line would be plastered upon his brow in strings, and if it meant the sacrifice of his trousers-crease, then it was high time to consider prudent covering from the storm.

Nodding absently to a neighbor, Fillmore returned to his apartment to fetch overshoes and bumbershoot.

While laboring to pull the recalcitrant galoshes over his black Bostonians, Fillmore had two thoughts, only one of which was laudable.

"Why not pursue this problem of the old ladies?" he asked himself. "The research I've done won't be wasted: I can find a good basis here, I should imagine, for a new dissertation topic."

Having at last stretched the rubbers over his shoes, he reached into the closet again for his austere black umbrella. Then he had his second thought, and withdrew his hand.

"Well, of course she said it wouldn't work, but let's see, all the same . . ." Entering his bedroom, he opened up the extra closet where he kept his curios and took out the peculiar object of his musings. It looked larger than he remembered, and its garish colors and devices, faded though they were, practically glowed in the drab, chilly bedroom.

Was there a catch along the pole to release the hood? Yes, there was and Fillmore pressed it. But nothing happened.

"Rose must have been right," he sighed. "The button's stuck. How Quintana's eyes would have popped!" Now that the decision was out of his hands, Fillmore told himself he never would have *really* walked into the department head's office carrying the outlandish rainguard. Yet it would have been a noble gesture, a vestigial symbol of dignity.

Even as he thought it, Fillmore laughed. Imagine this gaudy oddment being construed as dignified! Staring at himself in the mirror, he made a comical face and twirled the umbrella once around by the handle in Chaplinesque fashion.

There was a sudden snap. The release button popped out an eighth of an inch farther from the pole.

"Precisely so," said the magician. "The handle was never loose; it's a safety catch. Prevents the fool thing from slipping open by accident. Of course, it's not necessary on the later models. We've worked out all the bugs by now—"

Fillmore pressed the release and the umbrella snapped open. My God, he thought, it's bigger than I imagined, even considering how bulky it is . . .

The hood stretched out to the furthest corners of the room, blocking off the ceiling. It grew and grew, blotting from sight the entire room, the street below, the town. It hid the world.

Yet through the translucent material, Fillmore could still see the pale sunlight creeping through the rain-laved windowpane. But even as he watched, he saw the sunbeams grow stronger, and commence to beat and glow as if the pulse of the universe were behind and the umbrella-hood was the heart-wall of the cosmos.

The perimeter of the cloth was a single, seamless circle. But Fillmore, astonished, suddenly realized that, like a wing, it was fluctuating in the wind.

Wind?!

Gravity shifted: his stomach executed an Immelman turn. The umbrella was no longer above him. He was streaming head-first after its downward flight, and the wind plucked fiercely at him, trying to rip him away from the incredible instrument.

Then it reversed once more, and he soared into cacophonous night, alive with vague glints of color. Whether he was hurtling over some plain or through some void, he did not know, for he dared not look down. He clung with both hands to the umbrella-grip, and his arms began to ache. Fillmore fastened his gaze upon the bizarre shapes and colors emblazoned on the hood above, but he suddenly closed his eyes tight.

"I'm going mad," he thought, "or else the whole world's turned topsy-turvy!"

For the suddenly-sinister cabalistic symbols seemed as possessed by the elemental fury of flight as the umbrella itself.

To his vast surprise, all sensation of rising and falling ceased as soon as he closed his eyes. Above him, the umbrella folded up. His feet touched grass, and summer sun shone upon his wind-chapped cheeks.

Fillmore opened his eyes. As he did, a fanfare sounded from somewhere nearby. It was like the beginning of an overture.

CHAPTER THREE

It *was* an overture.

The merry strains of some sprightly gigue or horn-pipe seemed to shimmer on the sunny air: as Fillmore listened, amazed, entranced, the music passed through a transitory passage into a sweetly doleful refrain. Then, before his spirit could be more than minimally mellowed by the gentle melancholy of the subject, the music was off again in a sprightly run of violins and violas, overlarded with scampering trills of piccolo, flute and clarinet.

The only trouble with the delightful serenade was that it seemed to have no point of origin. It pervaded the air, rang about the teacher's ears, swelled up from the ground . . . but proceeded from no discernible source. Yet it was so gracious and pleasing to his ears that, for the first time in many dreary, disappointing months, Fillmore felt refreshed, at rest. The fact that he had just undergone some undefinable transference did not, for the moment, disturb him; he enjoyed the cool breezes and warm sun bathing his upturned face. He remained still until the last melodic strains died away into the whispered sibilance of the nearby zephyr and a not-too-distant seaside.

Fillmore was standing on a grassy knoll overlooking a rocky seacoast. In the distance, a calm sea bore up an anchored schooner. Along the horizon, a network of rockfaces, wattled with caves, described a jagged skyline; from some point directly in front of the nether cave-mouth, smoke ascended, but the roll of the grassy mound on which he stood cut off the source of the haze from his vision.

In the other direction, as far as Fillmore could see, a gentle meadowland rolled parallel to the stony abutments of the coast. The landscape was deserted, and the only movement was the bending of the grass-field under the caress of the breeze that carried warm summer smells to his nose. Overhead, a seagull wheeled lazily a moment, then dove towards the sea. At the perimeter of the water, the surf broke smoothly in places, while in others, the rocks sticking out into the sea kicked up spume that glinted like a shower of gems in the sunlight. The sky was pastel blue, noon-bright and cloudless.

Lowering the now-shut umbrella so that its point rested against the ground, Fillmore found himself surprisingly apathetic to the fact that he had just undergone an impossible polarity of physical circumstance: where he had been indoors, he was now in an unpopulated expanse; where it was raining, it was now sunny; where it had been autumn, it was now late spring or early summer. And Parker College was landlocked and hemmed in by the ancient Appalachians; but this unfamiliar seascape thrilled with the tang and promises of ocean voyages and far lands. He had always loved the sea, detested the claustrophobic mountains that enclosed him in with the petty systems and niggling tyrannies of his parochial life.

Thus, he experienced a curious emotional tranquility in the face of a circumstance that would have thoroughly disoriented another mortal. But Fillmore, nurtured on the fantasies and utopias of the imaginative fiction that he loved, was well prepared for magical transposition: unconsciously, he had longed for it so long that it rather seemed tardy, having come.

As he stood upon the bluff taking in unpolluted ocean air, he was aware, rationally at least, that he may have lost his faculties. But even in thought, he scoffed at the possibility of experiencing sensory impressions while simultaneously doubting their very existence. He was too much of a post-Nietzschean to negate himself in an Oriental wash of cosmic solipsism. "No," he told himself, "I've actually been propelled elsewhere." The umbrella clearly was the mode of transit . . . but what sort of propulsion might it represent? Spatial, temporal or dimensional?

He examined the device once more, seeking evidence of some recognizable mechanical principle employed in the intricacies of the instrument. But his scrutiny was unsuccessful. Fillmore decided to try it again, this time studying the mode of operation. He turned the handle, watched the catch pop out once more. He pressed it with his finger.

Nothing happened. Fillmore fiddled with the release, shoved the movable shaft forward up the pole, plucked at the folds of the hood. But the umbrella would not open again.

"I didn't engineer it that way," the magician remarked. "But apparently there are physical laws governing it. I've seen it myself. You've got to finish a sequence . . ."

Just as a graduate student pigeonholes interesting bits of information that crop up on tangents to the main thrust of his research, so Fillmore set aside for later musings the murky issue of his transposition and whether it was the product of superior technology, sinister sorcery or a deranged mentality.

The day was too lovely to let gloomy thoughts dominate him. Slipping off rubbers, slicker and scarf, he carelessly dropped them on the ground and began walking in the direction of the cave-pocked cliffside, swinging his umbrella as he spryly sprang over the re- silient earth of the green knoll. Overhead, the seagull, sated, circled lazily. The surf plashed with the pre- dictability of a preclassical passacaglia.

Walking, Fillmore began to hum light-heartedly to himself . . . a rare practice for the pedant. After some minutes, the hum grew into a kind of wordless caroling. He stopped, amazed, delighted; the corners of his mouth crinkled up. How long had it been since he'd sung to himself out loud?

Imagine what one of his sober-faced colleagues would think of such unorthodox behaviour! He laughed, considering the notion, and resolved what he might do should he come on some dour-visaged profes- sorial type upon his balmy seafront.

Fitting notion to action, he warbled in improvised recitative: "Good gentleman, I pray you tell me what clime this is? I prithee speak, oh speak, I pray you!"

"Why?" intoned a basso nearby. "Who are you who asks this question?"

Fillmore started. All blithe resolve collapsed miser- ably with the knowledge that he'd been heard, and evidently mocked. He blushed mightily.

By that time, Fillmore was standing on a sandy plain at the foot of the low bluff. The seaside was directly off and to his right. In the distance, he could

see the fire that produced the smoke wafting above
the cliff-wall. A group of people were huddled about
it, but they were too far away to distinguish.

The person who'd spoken—or rather chanted—was
much nearer, some twenty-five feet away and just
rounding a small out-cropping between the spot
where Fillmore stood and the sea.

The scholar gaped at the newcomer's outlandish appearance. A tall, portly man in his middle ages, he
walked in a curious swaggering manner that was almost a dance-step. He had flaming red hair, an immense bristling mustache jutting out several inches on
either side of his face and a Mephistophelean goatee
just above the rugged jawline. But his barb was what
astounded Fillmore: treading in calf-high hard-leather
black boots, the stranger wore purple, satiny slacks
partially obscured by a yellow vest, over which had
been draped a long purple coat (of a different shade
than the trousers) with huge brass buttons and reinforced cuffs. A lace ruffle encircled the bull-neck and
on the man's head was perched a flat black hat with
the lateral curve of a boomerang. Above his waist,
there was a leather belt fully four inches wide, buckled in front; in it was thrust a pair of single-shot pistols of so antique a design that Fillmore recognized
them at once. Yet they gleamed, both barrel and
wood, as if new-purchased.

When the other approached near enough for normal
converse, Fillmore spoke. "I beg your pardon, but I
seem to be lost. Where am I?"

"Cornwall," the other lilted, still chanting. "And
who are you?"

Fillmore was mildly annoyed. He'd gotten the
point; was there any necessity for the stranger to further mock his recent outburst of musical high spirits?

However, choosing to ignore the affront, he satisfied the stranger's curiosity by briefly identifying himself by name and occupation.

"If you will come with me," the other said, still intoning, "I will deem it a pleasure. Permit me to introduce myself: Samuel is my name." His voice fell on the last phrase, and the invisible strings described a two-note cadence.

Fillmore wasn't certain he wanted to accompany the odd stranger, but before he could express any objection, the fantastical Samuel had a pistol in each hand. With the merriest of smiles, he repeated his request. The scholar tried to put up his hands, but only succeeded with one, the umbrella being too heavy to loft single-limbed.

Stepping off in the direction Samuel indicated, they walked in silence. As they slogged along, Fillmore took occasional glances back at the bizarre figure. He certainly knew little enough about the customs of the Cornish (somewhere on the south coast of Britian, wasn't it?), but he doubted that they included the flamboyant costuming of his captor.

Before long, they came to a small precipice of rock just landward of the ring of people earlier spied. The various stone mounds cut them off from sight during the latter portion of his enforced walk.

At the foot of the precipice, Samuel bowed in courtly fashion, told Fillmore to be patient a moment, and—to the scholar's astonishment—rounded the rock and disappeared from view, leaving his captive unguarded.

Fillmore's initial impulse was to run. But not being an athlete, he doubted his chances in protracted pursuit across the havenless lea. So he did the next best thing: he hid. Climbing halfway up the face of the rock, he pressed himself as deep as he could into a shallow niche and awaited the development of events.

He hadn't long to wait. Presently, Samuel returned, followed by a small group of men dressed in similar fashion. One young man, obviously a person of some rank, was beardless and hatless; he wore a long face, and walked arm-in-arm with a stout woman in her mid-forties. She was wearing long skirts, impractical for the country and time of year, and had an ample corseted bodice and puffed shoulders.

"Well, Samuel?" the sad-faced youth asked. "Where is your prisoner?"

"Well, I left him here and requested that he wait," the other replied in a hurt voice. For once, he did not sing.

"Samuel," the woman asked, "did you ask him politely enough?"

"I was the embodiment of gentility!"

"But *did* you ask politely?" she persisted.

"Indeed, I did! Am I to blame because the chap hadn't the manners to wait? I took him most fair by the rocks below the bluff. You'd think he would have realized he was honor-bound to stay our coming." Shaking his head dolefully, Samuel looked away, scanning the skies with a vacant expression. He had the air of one grievously wronged. As his gaze passed near Fillmore's eyrie, the scholar squirmed as far back into the depression as the ungainly umbrella would permit. He had it behind his back, for fear its gaudiness would serve as telltale.

"I ask ye, Master Frederic," Samuel said, "is there aught for which I can be faulted?"

Frederic, the sad-faced youth, shook his head, and in a rich tenor voice, intoned, unaccompanied: "By your lights, there is no crime. Nor should I have wished any other outcome to the happenstance adventure. But, Samuel, I fear I must tell you . . ."

"Aye?"

The young man hesitated. In the brief silence, Fillmore, upon his perch, heard the strains of a rumtiddly-tum kind of music strike up from some invisible source.

"No," said Frederic, "I cannot fail in my duty to tell you, Samuel. Though it hurt your sensibilities, I must point out that no truly professional buccaneer would be as trusting or as kindhearted as you or the rest of our band appear to be!"

With that, the music swelled and Frederic continued his discourse in song:

> The man would a pirate be,
> And ply his craft upon the sea
> Must learn to play a villainous part,
> With stiff upper lip and an ossified heart.
> Though lasses crave quarter with wailing and
>   sighs,
> And maidens assail you with tears in their eyes,
> No mercy afford them—for oft I've heard say
> That women are pirates, and steal hearts away.

He broke into the refrain:

> To be a buccaneer—

which the rest of the group echoed with

"—'aneer—"

Frederic continued the chorus.

To be a buccaneer—
You must plunder and thunder
And send some ships under
And fill all your messmates with fear!

The other pirates—for it was by now apparent the
kind of peril Fillmore faced—joined in with Frederic
to repeat the chorus. Then the long-faced young man
sang a second verse to Samuel.

The man who would a pirate be,
And quest for gold upon the sea
Must wear a scowl instead of a grin,
And never wait by till his prey ask him in.
And once you've elected to follow our trade—
Be cunning and daring and never afraid;
But should you be lacking in ruthless éclat,
Just pick some attorney and pattern on that.
To be a buccaneer—
CHORUS: —'aneer.
FREDERIC: To be a buccaneer—
You must plunder and thunder
And send some ships under
And fill all your messmates with fear!

Joining in on the repeat of the chorus, the entire
band copied Samuel's rolling gait and hornpiped their
way around the rock and off to their camp, voices
fading in the distance. The last *pizzicatti* plunked in-
visibly after them, and the seaside again was silent
and deserted.

Fillmore climbed down with some difficulty, the
umbrella hindering the likelihood of a safe descent.
When he reached the ground at last, he slumped against

the pile, panting, as much winded as he was non-plussed.

For what he had just seen, there was nothing in Fillmore's philosophy to offer up a sensible explanation. Lacking the objective proof for determining whether he had gone mad, he had to content himself with the supposition that the things he'd seen and heard really existed.

Could the whole group be mad? But then, where did the music come from? A loudspeaker? Yet the perfect accord with which the pirates echoed Frederic's ostensibly spontaneous song was uncanny!

Fillmore laughed suddenly. Could it be that there was nothing more peculiar about the business than that he'd stumbled on some vacationing repertory company rehearsing at seaside, staying in character and, in true ensemble fashion, expanding and improvising on the dramatic material in which they were professionally involved?

If so, Fillmore was well aware of the show they were rehearsing. But he set the thought aside, not wishing to be reminded of a personally depressing subject.

He determined on a course of action: he would creep carefully round the stone and seek some safe vantage-point where he could study at greater leisure the comings and goings of this odd company.

Five minutes later, he lay in a V-notched cut in the loam overhanging the pirate's camp. Below, Samuel stood in front of the assemblage of thieves, telling his story to the leader of the band: a large, shovel-hatted individual seated on an ornate throne in the middle of the clearing. Over one eye, he wore a black patch, and a skull-and-crossbones grinned gauntly from the standard clutched in his knuckly right hand.

As Samuel unfolded his tale, Fillmore noted once again the pistols thrust into the buccaneer's belt; he began to question his theatrical-company theory.

Looking over the group, one by one, Fillmore noted that the sad-faced young man was absent. No sooner had he thought it than someone tapped him on the shoulder and he almost jumped out of the niche where he lay.

Whirling around and pushing himself to his feet with the aid of the umbrella-staff, Fillmore edged away from the ledge until he was out of sight of the pirates. He stared directly into the mournful eyes of young Frederic.

"Wh-what do you want?" he asked, clutching the umbrella for possible use as a weapon.

"Quick," Frederic replied, "there is no time! You must hurry away from here. Men who stick at no offenses—"

Scarcely had he uttered "offenses" than *he* jumped and whirled. Behind him was the stout woman Fillmore had seen upon the path.

"Ruth! What are you doing here?"

"I followed you, master," said the formidable woman. "I see you've caught the scamp our dunderheaded Samuel let go."

"Ruth, I intend to let him fly from here."

"Indeed?" Ruth asked, then stepped in front of Frederic and scrutinized Fillmore with calculating feminine eyes. "Are you married, man?" she asked.

"No."

"Frederic," Ruth told her companion, "I feel I am required to point out that you are a pirate until next week, and have a duty to serve the band to whom you are indentured."

"Thanks to you!" Frederic said bitterly. "You were supposed to apprentice me to a pilot, not a pirate!"

"Well," she whined, "I did not catch the word aright—"

"Through being hard of hearing," he finished, bored. "I note your affliction was remarkably short-lived. And pray do not sing me *that* song again of how you made the mistake! I've heard it more times than my stomach can take!" He emphasized the rhyme.

"Oh, is that so?" Ruth snarled. "Well, it just so happens that my deafness cleared up in the sea-air, Mr. Smarty! And as for my singing—"

"Please, please," Fillmore interrupted, clearing his throat, "haven't you forgotten about me?" He was beginning to enjoy his ridiculous predicament. A new theory had occurred to him, hardly original: but what if the entire experience really were a dream? In that case, he would just as soon have as much of it as possible before waking.

"Oh, terribly sorry," Frederic said. "Well, I suppose I *must* take you back down with us. Sorry for the inconvenience and all that—

> But I really must plunder
> And thunder and blunder
> And act like a true buccaneer.

He sang it unaccompanied, reaching high A on "true," after which he sniffed disdainfully at Ruth. Then, pointing to the descending path, he waited for Fillmore to begin downwards, before following with Ruth upon his arm.

CHAPTER FOUR

The pirate king, who introduced himself as Richard, demanded that Fillmore give over all his money. The aftermath of that action turned the teacher's suspicion concerning the buccaneers into absolute certainty in his mind.

Placing the contents of his pocket upon the flat stone directly in front of the chief pirate's throne, Fillmore leaned against his umbrella-shaft and shrugged.

"That's the lot of it: $34 and a few odd coins. You might have picked some more prosperous prey."

"Here, here," the pirate king rumbled, pulling at the waxy black mustache that curled up impressively almost to his hairline. "What kind of trumpery do ye seek to foist off on us, young man?" He reached out and wadded up a chunk of bills in his fist, surveying it with suspicion. "I've never seen the likes of such currency!"

"Why, it's solid American legal tender," Fillmore protested.

The other stood up and glowered down on him from his one good eye. But Fillmore stared back, suppressing a smile. It was certainly a *vivid* dream! "Hear me, stranger," the pirate commanded, "I spent me earliest maiden voyage in the New World, and I remember naught like this counterfeit ye've flaunted! Surely—"

"Here, here, Dick," Samuel rumbled, standing to the right of Fillmore, "the lad's right enough, even if he did insult me mightily. There's nothing else resembling money in his pockets."

"Indeed?" the king asked. "I should like to know how, then, he intended to get about in Cornwall? Or anyplace else in England for that matter!"

Fillmore held up a finger tentatively. "Your majesty, if you will permit me, I think I can explain my peculiar predicament." The scholar had, in fact, been doing some quick thinking and had come up with an idea which he proposed to put to the test: a method for gaining sympathy.

"Well," said the pirate, "we *are* a bit short for entertainment. Perhaps you might begin at the beginning and tell us your entire story."

"Very well," said Fillmore, "I am a professor—"

"No, no!" the king protested. "Begin when you were born and work forward!"

"I *was* going to allude to my birth," Fillmore said, "but if you wish it the long way around . . ."

"We do!" the pirates chorused in one voice.

"All right, then . . . I was born . . ." And Fillmore was off, covering all the chief details of his life: his boyhood in Philadelphia, the early demise of both parents in an accident, his eventual supervision by a disinterested aunt whose only redeeming feature was the immense library she kept and let him roam in. He passed on to his friendless, though scholastically distinguished adolescence, touched upon his cheerless college days, followed by graduate work and his most recent position—he already regarded it as a closed epoch of his life—as doctoral candidate and literary instructor. Finally, he described the purchase of the umbrella and his strange journey to the Cornish coast.

When he was done, Fillmore noted with satisfaction that, except for Ruth and Frederic, there wasn't a dry eye among the pirates. He asked innocently what had touched them about his tale.

The pirate king, sniffing, answered in an andante baritonic passage, "Although our dark career sometimes involves the crime of stealing, we rather think that we're not altogether void of feeling."

"The story that you've told," Samuel sang in continuation, "has robbed our hearts of joy—"

ALL: We pity you, poor fellow—

KING: For you are an o-o-orphan boy!

"Yes," said Fillmore, nodding gleefully, "I *am* an orphan boy."

The king looked at him oddly. The music ceased. "Well, I know you are, lad—but why didn't you sing it!"

Fillmore shrugged, chuckling to himself. He was right: these *were* physical embodiments of W.S. Gilbert's *Pirates of Penzance*! In the operetta, all the pirates, being orphans, were merciful to fellow unfortunates—and this outlandish throng followed suit, even to the extent of using a similar melodic response.

"Here, lad," said the king, waving a hand at Fillmore's pocket contents on the stone shelf, "take back your goods. And, as an orphan, you are automatically elected—"

"An honorary member of the band?" Fillmore asked smugly.

"That's right! How d'ye know?"

"Fey quality, I suppose," he replied, refraining from exposing a full rehearsal of the plot of *The Pirates of*

Penzance. Cassandras, he recalled, are rarely believed and certainly never popular . . .

"Look here, Richard," Frederic addressed the chief of pirates from the door of an adjacent hut, "we can't allow the poor bloke to roam about without money, now can we?"

The other was vigorously shaking his head. "No, no, Frederic, I was coming to that. What do ye say, men, to staking this unfortunate fellow from our coffers?"

The rest of the pirates cheered the suggestion mightily, and within a matter of moments, Fillmore found himself laden down with gems and trinkets, rolls of pounds sterling and clinking handsful of crowns and shillings.

The untypical piratical business attended to, the dazed scholar found himself the centre of attention. On all sides, pirates young and old, tender and toothless, vied for his autograph. They deafened him with questions, shook his hand, bent his ear with sea tales, made him tipsy with bottles of grog passed hand to hand.

The day wore on, and someone scared up meat for a stew-pot. The scholar, finding himself curiosity-of-the-day, was easily pressed into staying for dinner, which promised to be a feast.

The firelight flickered gently, and the sounds of a guitar clung upon the evening air like clusters of musical grapes. This time, the source of music was apparent: an elderly pirate in golden pantaloons, gypsy bandana and wine-scarlet coat serenaded the drowsy company ringed about the slowly dying flames. Along the circle of faces the alternating lights and darks of fire and night played hide-and-seek. Here a crew member tipped a bottle up to his mouth, the glass

catching the glint of reflected light. There a chubby buccaneer snored off a tipsy sleep, his many chins pillowed on his capacious breast as he leaned against a pile of stolen carpeting. Everywhere the celebrants talked to one another in whispering groups of twos and threes.

Fillmore was on the pirate chieftain's left hand and, at the moment, held earnest converse with the maid-of-all-work, Ruth. Frederic was on her extreme side, brooding in his cups.

"But why did you do it?" the scholar asked with great intensity.

Ruth shrugged, clasping her hands in front of her broad midriff. "I was a member of this band myself for many years. It was Samuel's idea—he's my uncle—to seek employ in town where I could snatch some little cherub. But it . . . well, it didn't quite work out like that. Frederic was going to be apprenticed, anyway. I missed the carefree life of a pirate's helper. So I simply combined the two projects. Alas . . . it slipped my mind that we wanted to ransom off the youth." She sighed profoundly, then swallowed half-a-tankard of ale. Wiping her lips, she cast a wary eye on Frederic, to see whether he was paying attention. But he seemed to be off in some world of his own.

Fillmore could not resist pursuing the line of his contention. Lowering his voice and bending his head closer to Ruth's ear, he asked whether she were truly in love with her charge, young Frederic.

"Hardly," she shrugged. "He's a child, for heaven's sake! I like maturer men," Ruth explained, pinching Fillmore playfully on the cheek.

Hardly noticing, he persisted: "Yet I understand the two of you are betrothed?"

"So you may have heard. But the truth is, I've at

last wearied of this hardy existence. I'm fully forty-seven years old, though you wouldn't believe it to look at me." She paused, waiting for corroboration. Getting none, she proceeded, a little testy. "Anyway, this stripling by my side is the sole ticket I've got back to town, to a life of idle leisure. I'll tolerate him, I will, if I can get what I want."

"Exactly what I suspected!" Fillmore exclaimed happily. "I *knew* your affection for him disappeared much too swiftly at the end of Act One—"

"What the deuce are you talking about?" Ruth asked, mystified.

"Never mind!" the scholar happily replied. "The important thing is that you don't love *him* at all!"

Ruth studied him shrewdly. "Does it mean all that much to you, then?"

"Why, you cannot imagine how that news pleases me! It's uplifted my spirits tremendously!" Perhaps Fillmore would have been a trifle less enthusiastic had he been a trifle more sober. But he was and he wasn't—so he opened the way for what was to follow.

Which was Ruth: without warning, the massive woman flung herself into his arms, knocking the wind from his chest like a pair of bellows squashed by a falling rock.

"Adrian, my love!" she exclaimed. "Say no more! I am yours!"

Sputtering, the professor would have protested the hasty dedication Ruth made of herself . . . but the matter was wrested from his control with alarming rapidity.

"Friends!" Frederic shouted lustily, waking even the chubby pirate. "Good news!" The young man, in a flash, had come out of his introspective trance; he leaped to his feet and called out in a heartier manner

THE INCREDIBLE UMBRELLA   49

than he'd displayed up to that time. "Good news, messmates! Our honorary brother has become betrothed!"

Pirates rushed upon the pair—Fillmore and Ruth—pummeling them on the back, shaking hands, expressing vociferous good wishes. So great was the din, that two sounds were entirely drowned out.

The first was Fillmore's thin, protesting voice. "*No!*" he cried, "this is a dreadful mistake! I don't want to marry anybody!"

The second sound lost in the bustle and brouhaha was the whine of a bullet ricocheting off the surrounding cliff-face.

CHAPTER FIVE

It was a most peculiar fight.

The assailants, concealed behind every looming precipice and stone-pile, opened fire without warning (though they seemed to take pains not to injure anyone). The noise was deafening, as each bullet echoed amongst the crags and crevices.

The pirates, taken unawares, were panic-stricken—facing, as they were, unseen foes protected by the night and a superior position. The brigands, forgetting all about Fillmore and Ruth, streamed off, dove, ran in circles, all the while grabbing loot and weapons. Everyone shouted imprecations, warnings, instructions; no-one heeded the pirate-king standing in the center of the clearing waving his arms wildly and shouting for obedience.

Over the whole confused scene roared the *prestissimo* clamor of brass and galloping strings, shrieking woodwinds and pulse-quickening tympani—a blustering tone-poem to the spirit of strife. It tore at Fillmore's eardrums.

At his sleeve, Ruth—a knife in her left hand and a pistol in the other—plucked insistently. She pointed at the largest tent across the clearing from the spot where she and Fillmore were standing. "Quick! Over there!" she cried. "The tent behind the throne—quick, beloved! There is additional weaponry inside. Get yourself firearms, dirks and life-preservers . . . you may want to hit!" She howled the command with the delirious joy of one long deprived of a favorite sport. Pushing him with all her might, the blood-thirsty Ruth nearly sent her hapless prey sprawling.

Fillmore wasted no time in following her orders—inasmuch as they provided him an opportunity to escape her proprietary grasp. He ran across the clearing, keeping far away from the illuminating flames. Confusing shapes loomed out of darkness and were swallowed up again; someone bumped into his shoulder with a sharp instrument and scratched him slightly. Samuel, somewhere behind him, bellowed out disregarded commands.

The music's din suddenly paused on a tense tremolo just as Fillmore reached the tent. Looking back, he saw the pirate-king standing erect by his throne, the Jolly Roger defiantly aloft in his fist-grasp. Samuel stood next to him, broadsword in one hand, a pistol in the other. Across the nearly extinguished fire stood Frederic, arms akimbo, looking very bored. Ruth, next to him and armed to the teeth, was chiding the lad for his indifference. No one else was in the clearing—but in the shadows and behind each tent-flap, Fillmore could espy the terrified gaze of the cowed band of brigands.

The bullets ceased. Except for the anxious sawing of the invisible strings, all was silent. Fillmore held his breath.

Then a supercilious voice sneered at them from some elevated, night-cloaked vantage-point. "Lay down your arms, pirates! We charge you yield in the name of Her Majesty's Navy!"

"Who are you?" the pirate shouted.

"Sir Joseph Porter, K.C.B.!" the other sneered. "And if you do not do as you are told, I have a crewful of man-o'-war's-men available to enforce my will! Surrender, pirates!"

His words produced an extraordinary effect. Throwing down their arms, the pirate chieftain and Samuel shouted to their men to scatter; then the pair rushed pellmell off to the safety of the hillside. The concealed pirates followed suit, swarming like ants into the many cave-mouths riddling the rock-face. Frederic followed at a lope, still rather bored by the entire proceedings. The only animation he showed, even momentarily, was a brief, longing glance that he cast back in the direction of the unseen naval company. Bullets began to fly once more.

Ruth rounded the fireside and confronted Fillmore. "Well, aren't you coming?"

"Why is everyone running? Isn't anyone going to fight?"

"Bah!" she sneered. "They're cowards all! Afraid to be captured by Sir Joseph."

"Why?"

"Don't you know?" she asked, eyebrows raised. "No, I suppose you wouldn't, being a stranger. Sir Joseph's got the longest and dullest tale of how he got to be ruler of the queen's navy, and he sings it at every possible opportunity. Besides, he never goes anywhere without his entire family—the distaff portion, at any rate! One's own relatives are quite boring enough: someone else's are positively intolerable!"

The situation was more complicated than Fillmore imagined possible, and he had little leisure to reflect on it. The important thing at the moment was to escape from the domineering Ruth.

"Well?" she barked at him, oblivious to the bullets whizzing about her head. "Are you coming with me, lad?" Her tone left little doubt about his fate if he refused.

"Yes, certainly . . . ah . . . love," he replied. "But I haven't had an opportunity to arm myself as you suggested."

"Well, then, be quick about it!" she snapped, pistol raised in his direction. Around them, the cacophonous battle-music was raging once more.

"I'll be just a second," said Fillmore, entering the weapons-tent. Moving with great rapidity, he snatched up the sharpest-looking dagger and made a long, noiseless lateral cut in the back wall of the canvas enclosure. Withdrawing the point, he thrust again some inches above the center of the slit and cut downward, stopping by necessity at the juncture. Next he jabbed the dagger-point into the bottom of the flap.

"What's taking you so long?" Ruth yelped. "Don't pick and choose—grab the first thing you can lay your hands on!"

"I . . . I'm loading up!" he retorted. "I'll just be another ten seconds!"

"We'll see!" she snarled. "One . . . two . . . three . . . four . . ."

Fillmore sliced upward along the canvas, until the blade met the lateral cut.

"Five . . . six . . . seven . . eight . . ."

"No fair!" he thought, plunging through the opening. She should be adding "a-thousand" after each number to make them equivalent to a full sec—

"Nine . . . *ten!*" shouted Ruth, storming into the tent—just in time to see the scholar withdraw his right leg and light out for the hillside.

With a bellow of rage, she fired at his silhouette, etched dark against a blacker night. But the shot went wild.

Fillmore ran faster than he'd done in years. Even when he was sure that Ruth no longer pursued him, he continued to flee, paying no attention whatsoever to direction. Suddenly, he collided into something hard and rebounded backwards; the dagger went flying off into the night. Groaning, he rubbed his injured nose and inched forward.

The obstruction he'd encountered was a tree-trunk. Fillmore slumped down on the grass and leaned against the bole, waiting for the pain to subside. Once the ache in his head abated to the level of a dull throb, he began to assess his situation. It wasn't *too* bad, all things considered: the pirates were concealed and perhaps by now Ruth had joined them. As for the navy, they wouldn't even be aware of his exis—

A thought hit him like a slap across the face: where was the umbrella?! He leapt to his feet, horrified; it was gone.

With an awful pang, he realized it must still be on the ground by the fire where he'd put it down. He'd forgotten all about it ever since the business with Ruth began.

It was a desperate idea to return for it, but the fugitive had no alternative. The umbrella was the only conceivable chance he had to escape from this rapidly-palling world, the only possible bridge back to his own place and time.

Creeping back the way he came, Fillmore attempted to retrace his steps. The music had stopped, and the only sound was the distant sussuration of the waves. He ran into another tree, gently enough this time. He became thoroughly disoriented. Which way should he go? Was the camp in *that* direction? Or was it the other way? Why couldn't he see the glowing embers of the fire? How far could he have run, anyway . . . ?

Then, a disconcerting thought occurred to him. All that afternoon, he'd noticed no hint of woodland on the open meadow. Yet he was now hiding behind a tree-bole, one of many in the immediate vicinity. His frantic run in the dark must have taken him further landward than he'd calculated. How would he find his way back without a light?

As if in answer to his thoughts, the blinding spill of an open lantern cut across the night, dazzling him momentarily. A familiar tenor voice rang out.

"Hold, rascal! Just put those hands high in the air, if you will!"

Fillmore complied, waiting for the newcomer to advance. The lantern swung in a slow arc and the other drew near enough for the scholar to make out his face . . . as well as the firearm leveled at his own breast.

"Frederic," he said, surprised, "what are you doing in that outfit?"

"I beg your pardon, sir!" said the other, affronted. "My name ain't Fred, and this *is* my proper uniform as an able-bodied seaman!"

In the lantern-glow, Fillmore studied the other. It was impossible: he looked exactly like the young pirate and spoke in the same light upper register. But the sailor was clad in the simple shirt and bell-bottoms of a humble foremast hand; on his head was stuck a white cap with blue horizontal stripe and a tongue of ribbon protruding from in back. Around the base of the cap, superimposed in white upon the lateral stripe was a neat legend: H.M.S. PINAFORE.

"What's your name, sailor?" Fillmore asked.

"Rackstraw's the name. Ralph Rackstraw." But he pronounced it 'Rafe.' "A.B.S., Her Majesty's Navy. Now identify yourself!"

Fillmore calculated his chances quickly. This seaman, evidently part of a search-party, must have been told off to round up the pirates: it was likely he believed Fillmore to be part of the brigand-band. How could he discourage that notion?

Fillmore briefly told his story, but Rackstraw listened with obvious disbelief. He looked especially dubious when the scholar asserted that he'd been captured by the pirates. "And they've stolen a valuable piece of my property which I simply have to get back!"

"Pray tell," Rackstraw said, a little too politely. "Now if you'll just come with me, I'll take you to my captain who is, even now, at the pirate's lair. You can tell *him* your story. This way—here, I'll just take your wrist and guide you . . ."

It was clear the seaman didn't credit a word he'd said. Following unwillingly, Fillmore desperately tried to think of a way to gain the sailor's confidence. Rackstraw . . . Rafe Rackstraw . . . what was he like in H.M.S. *Pinafore*?

Of course! the scholar thought, snapping his fingers. In the operetta, Rafe is in love with the captain's daughter. But he's afraid to court her because of the disparity in their social stations . . .

"I can give you good advice," he told the sailor abruptly.

"About what?" Rackstraw asked unenthusiastically.

"About love."

"What *are* you talking about?"

"About you," Fillmore winked, though it went unnoticed in the darkness. "I know a secret concerning you and a certain young lady."

The sailor stopped, eyed his captive suspiciously. "Indeed? And how d'ye know *anything* about me, since we're strangers?"

"Bit of a fey quality, I fancy."

"Well, well," the sailor grumbled, "and just *what* do you know?"

"Let's say this much," Fillmore told Rackstraw. "You are in love with a lovely young girl of high rank and position."

"Ay? What else?" the other asked, surprised.

"Have no fear, I won't divulge your secret." Privately, Fillmore wondered what would happen if he *did* tip off Rafe's love for his captain's daughter too soon? Would the very underpinnings of this mad universe crumble? "What I want to do is advise you to keep up your hopes. Things are not so black as they seem."

"They're not?" Rackstraw asked ardently. "These are the first encouraging words I've heard since this affair grew too hot for me to bear! But how can you prophesy thus? The lady doesn't even know that I exist."

"You're wrong there," Fillmore answered. "She loves you with a passion equal to your own for her."

The sailor whirled around in a merry figure, the lantern flickering in a sudden flare-up as he did. Fillmore felt obliged to warn him about it, simultaneously requesting that he moderate his whoopings.

Checking his enthusiasm, Rafe began walking briskly forward once more, practically dragging Fillmore by the wrist.

In the distance, the scholar could see the newly-lit fire of the campsite; in its glow, he made out blue-coated and white-shirted officers and tars. The battle music had long since climaxed and died.

At his side, Rafe mumbled happily to himself. "Ah, if I might only believe these tidings, how glad I would be! But what could I do to advance my case?"

"Take my advice," Fillmore answered, unsolicited. "Speak to her at your earliest opportunity."

"But if she spurns me?"

"Well," said Fillmore, smiling at the notion of putting words into Rackstraw's mouth, "all I can say is that your love is as good as any other's! Is not your heart as true as another's? Have you not hands and eyes and ears and limbs like another?" He got the little speech from *Pinafore* almost letter-perfect, having himself played the part of Rafe—woeful miscasting!—once many years before in junior high school.

"Aye, aye!" the sailor shouted. "What you say is true, friend! I'll speak to her at the first opportunity! Friend, your hand." He held out his weather-tanned right arm, sinewy and bare to the elbow, and shook Fillmore's heartily.

There, that's done! thought the scholar. No more nonsense about my status with this Rackstraw. . .

The two drew up short, having reached the campsite. Stepping forward briskly, Rackstraw smartly saluted a gold-epaulleted figure in captain's hat and dress blues.

"Captain Corcoran, sir?"

"Aye, Rafe?"

"Rackstraw reporting!"

"So I see," said the captain, peering over the seaman's shoulder at the oddly-dressed personage just behind. "Have you captured one of the blighters?"

"Aye, aye, sir! The queer-looking pirate we saw grappling with the fat woman."

The captain strode up to the dumbfounded Fillmore. "Sir," he said, "I arrest you in the name of Queen Victoria! Clap him in irons!"

Several sailors appeared and grabbed the scholar firmly by the arms.

The captive protested volubly, glancing about wildly for his umbrella. It was nowhere in sight.

"Here, here, my good fellow," Corcoran admonished. "It's quite obvious that you are a pirate, don't try to deny it!"

"Prove it!" Fillmore challenged.

"Very well," said the captain, sticking his hand inside the other's jacket pocket and withdrawing a large quantity of notes and gems. "Why, man, your pockets all are fair bulging with loot! If you want to pass for innocent, you *must* do better than this."

Fillmore looked down at the riches, horrified: he'd forgotten the probably-stolen goods and monies pressed upon him earlier by the tender-hearted pirates. The evidence was most incriminating.

His guards pulled at him roughly, impelling him in the direction of the seaside, where several dinghies were beached.

As he passed Rackstraw, Fillmore glowered. The sailor shrugged, holding up his hands in a "what-can-I-tell-you" attitude.

"Duty's duty," the sailor said. "But thanks for the advice, all the same."

CHAPTER SIX

It was a rare morning, even for July. The sea-breeze gently fanned the sailors' cheeks. The sun, already bright, shed just enough warmth to take the chill out of the early air. The sea was calm and the surface of the water rippled gently in a wind strong enough to waft the ship on her homeward journey, yet sufficiently mild to caress, rather than buffet the crewmen working on deck.

The *Pinafore* was a-bustle with activity, as Captain Corcoran plotted out the trip back to Portsmouth and the sailors hurried to meet the tide. As they went about their nautical duties, they sang a slow but lusty *a cappella* oceanic hymn:

> Up merry mates, the anchor weigh!
> Unfurl the sheets and spare no toil.
> This is the sailor's happiest day—
> Homeward we turn from foreign soil!

Down below, one of the ship's passengers failed to appreciate the musicale.

"Foreign soil, indeed!" Fillmore sniffed, sitting on his hard bunk in the brig. "These insular British . . . they've only sailed from Portsmouth to Penzance, hardly an ocean voyage! Bah!"

Oblivious to their enforced guest's displeasure, the sailors took up the refrain again:

Back to the homes so far away—
Back to the girls who for us sighed—
Homeward we sail, and home we'll stay
. . . Until the turning of the tide!

"Blah-blah blah blah-blah-blah blah blah blah!" yelled Fillmore through the one porthole. But his mockery went unheeded.

Any thought of enjoying his adventure had left him during the night: he was sore and stiff from trying to rest on the unyielding cot chained to the brig's bulkhead. The rocking of the ship did not sit well on his stomach, either, and the provender afforded him was fit only to dump through the porthole—causing, no doubt, the demise of any hapless fish near enough to partake of the slop.

As near as Fillmore could tell, the captain of the *Pinafore* intended sailing back to Portsmouth, where the captive would be handed over to the authorities to be transported to London. There, he would be tried for piracy.

It was apparent by the contiguity—within the space of one day—of characters both from *Pinafore* and *Pirates of Penzance* that he'd gotten himself stuck in a Gilbert & Sullivan world. All ideas of madness or dreaming had been scuttled: his joints ached too powerfully to question the objective reality of his whereabouts. *Why* he should be in such a world was another issue entirely; he could easily accept a dimensional transfer via the missing umbrella into many sorcerous, idyllic or even familiarly mechanistic societies. But a

musical world patterned on fourteen theatrical operet-
'tas? It was absurd to the *nth*!

Under other conditions, the opportunity to investi-
gate the Gilbertian cosmos might be charming
enough. But Fillmore was finding himself too put-
upon a figure in the melodramatic churnings of the
plot he'd gotten stuck inside: first threatened by pirates, then by marriage; now confined to horrendously
filthy quarters with no future prospects but trial for
piracy and likely enough, subsequent hanging.

Any inclination to regard the entire business as too
silly for notice was fast quelled whenever the ship
rode an occasional swell and the brig lurched sicken-
ingly. Too, Fillmore remembered an admonition that
had been given to the hero of a science-fiction book
he'd once read. In it, the protagonist found himself
unexplainably in an alien world; asking a super-
computer to assist him, the metal brain warned, "Do
not underestimate the danger of your position. If you
die here, you will stay dead!"

He must get off the ship somehow, that much he
knew. How to do it was another matter. Afterwards!
Well, *that* he *had* figured out . . . wasn't the inscription on the umbrella 70 sm—? During the night, Fillmore deciphered what it probably meant.

He must reach London and seek professional advice. But first, he had to work his way out of the present predicament. And that meant some serious
thought.

The key must lie in the workings of this topsy-turvy
universe, the scholar told himself for the fiftieth time
in the past hour. If music can start up from no deter-
minate source, and if individuals can blend their
thoughts in perfect harmony, then there must be other

peculiarities that, once grasped, could be wrested to his purpose.

"Peculiarities?" the sorcerer asked with surprise. "But my good man, our people study music from very babyhood. It is expected of them. To speak without an occasional chorus or solo is as unthinkable as to imagine that God did not put his Holy Orchestra above to manifest His Will to us! The music is Holy Tone, my lad, showing us the way to interpret His Intentions!" His face took on the fixed expression of one who dare not be contradicted on an axiom of faith.

The single victory Fillmore had enjoyed—that of the pirates' good will and ill-sequeled generosity—was based upon the artifice of mentioning his orphancy: it was a device that employed the very über-knowledge that the scholar possessed concerning the G&S world he was in. It took advantage of one of its topsy-turvy values: that black-hearted pirates might be emotionally-tender little children within.

Hold on! That concept bore further examination. If, indeed, the pirates were gentle fellows, what might that mean in terms of the entire complex of laws governing G&S-land?

Fillmore thought of all the villains he could bring to mind: there was Sir Despard Murgatroyd in *Ruddigore:* a noble, principled gentleman. What about Don Alhambra in *The Gondoliers*? Hardly a villain. Neither was the loutish Wilfred in *The Yeomen of the Guard.* In fact, Fillmore realized with some surprise, there were scarcely any real villains at all in the Gilbert & Sullivan operettas.

Heroes? Ah, that was another matter . . . the lot of them were shallow, vain and spiteful: from the de-

fendant in *Trial by Jury* through the abominable
Colonel Fairfax in *The Yeomen*—

Good God! Fillmore mused, I'm beginning to sound
like Quiller-Grouch. Yet there was considerable truth
in what he'd asserted: look at his own brief experi-
ences on this side of the umbrella—so to speak. The
pirates themselves had treated him nicely enough. But
the noble Frederic got him into the mess with Ruth
by shouting out the nuptial news with suspicious alac-
rity.

And that two-faced Rafe Rackstraw was responsible
for his present predicament. It was pretty obvious,
was it not, that Fillmore had made a grave tactical
error in trusting the "heroic" seaman?

Better if he'd cast his lot with a villain . . .

And the idea Fillmore had been chasing around inside his brain finally held still long enough to apprehend it.

Dashing over to the barred door of the brig, Fillmore shouted until the watch came back to see what
he wanted.

"'ere now," said the tar, "you'll do well to keep
down the din."

"I'd like some company," Fillmore confided.

"Oh, is 'at so? And who, pray tell, would you like
me to summon? Perhaps Sir Joseph himself? I'll call a
special party to row to his yacht and fetch him over
straight!"

Not at all, not at all," the scholar demurred. "But if
I'm not mistaken you have a sailor aboard, do you not,
who answers to the name of Deadeye?"

The sailor shuddered. "Is it Dick Deadeye ye're
wanting? Faith, and you'll be welcome to *him*, right
enough! I'll fetch 'im straightaway."

"And see we're not disturbed!" Fillmore shouted.

"That you won't be," the sailor called over his shoulder. "Not with *him* about!"

"It's a beast of a name, ain't it?" Dick Deadeye said, squinting at Fillmore with his one good eye.

The scholar, bored, repeated the expected response for the third time in half as many hours. "It's not a nice name, no."

"I'm ugly, too, ain't I?" he snarled, wiping his hairy hand across an unshaven chin.

"You *are* certainly plain."

"And I'm three-cornered too, ain't I?"

Fillmore nodded, idly wondering just what it meant to be "three-cornered." Perhaps it alluded to Deadeye's habit of walking in a crouching manner, his elbows and knees presenting sharp angles with the bend of his back.

"*I said I'm three-cornered, ain't I?*"

"You certainly are triangular."

"Ha-ha," the villain laughed. "That's it. I'm ugly, and you hate me for it, don't you?"

"I do *not* hate you," said the scholar for the umpteenth time. "Where I come from, physical beauty is not a necessary attribute to popularity!" He shuddered as he said it, and kept his fingers crossed.

"So you did, so you did," the other answered, "but what of it? You want a favor of me, do you not?"

"Now that you mention it—"

The sailor sniffed angrily. "I *thought* as much! I'll say good-bye!" He began to gesture toward the distant guard. Before he could get his attention, Fillmore yanked down his arm.

"See here!" he said. "It's not so awful. Simply find me my umbrella and help me escape!"

"Ha! Ye call that *simple*."

"I have it all planned . . . arrange to take the watch down here in the brig. Do it just outside of Portsmouth. Slip in and take the valuables they confiscated from me. Keep them for your own. All I want is a few odd pound-notes and the umbrella. *Especially* the umbrella."

"How will I explain your disappearance?" Deadeye asked dubiously. "There's no chance you could get the keys and overpower me."

Fillmore shook his head. "Not necessary. Claim you saw me vanish before your very eyes. Impute it to magic. No-one will doubt your word, if you give it with sufficient malevolence . . ."

"Naah, naah," the other said vehemently, pacing from side to side in the narrow brig. "It's too great a risk. And I get nothing from it."

"I said you could keep the money and jewels."

Sneering, the seaman turned a twisted, baleful expression upon Fillmore. "Money!" he spat. "What good would that do me, eh? Would it fix my face, mend my halting walk?"

The questions were unanswerable. Fillmore said nothing for some time; instead, he watched the bitter tar stride back and forth, back and forth, two paces one way, two paces the other—

"Think of it this way," Fillmore said at last. "Helping me escape will be a blow against a callous society which scorns you and keeps you type-cast as a blackguard."

The sailor stopped pacing. Saying nothing, he stared for a long time through the porthole at the face of the afternoon sky. The minutes passed, but Dick Deadeye said nothing. Fillmore became fidgety and, at last, decided he had better break the silence. But just as he cleared his throat to speak, the other finally addressed him, without turning.

"There's truth in what you say, friend." Deadeye's voice was a little higher in pitch than normal, but otherwise he had himself in full control. "I've considered your plan, and I'll help you in it."

Fillmore caught his breath, rose from the bunk. "How soon will we be in Portsmouth?"

"If we catch the tide," said Deadeye, turning, "we should weigh anchor there this very evening, or tomorrow morning at the latest."

"Then it must be tonight," said Fillmore, expressing the obvious. "Can you get watch?"

"Aye—it's my regular round this night," said Deadeye. "Be prepared for my coming, and I'll be brisk to prepare your going."

A whining bass-line slithered through the gloom of the brig. My God, Fillmore thought, the damned music even extends down here!

Deadeye sang in a sly, insinuating fashion:

Good fellow, I'll assist you in your leaving;
  Sing hey, the mystic fellow that you are!
I'll fetch you your umbrella late this evening.
  Sing hey, the mystic fellow and the tar!
    The mystic, mystic fellow,
    The mystic, mystic fellow,
  Sing hey, the mystic fellow and the tar!

He looked at Fillmore a little sourly, and the teacher supposed he should have joined in on the chorus. But it had been too many years since he'd been involved in amateur theatricals, and he wasn't about to start now—

"Well?" Deadeye grunted. "Ain't you gonna sing your verse?"

Fillmore groaned inwardly. For the love of God, he thought, the song is in response-and-reply form: it takes a minimum of two verses to complete it. Though the scholar was completely unenthusiastic about joining in on the fun-and-games, he worried that 1) Deadeye might refuse after all if Fillmore didn't return the expected polite answer and 2) his refusal to sing might somehow damage the very fabric of this strange universe into which he'd been tumbled.

Gesturing with resigned good will, he did his best to think up a few appropriate rhymes. It was easier than he imagined possible. But Fillmore held on to some shred of individuality by talking his verse in a kind of *singspiel:*

> Kind sailor, I appreciate your daring—
>   Sing hey, the doughty sailor that you are!
> Be sure you snatch it when there's no-one
>   staring . . .
>   Sing hey, the mystic fellow and the tar!
>   The mystic, mystic fellow,
>   The mystic, mystic fellow,
>   Sing hey, the mystic fellow and the tar!

Dick Deadeye joined him in the chorus this time. At the end, the sinister bass rounded out the musical thought and the duo solemnly shook hands like a pair of soloists at the end of a concert.

"Just out of curiosity," Deadeye asked, "what will you do once you've escaped?"

"Head towards London," Fillmore replied. "There's a sorcerer there, I've heard, who'll help me quit this strange sphere, I hope."

"I see," the sailor said. "Then—"

The bass accompaniment, which had not quite died away, swelled up afresh. Deadeye went into a quick finale, which Fillmore instantly recognized. He had no choice but to join right in.

DEADEYE: This very night
        With bated breath—
FILLMORE: —And muffled oar—
DEADEYE: Without a light,
        As still as death—
FILLMORE: —I'll steal ashore!
        I'll flee from here
        And seek to find—
DEADEYE: —The proper one—
FILLMORE: A sorcerer
        Who'll ease my mind—
DEADEYE: —And get ye gone!

They repeated it thrice, gathering speed as they sang (or, in Fillmore's case, declaimed) until they reached the final line once more. They uttered it in unison and, in Fillmore's version, it came out "And get *me* gone!" It sounded just like a first-act finale.

The bright flourishes that rushed to a final tonic-dominant alternation were so loud and bombastic that Fillmore feared they would attract the attention of the guard or, for that matter, anyone above them on deck.

"Impossible!" the sorcerer exclaimed. "We value our privacy! Listen in on someone else's musical statements? Not done, my lad! As soon imagine some nightmare society whose police listened in unan-

nounced at a gentleman's own home! You see what I mean? It's simply not done!" The little merchant-magician shook his head from side to side in utter disbelief. "Simply isn't done," he repeated.

CHAPTER SEVEN

How he got on the gondola, Fillmore had no idea, but it was a picturesque trip. The twin gondoliers sang out the attractions as they glided past in no discernibly logical order: "Castle Adamant . . . Tower of London . . . Site of the Statutory Duel . . . Utopia . . . Mount Olympus (!) . . . Castle Bunthorne . . ."

And then the scenery shimmered and shifted and he was walking through a quaint fishing village. He spied another castle in the distance. It played a coquette's game. As he approached, it retreated. He veered toward the coastline, and suddenly the place planted itself squarely in his path.

A bevy of maidens in flowery array scattered rose-petals where he walked. They sang:

> Oh, happy the lily when kissed by the bee,
> And, sipping tranquilly, quite happy is he!

Fillmore could not imagine how he reached the village. Somehow he was certain it was in Cornwall, yet he could not recall jumping ship. For that matter, the *Pinafore* was already some distance away from . . .
From?
His thoughts were thoroughly muddled.

At least the castle was over its bout of diffidence. Suddenly

> SCENE.—*Picture Gallery in Ruddigore Castle. The walls are covered with full-length portrait frames, but where the pictures should be are only blank spaces reminiscent of the famous uncompleted painting of George Washington. A single portrait stands completed, that of a bishop . . . Sir Desmond Murgatroyd, Sixteenth Baronet of that accursèd line of noblemen.*

SIR DESMOND (*popping his head momentarily out of the canvas*) : It's a wretched likeness!

A slim, medium-sized gentleman with graying hair and grandiloquent airs entered. He was clad in the respectable at-home-wear of a British country squire.

"Let me guess," Fillmore murmured. "You are Sir Ruthven Murgatroyd, the latest Lord of the line?"

By way of reply, there was a tremendous orchestral crash and the other began to sing melodramatically. Fillmore recognized the melody as the duet which begins Act II of *Ruddigore*, Gilbert's spoof on nineteenth-century melodrama.

> RUTHVEN:
>
> I once was a thoroughly wicked young Bart.
> Because I was accursed!
> A crime every day I had to commit
> And so I did my worst!

My turn, Fillmore thought with resignation. He sang.

FILLMORE:

For if you refused, in horrible pain
You'd die—I know the tale!
This curse was enforced by all of the ghosts
Of every Murgatroyd male!

(Suddenly Fillmore felt strange. If he could have described the sensation in a word, he might have chosen *fixed*.)

Murgatroyd stopped singing momentarily to eye the professor with surprise and suspicion. "How did ye know about my spectral ancestors?"

Fillmore shrugged. "Bit of a fey quality, I fancy."

"It's true," Murgatroyd nodded, leaning against the bishop's portrait-frame. "The curse temporarily separated me from my true love, Rose Maybud. But then it occurred to me that sooner or later, every Murgatroyd vows to sin no more. On the day he says that say, he dies. Or used to."

"Yes, I know," said Fillmore. "You reasoned that deciding not to commit one's daily crime was tantamount to suicide, but suicide is itself a crime, so no Murgatroyd should ever have died at all."

"Quite. And as a result, all my forefathers immediately returned to life—"

Sir Desmond, the bishop, again stuck his astral noggin out of his frame. "All but one! Bishops don't commit suicide!"

His descendant ignored him. "And now the castle is full of Murgatroyds, eating me into ruin, swearing and gaming and hunting all the foxes in the counrty! It's a dreadful bore!"

"Well," Fillmore philosophically observed, "at least you and Rose Maybud were united in matrimony."

The same thundering *tutti* sounded.

"Not so," said Murgatroyd, with a heart-felt yet rather exaggerated sigh . . .

RUTHVEN:

I once was a happily-married Lord
I'm now lovelorn and glum
My wife went and left me, to*tal*ly bereft me,
And now my word is Mum!

Fillmore winced. Typical Gilbertian trick: when nothing else rhymes, stick anything in at all. And then he realized it was his turn again. *What should I sing? The theme this set is personal misfortune* . . .

FILLMORE:

And I who was once a modest scho*lar*
Am totally unemployed,
Extremely befuddled and thoroughly muddled
And more than a bit annoyed!

(As he sang, he felt odder and odder. He almost sensed himself condensed, notated on a two-dimensional plane. "Shades of *Flatland*," he mused.)

RUTHVEN (*speaking*):
Well, we *were* married, Rose and I. But then she grew restless and took to studying at an adjacent woman's university. Eventually her study of old lore and metaphysics led her to consult a sorcerer who sold her— (*He stops suddenly.*)

FILLMORE:
Sold her what?

RUTHVEN (*pale with rage*):
AH-HAH! SIRRAH! I HAVE YOU NOW! MARRIAGE-DESTROYER!

FILLMORE:
What the *deuce* are you talking about?

Murgatroyd points to Fillmore's umbrella.
"Odd," the professor thought to himself, "I didn't have it a moment ago . . ."

RUTHVEN:
It is the very instrument which stole her from me! I shall punish thee, knave!

FILLMORE:
You already are! Dreadful over-acting!

RUTHVEN:
Revenge!

> *Sir Ruthven Murgatroyd ties Fillmore to a post with a good stout rope . . . and then makes hideous faces at him. After a moment of this, he stops and unties the professor, gleefully chortling all the while.*

RUTHVEN:
I'll wager you've been taught a lesson you shan't forget, rascal! (*Anxiously*) I trust you did not find me too over-bearingly rude?

*   *   *   *   *

Fillmore was just about to answer when someone shook him. He woke with a start.

He was on the cot of the *Pinafore* brig. Dick Deadeye stood over him, gently nudging his shoulder.

" 'Tis time, mate! Heave to and prepare to disembark!"

The teacher arose and gratefully took the umbrella which Deadeye, good as his word, snatched when no-one above deck was staring.

"Bit of a strange dream," J. Adrian Fillmore murmured. "I wonder what it meant?"

"I should say," the sorcerer reflected, *"that it was not so much a dream as a warning . . ."*

CHAPTER EIGHT

The diminutive executioner bowed low and, smiling graciously, indicated a grillwork bench overlooking the placid pool. Satisfied that the stranger with the preposterous parasol was at ease, he picked up his gleaming, untarnished headsman's axe and, toddling back over the delicate arch spanning the pond, nodded to a bevy of pale-skinned, tittering maidens whose lovely faces were hidden by delicate fans. Then, rounding the circular perimeter of a ruby-hued pagoda, the peculiar Japanese disappeared from sight.

Fillmore, heaving a profound sigh, felt comfortable for the first time in days. He rested his eyes on the odd-shaped vegetation that lent a somewhat theatrical aura to the pleasant Oriental hideaway.

His escape from the *Pinafore* came off without a hitch. But hiking sixty miles in just under two days—sleeping in fields, keeping out of sight of the constabulary—sapped his strength and wore holes in his shoes. Only once, though, did he draw a suspicious stare: on a meadow just south of London, his garish umbrella got a squint-eyed glance from a crimson-coated Grenadier who, fortunately, was busy marching with his fellows at the time. They, in turn, were in the van of a magnificent procession of peers busily stomping all over the greensward, singing and sneering and trampling down the wildflowers. It was the only close shave; otherwise, the flight had been quite uneventful.

Now it was sheerest luxury to rest his aching joints in this quaint reproduction of a Japanese village that he'd found below Hyde Park on Knightsbridge. Some sort of ethnic exposition, it was a nicely secluded place for Fillmore to revitalize himself.

He'd stopped the headsman for directions to St. Mary's Axe, guessing who the little hatchet man must be—surely there could be no more perfect individual to ask. Ko-Ko, the Lord High Executioner of *The Mikado*, was the meekest of men (he'd never beheaded a soul). Furthermore, it would be extremely unlikely for the little Japanese to be the least bit concerned or aware about fugitive Occidental "pirates."

Ko-Ko returned. "So sorry not to be able to assist you personally. I am totally unaware of London geography. However, my wife is coming to answer your question. I think you'd better kneel."

His wife? Fillmore wondered. But Ko-Ko, in the operetta, wasn't married. No . . . wait a minute . . . at the *very end* . . .

Just then, a ferocious Oriental woman of huge proportions stormed across the bridge over the pool, heading in the scholar's direction. The reinforced customs of a lifetime die hard, so he rose to his feet, gaping with dismay at the formidable female. Like her husband, she was dressed primarily in black; her kimono, cinched at the waist with a blood-red belt, was capacious. Black, beetling brows lowered above a thin, cruel mouth and her hair, stuck all over with knitting needles, looked like some infernal spiky cactus.

Good God! the professor thought, his sense of secu-

rity instantly evanescing, it's Katisha, the one *real* villain in all the G&S operettas! *She's* the one that Ko-Ko marries at the very end of the show. But that meant that the two of them here were living *beyond* the final scene that Gilbert wrote! What—

"Down on your knees, swine!" she bellowed, approaching him and Ko-Ko. Quailing, Fillmore instantly complied. "How *dare* you stand in my presence?" she roared. "Do you not know who I am?!"

"I think so," the scholar muttered. "You're Katisha, daughter-in-law elect to the Mikado."

"Not any more," the frightful apparition howled, gnashing her teeth. "Just when I was conditioning the Mikado's son to love me—"

"It's a lengthy process," Ko-Ko remarked.

"Silence, worm!" she snarled, kicking at him. Ko-Ko dodged with practiced agility. "Well," she continued, "just as Nanki-Poo was in my pow—in my arms, a shameless hussy stole him. So I went mad and married this insignificant termite instead!"

Making fun of an old lady in love, indeed! Fillmore shuddered, recalling Quiller-Couch's accusation. As soon make sport of a tornado!

A nervous orchestral figure struck up and Katisha continued her complaint in song:

> My life at court
> Has been cut short
> Because I'm wed
> To this dunderhead!
> This conjugal pest
> Has filled my breast
> With flames of hate
> For my marital state.
> So if I'm rude

And tend to brood,
It would be shrewd
Not to intrude,
Not to intrude—

Ko-Ko attempted to intervene:

Beloved wife,
No need for strife
Or quarrel, dear,
Is needed here,
Is needed here!
This passer-by
Did catch my eye
And asked a way
I could not say:
He doth entreat
Of us, my sweet,
Directions meet
To find a street.

"*What?!*" shrieked Katisha. "You dared disturb my rest because some vagabond wishes to inquire directions?"

"Yes," Fillmore replied fearfully. "Trying to find 70 St. Mary's Axe. Some of the residents elide it—70 Simmery Axe . . . ?"

The virago glowered at him, but said nothing. Ko-Ko leaned against his official chopper, staring at Fillmore with perplexed anticipation.

Here we go again! the scholar groaned inwardly. The verses they sang are part of a patter *trio*. If I don't respond, they'll just stand there gawping at me.

Then it occurred to him: how many adolescent parties had he spent, tipsy, trying to find a third voice for an impromptu rendition of this very trio? And here was a chance to sing along with one of the original characters . . . how could he resist?

"I wish you had, all the same," said the sorcerer, shaking his head. "As long as you confined yourself to rhythmic declamation, you were in comparatively little danger. But once you started singing . . . . well, well, how could you know?"

FILLMORE:

If you'll excuse
The time that you'll lose,
I'm desperate to know
Which way to go
To find the shop
Where I must stop:
A store a djinn,
A djinn
Is said to live in.
A place of spells
And witches and knells.
A man named Wells
Presides there and sells.

"There! I've finally played their silly game," the scholar thought, mightily pleased with himself.

But his recital created an unexpected effect on his auditors. Katisha, snatching up the skirts of her kimono, ran along to the main archway of the replicatory village. Clapping her hands, she bellowed out something in Japanese.

"What's wrong?" Fillmore asked Ko-Ko, who was staring at him in great dismay.

"I'm afraid," said the executioner, pale face turning even whiter, "you've run afoul of one of our Mikado's innumerable laws. Anyone who practices magic, or seeks to practice magic, or even *thinks* about practicing it is a criminal, according to our ruler's stern decree!" Glancing in Katisha's direction, Ko-Ko continued the patter trio:

> Oh, dear,
> I fear
> There's danger near!
> Our emper-or
> Had decreed war
> On magic lore.
> I fear, what's more,
> Bad luck's in store
> For you, Fillmore!

This was the worst predicament yet, the scholar realized with horror. The dire threats of torture and death that run beneath the surface gaiety of *The Mikado* give that operetta, joyous though it is, an underlying somberness of tone unique in the series. What might the Mikado's punishment be for seeking to consort with a sorcerer? The penalty, of course, would fit the crime—would it be something lingering, perhaps with a wizard's-kettle filled with boiling oil a necessary ingredient?

"Well," the professor told himself, "I'm not about to find out." Snatching up his umbrella, he raced around the corner of a purple pagoda . . . but the way was cut off by a huge company of fierce samurai who, in answer to Katisha's shouted commands, were running towards him, whirling their giant swords menacingly.

Spinning, Fillmore lit out in another direction. But

it was no use: more warriors clad in black togas were coming at him that way as well. He turned this way and that: everywhere, hordes of samurai with hideous expressions on their faces and hair tied in severe back-knots swarmed forth from every nook and alleyway. Their bloodthirsty cries startled women, set children to weeping. Many bystanders hurried indoors, heads ducked low as they dashed for sanctuary.

Fillmore halted in his tracks. It was clearly a case of stand fast, or be snipped by snickersnees. Breathing hard, he faced the terrible Katisha who was striding toward him with a cruel smile on her face.

The music, which had mocked his abortive flight with a programmatic episode depicting pursuit, returned to the familiar strains of the patter trio and Katisha sneered her second refrain.

KATISHA:

And so
Although
You're ready to go
Upon your quest,
I must protest
(It is no jest):
For your crime confessed,
As you may have guessed,
I now arrest—

FILLMORE (*defiantly*):

I'll go
And show
Both friend and foe
How much I dare.
I'm well aware

> You don't much care—
> —It's my affair—
> Yet I declare
> I'll take my share
> Although ill I'll fare.

He wasn't really feeling all *that* courageous, but the sentiments were easy to express in the obligatory trio part for which he was responsible.

The entire Japanese village immediately joined in for the coda. Samurai, geishas, water-carriers, rickshaw-runners, sushi-shop chefs, Katisha and Ko-Ko all roared out an ominous prediction of Fillmore's potential punishment:

> To sit in solemn silence in a dull dark dock,
> In a pestilential prison with a life-long lock,
> Awaiting the sensation of a short, sharp shock
> For a cheap and chippy chopper on a big black
>   block.

The mixed chorus was so loud that the noise could be heard all the way across the length and breadth of Hyde Park.

CHAPTER NINE

So, for the second time in as many days, J. Adrian Fillmore found himself shut up in a prison cell.

The new one, at least, was more comfortable than the space-starved brig, but otherwise the conditions were just as bad and the food equally unpalatable. Being on dry land, of course, was an improvement over the queasy movement of the anchored ship, but the Fleet more than offset the advantage by the uncleanly squalor in which it was allowed to be maintained.

Luckily for him, the Mikado's jurisdiction did not extend to England, a fact which might not have helped much if Katisha's will had prevailed. But the conscientious Ko-Ko brought the matter before Commons, and Fillmore—as a vaguely American citizen (in the eyes of the G&S world's citizenry)—was released from the shrewish woman's custody. However, he was immediately rearrested for piracy; it was for that alleged crime that he now languished in jail, awaiting the time of his trial.

Several weeks elapsed in the interim. As near as he could reckon (for no one kept him informed about the time), his day in court should be almost at hand. In the meantime, much must have transpired in the topsy-turvy kingdom on the other side of Fillmore's cell-window. He imagined paragraphs got into all the papers about his supposed crimes, capture and forthcoming trial, but the matter failed to interest him.

What was more intriguing to his scholar's mind was that the familiar plots of at least three Gilbert & Sullivan operettas had run their course since he'd first come over with the umbrella (now one of the prosecutor's exhibits). In fact, in the case of *The Mikado*, the story as Fillmore remembered it had already ended.

What about *H.M.S. Pinafore?* The ship docked at Portsmouth weeks ago, with Rafe Rackstraw preparing even then to speak to the captain's daughter. Thus, by now, the scholar realized, the couple must be married and Rafe and Captain Corcoran—as in the operetta—would have changed places with each other. But it made little difference which one testified against him: the captain-turned-seaman who honestly believed he was guilty, or the sailor-turned-captain whose personal gratitude towards Fillmore would certainly not stand in the way of Rackstraw condemning the accused.

As for *The Pirates of Penzance*, their destinies would also have been worked out long before Fillmore stood trial.

Evidently, the conclusion of story-lines as Fillmore knew them had no negative effect whatsoever on the world he was stuck in. But there was one plot, if ended, that mightily worried him: what if the story of *The Sorcerer* terminated? In that case, whether the scholar won his freedom or no, he was still in prison, albeit a larger one . . .

He could not ignore the irony of the notion. Life at Parker College—reclusive, unchallenging, emotionally *and* physically frustrating—was itself an incarceration for Fillmore. Yet escape, for which he'd so long pined, was decidedly worse—at least in the Gilbertian cosmos, where he'd been shot at, smothered with unsolicited ardor, forced to turn fugitive and, at the last, threatened with loss of life as well as liberty.

In all those picaresque romances he'd devoured with unexpressed longing, high adventure was supposed to be one exhilarating round of ample bosoms, intrepid treks over enemy territory, duels of wits and swords in which virtue ultimately triumphed. But in fact, he bitterly recalled, there had been few enough wits to challenge, and the distaff opportunities had been non-existent. (For that matter, in the Gilbertian scheme of things, the heroines Fillmore might meet would only turn out to be vain, emptyheaded little egotists.) As for the cross-country trip, there simply was nothing charming in snatching bits of food on the run and sleeping out-of-doors in the same underwear.

The real disappointment about his plight was the absence of joy in the grotesque world he'd landed in. It was characteristically paradoxical that he'd undergone such turmoil and discomfort in a milieu which had, in his own time, provided such delicious enjoyment during leisure hours. The answer, though, was obvious on reflection (for which he had ample time in his present state). Once, at a faculty supper for a visiting G&S star, Fillmore heard the thespian vigorously emphasize the secret of playing Gilbert & Sullivan: "You must never, *never* play for laughs! Gilbert's characters are quite serious in what they say, do and sing—that's what makes them so funny. If you 'camp' up Gilbert, you sacrifice the wit and fun for cheap college-frat inanities."

Then what could the scholar expect in a world conforming to the G&S system of logic? No doubt some impartial observer might find a degree of drollery in his troubles, just as Fillmore might chuckle at the observer if their positions were reversed. But there was no bright side to being cast as victim.

Victim . . . that was the word to hold onto, he mused. Up till now, Fillmore had played too passive a role in events involving himself. Even when engineering the escape from the *Pinafore* brig, he'd experienced a curious detachment from circumstances . . .

And look where it had gotten him! No, he must review his strategy and plan to react more directly, more emotionally in his future trial. Having broken the singing barrier with Katisha and Ko-Ko, he had no intention of letting up when—

With a croaking groan and muffled clang, the door to his cell suddenly burst open, dispelling a dense dust-fog that made him cough and choke. An elderly, gnarled turn-key stood in the entrance.

"Up, lad," he rasped in a tone harmonically attuned to the protestations of the door-hinges, "it's time to go to trial."

"What? Just like *that?* Without warning—at this hour of the morning, and without breakfast?"

"I'll keep it warm for ye. Shouldn't take long to toss you back."

Sliding off the bunk and into his shoes, the prisoner dryly thanked the jailer for his vote of confidence. Lacing up, Fillmore stood and walked stiffly through the cell-door, blinking at the unaccustomed brightness of the prison corridor.

CHAPTER TEN

On this day of the month, the 25th
in the year 1875,
in the City and County of London
Shall be tried at 10 a.m. in Old Bailey
The criminal action of

VICTORIA REGINA

VS.

J. ADRIAN FILLMORE

on the charges of piracy and eluding justice.

FOR THE STATE: *The Hon. Samuel T. Cellier.*

FOR THE DEFENSE: *Defendant will be self-represented.*

THE RT. HON. RICHARD D. CARTE PRESIDING.

SCENE.—*A Court of Justice.*
Barristers, Attorneys and Jurymen discovered.

CHORUS

Hark, the hour of ten is sounding:
Heart with anxious fear is bounding,
Hall of justice crowds surrounding,
Breathing hope and fear—
For today in this arena,

Summoned by a stern subpoena,
Fillmore, sued by V. Regina,
    Shortly will appear.

He was, in fact, already there, but that did not for a
moment interfere with their caroling. He looked
around with great interest at the bustling courtroom,
which had already taken up a modified opening chorus from *Trial by Jury*, Gilbert's only one-act operetta. Studying the assemblage, Fillmore was reminded of the equally-preposterous trial scene in
Dickens' *Pickwick Papers*. He recalled a little of one
descriptive passage: "There were already a pretty
large sprinkling of spectators in the gallery, and a nu-
merous muster of gentlemen in wigs, in the barristers'
seats: who presented, as a body, all that pleasing and
extensive variety of nose and whisker for which the
bar of England is so justly celebrated . . . The
whole, to the great wonderment of Mr. Pickwick, were
divided into little groups, who were chatting and discussing the news of the day in the most unfeeling
manner possible—just as if no trial at all were coming
on."

Fillmore's seat was to the left and in front of the
judge's bench—as yet unoccupied. He was grateful to
be allowed, in his capacity as counsel for the defense,
to sit there, avoiding the dock. He was relieved that
he would not have to spend the entire morning under
the collective scrutiny of the tatty onlookers who
jammed the place.

Counsel for the Crown entered. Fillmore, rising to
his feet, gasped when he saw the tall, portly figure in
black legal robes stride up to the right-hand anterior
table and drop a pile of musty old lawbooks upon it.

There was no mistaking the flaming red hair and jutting mustache—the prosecutor was Samuel, the lieutenant of the Penzance pirates! Crossing the brief distance between the two tables, the brigand smiled brightly at Fillmore and stretched out his hand.

"Delightful to see you again, my good fellow!" he told the flabbergasted scholar. "Hope you won't take umbrage at anything I say later on, you know. Just doing a job and all that."

"But . . . but . . ." Stammering, Fillmore could not express his thought. He gestured in wild circles with both hands.

Samuel laughed. "Daresay you're wondering what I'm doing here, eh? Long story, my lad! Let the judge tell it. Here he is now—"

Fillmore turned, following Samuel's pointing finger. A majestic entrance hymn was struck up by the members of the jury, and in came the presiding judge.

It was the pirate king.

Draped in flowing judicatory attire, he looked the soul of respectability—although the black patch over his eye still seemed slightly sinister. On his head, instead of his jolly-roger bonnet, the judge wore a frizzy white wig.

"What the devil?" cried Fillmore. "How can they possibly have assigned *you* to judge my case?"

The ex-pirate sat and beamed a paternal smile at the defendant. "Why, lad, it's a jolly day! Never expected to see ye again!"

"I repeat . . . *how can you be my judge?*"

His honor looked a little hurt at the question. "Why, young man, someone has to do it. Why not me? If you'd like to know the manner of my ascendancy, then lend an ear."

Before the defendant could protest, the invisible orchestra struck up a lively introduction and the pirate-
cum-judge commenced to sing:

> When Fred'ric turnèd twenty-and-one
> He embracèd the tenets of justice;
> He swore his piratical doings were done
> And he'd seek out our band just to bust us—
> So he headed a handful of laddies in blue,
> And he sent forth these constabulary
> To the Cornwallish coast and the lair of my crew
> Whom they promptly proceeded to harry.

(The jurors and spectators echoed the last couplet).

> We fought strong and hard, but scarce did
>   we win,
> When events took a turn unexpected—
> For the bobbies cried, 'Yield! To the queen,
>   give in!'
> And my men promptly genu-u-flected.
> But the tide soon turned when we told them
>   the news
> That once we'd been Peers of this Nation—
> So our crimes, they said, they'd politely excuse
> If we'd only resume our station.

JURORS & SPECTATORS: So their crimes, they said,
they'd politely excuse
If they'd only resume their station.
JUDGE: So now I'm a judge!
ALL: And a good judge, too!
JUDGE: Yes, now I'm a judge!
ALL: And a good judge, too!

JUDGE: Though homeward as you trudge,
          My sinecure you grudge—
          Yet I'll live and die a judge!
ALL: And a good judge, too!
SAMUEL rises.
RECIT—SAMUEL
Swear thou the jury!
AN USHER: Kneel, jurymen, oh, kneel!
    (All the jury kneel in the jury-box and so are hidden from the audience.)

While the swearing-in took its course, Fillmore slumped down in his seat, frantically trying to assess the ridiculous situation. He supposed nothing more truly Gilbertian could have transpired than that he be prosecuted and judged by the very criminals who'd pressed the incriminating money and jewels on him in the first place.

The only encouraging thing he noted was the absence of that same evidence upon the exhibit table just beneath the judge's elevated bench. Good old Dick Deadeye surely must have remained steadfast by getting rid of the gems and specie found on Fillmore. The only object on the prosecutor's table, the scholar saw with some relief, was his umbrella.

Samuel rose. After a few brief remarks concerning the two charges leveled against the defendant, he pointed out 1) the absence of any pirated property, save for one peculiar parasol—a filched fashion accessory, no doubt. The loot, of course, must have been hidden away during accused's flight. As for 2), the red-haired counsel explained that the *Pinafore* was off at sea once more, but various documents in his possession attested to accused's being taken in Cornwall with the stolen goods.

As he concluded his latter point, a restrained little air sneaked under as he spoke. Without changing rhythm or timbre, he passed from prose to lyric . . .

> With a sense of deep emotion,
> I approach this heinous case;
> For I hadn't any notion
> Any thief could be so base!
> He was caught with pockets swollen,
> Stuffed with jewelry and cash he'd stolen.

ALL: He was caught, & c.

(Fillmore was beginning to feel decidedly strange. If he could have described the sensation in a single word, he might have chosen *fixed.*)

COUNSEL:

> Picture now his crime denying,
> Though he's guilty as can be—
> This the charge we now are trying:
> Fillmore for high piracee!
> Doubly criminal, this raptor,
> For he broke away from capture!

ALL: Doubly criminal, & c.
  (*All the jury rise as one man.*)
JURY   (shaking their fists at Fillmore):
    Monster! Monster! Dread our ire!
    Quail thou, thief! Thou criminal and liar!
    Come! Substantial punishment!
    Substantial pun—
FILLMORE (*leaping up*):
    Silence in court!

(The defendant controls himself with great difficulty.)

SONG—DEFENDANT

Oh, gentlemen, listen, I pray,
Though I own that my temper is flaming.
No vestige of truth ever lay
In what learned counsel is claiming.
And it's every prisoner's right
When falsely arrested with booty
To do what he can to take flight—
In fact, I would call it a duty!
Ah!
And as for the jewelry and pelf
They claim that they found in my pocket—
They came from our good Judge himself:
'Tis *he* that should be on the docket!

ALL: Ah!
And as for the—

Swept up in the forward thrust of the trial, feeling very odd indeed, J. Adrian Fillmore would have plunged ahead in a second verse of his accusatory defense, but just then someone nudged him from behind. While the rest of the courtroom parroted his refrain, he turned to see what was wanted.

A big policeman pushed a small neatly-folded piece of paper at him, and whispered, "Little gentleman in the back insisted I get this to you immediately."

Thanking the policeman, Fillmore took the note and scanned the crowd in vain for its author. He unfolded it hurriedly, since it was almost time for his second verse. But what he saw written thereon stopped him

in mid-syllable. The music died away and judge,
counsel, jury and the rest of those assembled in the
courtroom stared at him in vast puzzlement.

The note was written in a big, flamboyant flourish.
It said:

> If you ever want the umbrella to operate for you
> again, restrict yourself to speech—or, at worst,
> declamation to music!
> But, for heaven's sake, *don't sing!*

At the bottom was scrawled the initials: JWW.

So the sorcerer himself had sought him out! Hearing of the trial, or reading about it in the papers, the
merchant magician must have instantly recognized the
umbrella as an instrument of his own manufacture.

What could the note mean? Evidently, Fillmore
stood in some kind of danger of which he was unaware. But if it was connected with the operation of
the umbrella, then he would do well to heed its man-
ufacturer's warning . . .

Turning to face the bench, the scholar begged to be
excused from continuing his defense in song.

The judge looked genuinely puzzled. "It's your privilege, of course," he explained, "but I can't imagine
why you chose to stop. You were doing so well . . ."

There was a murmur of assent from the jury, and
Fillmore noted with satisfaction that even Samuel
slyly winked at him. But he stood fast.

"Many thanks for these kind words," he told the
judge, "but I feel I will be more in my element if I
carry on in prose, Your Honor. Now, the case as I understand it is this: I am accused of piracy, a charge

which I flatly deny. Secondly, I am guilty of escaping from the custody of—"

"Oh, I think perhaps we may forget about *that*," the judge said. "Your point is well taken: duty of the captured to try to make a bolt for it, and all that. What d'ye think?" he added, looking in the direction of the jury. They all nodded their heads vigorously.

"But, m'boy," His Honor continued, "I'm afraid we can't forget about this piracy business. The gold and jewels and monies given you were all taken on the High Seas . . . and you *were* an honorary member of our band (pardon, hem!: our *former* band) of pirates."

"Yes," Fillmore protested, "but *I* didn't take the loot! It was all stolen long before I saw it."

"It was stolen all the same," Samuel remarked.

"Oh, ay," the foreman of the jury grumbled, but the judge held his finger up to his lips. Then, looking down with benevolence at the defendant, the arbiter clasped his hands across his breast and rocked for a moment in meditation.

"The point, you see," he said at last, "is not who stole the goods, but rather, who finally profited by them. We pirates all reformed and would have returned our ill-got gains. But there was a substantial cache that you'd taken with you, and since you never were a peer, there is no legal recourse but to prosecute you for receiving stolen goods and using them to your ends."

That, thought Fillmore is already a different charge than the legal definition of piracy—but the brand of justice meted out in a Gilbertian courtroom is too unorthodox to waste precious time haggling over such a point. What he must do, instead, is confront the court with the same sort of chop-logic it was wielding against him. . . .

"Is it quite certain, then," Fillmore asked slyly, "that you are absolutely resolved that possession of loot is tantamount to piracy?"

"Quite certain," the judge said.

"We are so resolved," Samuel replied, almost simultaneously. The members of the jury vigorously nodded their collective heads.

"Will nothing shake you?" Fillmore inquired.

"Nothing," was the unanimous answer. "We are adamant."

"Very good, then. In that case, I must demand that my accomplices in this offense be apprehended and tried along with me."

A murmur filled the courtroom. The judge rapped for silence, then stared at Fillmore with knitted brows. "How's this, lad, how's this? Are ye confessing?"

"Only within the rigid limits of your definition of the crime."

"Come now, laddie. I know right well ye'd no partners in this mishap."

The scholar, enjoying the confusion he'd implanted, rounded the table and paused to pour himself a glass of water. Taking his time swallowing it, he let his long-dormant theatrical predilection come forward. He sensed the moment when suspense amongst the jurors had built to an optimum level. Setting down the water-glass carefully, Fillmore glowered at the jury, then—suddenly whirling on the judge—dramatically pointed a finger skyward.

"I put it to the court," he said in ringing tones: "Are not those who take possession of stolen property and

bear it off culpable under the very principle of justice which condemns me?!"

"Yes, yes, I suppose so," said the presiding official, leaning so far over his lofty perch that his wig slid down over his eyes. "But who do ye accuse of such conspiracy?"

Drawing in a deep breath, Fillmore said, "the captain and crew of the *Pinafore!*"

A mighty burst of babbling, shouts and exclamations swelled up and rode an angry crest. Samuel, hopping to his feet, protested volubly. The spectators in the gallery above and behind Fillmore were divided between titterers and hissers.

His Honor adjusted his top-knot so that he could direct his single-eyed glare full upon the prisoner.

"That is an extremely serious accusation!" he fumed.

"Consider! Where is the remnant of the piratical plunder? Do *I* have it? No! Do you have it any longer! No! But who took it from me? Captain—now ablebodied seaman—Corcoran!"

"The loot vanished when you did!" Samuel snapped.

"That's what *they* tell you! But where am I? In prison! And where is the *Pinafore?* Far off in some foreign sea, that's where!"

"It's true!" shouted a voice from the back of the hall. "Why didn't the blighters show up to testify?"

A chorus of voices hushed the objector, but the point was made. An undertone of murmuring dissent swept the court.

"Damme," cried the judge, rapping for order. "I simply cannot arrest the entire ship! Especially when they ain't even here . . ."

"Nothing simpler," said Fillmore, who'd been waiting for the moment to thrust home. "The subtleties of

the legal mind should be equal to the emergency.
Here we have established a precedent—"

"*We have?*" the judge asked, perplexed.

"Yes! You pirates, being absolved from your crimes,
have resumed your former station, leaving the burden
of guilt to rest on my shoulders. Thus, all you have to
do is quit me of blame and affix responsibility on the
Pinafore company."

"But we cannot promulgate such a scandal!"

"You won't have to," Fillmore explained. "When
they come back to Portsmouth, find out what disposi-
tion was made of the treasure . . . ask a sailor by the
name of Dick Deadeye for the particulars . . . then
simply absolve the lot of them and try to convict
whoever has the cache by then. You can go on indefinitely!"

"Well, well," the ex-pirate mused, toying with his
gavel, "that seems a workable proposition. I don't like
it, mind—but . . ." Looking at the jury, he shrugged.
"Well, Mr. Foreman, I think we'll have to accept defendant's solution, won't we?"

The twelve good men and true wrangled among
themselves for a moment, then the foreman rose and
said they could not agree on a decision.

The judge, seized by a sudden fit of pique, ripped
off his bothersome wig and flung it in their direction.
Glancing at Fillmore, he asked sarcastically whether
defendant would mind if the bench sang? Getting no
opposition, His Honor swept off the papers and lawbooks from his desk in a rage, and embarked upon a
musical tirade:

> All these legal tangles tease me!
> His proposal doesn't please me!
> Yet I'm stumped for things to say

To explain his point away!
Barristers, and you attorneys,
Set out on your homeward journeys;
Gentle, simple-minded jury—
Get ye gone, and check your fury.
Put your briefs upon the shelf—
I will free the man myself!

A triumphal chord sounded; the jurors all applauded and came out of the box, thronging Fillmore to shake his hand. Samuel slapped him on the back and exclaimed how glad he was that justice had been done.

Remembering the admonition of the note, Fillmore restricted himself to speaking as the inevitable finale was stuck up by the omnipresent invisible orchestra:

Oh, joy unsated!
I'm vindicated.
I'm quite elated
And in the clear!

Suddenly, there was a commotion at the back of the court. The doors burst open and a large, dowdy woman in billowing, multi-pleated dress and an imposing hat rushed up the aisle. Pushing through the milling crowd, she made her way to the newly-freed scholar who was at the exhibit table gathering up his umbrella.

With horror, he saw it was Ruth. She threw her arms around him and crushed him to her breast.

Singing, she took up the finale:

At last I've found you;
With love I will surround you.

My arms impound you
And clutch you near.

SAMUEL:
I wonder whether
They'll live together
In marriage tether
In manner true?

The judge, descending, thoughtfully grasped Fillmore by the arm and yanked him away from the importunate female. Pushing him up the aisle, he offered advice that the other had every intention of heeding.

JUDGE:
I would not stay, sir!
You'll rue the day, sir.
I'd run away, sir,
If I were you!

Though I am a judge.
ALL:
And a good judge, too!
JUDGE:
Though I am a judge—
ALL:
And a good judge, too!
JUDGE:
I'll tell you all the truth:
If I had to marry Ruth—
I would sooner lose a tooth!
ALL:
And a good tooth, too!

Dashing into the outside corridor, Fillmore saw the judge push the courtroom door shut behind him—not altogether unlike the closing of a curtain at a play. As the portal slammed tight, the scholar could hear the final dominant chord sustained by the universal accompaniment.

Fillmore spared no time in quitting the building. Outside, a dapper little monocled man in striped trousers, cutaway morning coat and brushed top-hat stepped up to him, bowed low, and held out his wallet for inspection.

In it was the ornately-drawn business card which Fillmore later would receive a copy of:

JOHN WELLINGTON WELLS
President,
J. W. Wells & Co.,
Family Sorcerers.
If anyone anything lacks,
He'll find it already in stacks
at
70 ST. MARY'S AXE, LONDON
("SIMMERY AXE")

PROLOGUE

"The biggest danger you faced was subsumption,"
Wells told his guest. "You were beginning to accept
the axioms and tenets upon which my world is formu-
lated. A little more singing and you could have found
yourself permanently stuck here."

"But why?" Fillmore asked, "did you engineer such
a danger into your umbrella?"

"I didn't. The instrument—which I must admit is far
beyond my comprehension—operates on principles
and universal dictums that I've never been able to
completely pin down in the limited uses I've made of
the umbrella."

"Oh? So you've been elsewhere? In other dimensions?"

"Whatever you call them," the magician replied,
nodding his head sagely. "I've found worlds parallel to
this one, but with many intriguing variations in living-
style. In point of fact, the umbrella actually comes
from one of them—"

"Impossible," the scholar scoffed, rising to stretch
after his long sedentary session. "How could you have
reached another dimension without the umbrella?"

John Wellington Wells giggled. "You forget I'm a
sorcerer, lad! One time I wafted myself into an alien
universe, spied upon a master mathematician explain-

ing the principles of this very device to an associate. But when I heard what purpose the inventor had in mind for his cosmic-travel engine (so to speak), I stole it away. Then it was a relatively simple matter to analyze its working parts and manufacture more of them. Of course, I've been most discreet in seeing that only the *right* people get possession of them . . ."

Fillmore looked thoughtfully at the frayed and faded instrument propped up in a corner of the room. "I wonder how that one found its way to Rose's junkshop?"

The little man shrugged. "It's anyone's guess. Perhaps its owner allowed himself to be subsumed in your own world."

"Who would do a thing like *that*?"

"Someone tone-deaf, perhaps. Such people are *our* 'handicappeds.' But we are disgressing, are we not? I was discussing the properties and peculiarities of my traveling-wands. Normally, I furnish customers with adequate printed instructions. Since you have had no such briefing, I had better explain a most important factor in use of the instrument."

"Which is?" asked Fillmore.

"There is a very fine line between participation and subsumption. For some reason, when you make a dimensional hop with the umbrella, you must complete a sequence. You have to participate in some basic block of activity . . ."

The scholar nodded. "My adventures followed the developing logic of an operetta. I had to solve the chief plot dilemma before the finale could be attained, and the umbrella would work again."

"Yes," said Wells, "and you must now hurry in your departure, before a new sequence involving you gets under way." Rising and strolling to the piano, he played a few random notes while he collected his thoughts. "What I am trying to say," he continued, "is that the participation in other climes will be vastly different from this world. It won't always be so obvious as to what may ensnare you permanently . . ."

"Then how can I protect myself?"

"By doing what you did here: try to figure out the underlying postulates of the world you're in, and manipulate them without accepting them. Do you understand?"

The professor nodded, then walked over to the umbrella and picked it up. "The only thing that bothers me is the degree to which I was put-upon here, even when I wasn't singing."

"Ah, yes," said Wells, nodding sagely. "You yourself sensed the cheat. Man tends to remain stable in whatever dimension he inhabits. You must really try not to allow yourself to be victimized, you know!"

"But what can I do about it?"

"Don't know exactly. You'll think of something. It's a matter of identity, more than anything, I believe. If you really accept yourself in a certain kind of role, the chances are you'll *be* it."

Fillmore shrugged. "Well, I'll have to think it over." He held the umbrella aloft, point towards the ceiling. "How do you make this thing go where you want it, anyhow?"

Wells put a finger in the air in an instructory attitude. "It is absolutely essential to fix the kind of place in mind where you want to travel."

"But I wasn't thinking of anything in particular when I opened it!"

"Then it just picked up whatever you were musing about at the time. Do you recall what it was?"

The scholar slapped his forehead with an open

palm. "Of course! Gilbert and Sullivan! The old ladies in love and all that!"

"What *is* this gilbertandsullivan, anyway?" the sorcerer asked. "You mentioned it many times in your narrative."

"They wrote the operettas which certain events in this world echo. But you mean to tell me you've never even heard of them?"

"No, but why should I? You must remember that in our own world, we have our own objective realities. Your world is the only one I've heard of, up to now, that bears any relationship to mine—but it's so prosaic-sounding, I don't think I shall ever visit it. But . . ." The dapper little merchant paused, a worried frown creasing the corners of his eyes.

"Yes?" Fillmore prompted, putting his umbrella back down.

"Well . . . I said I wouldn't ask this sort of thing, but . . . well, dash it, you so much as hinted to me that my fate is rather dreary, according to the operetta that you know."

Fillmore fidgeted. "Well . . . ah, what happens in *The Sorcerer* is that you sell a love-philtre to a young man who will use it indiscriminately on his entire village. And then, in order to straighten out the mess, you—in the operetta—sacrifice yourself to Ahrimanes to break the spell."

"Oh, is *that* all?" laughed the sorcerer, relieved. "*That* happened to me some time ago. I made up that whole silly business of sacrificing myself! Fact is, it was an easy spell to remove—but I didn't want to get involved in any lawsuits."

It was the scholar's turn to laugh. "Thank heavens— it is the one really unsatisfactory ending in the whole G&S series . . ."

* * *

"Well," Wells asked, "are you ready to take flight?"

"Ready!" said the other, holding up the umbrella again and releasing the catch.

"Do you know where you want to go?"

"Well, I'm a little torn between home or seeking out the one man who could unriddle the mystery of this umbrella."

"Which mystery are you talking about?" asked the sorcerer.

"Why it takes the user to literary, rather than actual, dimensions."

"Well," said Wells, "as I've said, all the places *I've* been to have been actual enough. But what enlightened genius are you referring to? What man could possibly unravel the enigma of my marvelous umbrella?"

But the little magician never learned the answer. There was a sudden rap at the front door of the shop, which Wells had locked so he could hear his guest's tale undisturbed.

Looking through the entryway to the back room, the two men saw who was knocking. Fillmore paled. Crying out a hurried farewell, he pressed the button of the dimensional-transfer machine . . .

"*Wait!*" the magician shouted. But J. Adrian Fillmore was no longer there. Both he and the umbrella, Wells knew, were sweeping the stars away from some heavenly threshold in the precipitate fury of their flight.

There were two people at the front door: Ruth, and a small, bald-headed civil servant, dry in manner and parched of spirit.

"Where is he?" the shrew demanded, but the wizened functionary hushed her.

"By law," he said, "you should not even be here while I deliver this, madam."

"Deliver what?" asked Wells.

"Subpoena for one J. Adrian Fillmore."

"On what charges?"

"What else?" Ruth snapped. "Breach of promise of marriage!"

"Oh, dear," the sorcerer mumbled to himself, "another sequence! I *do* hope he got away in time . . ."

But Fillmore's thoughts were confused when he pressed the umbrella catch. Vivid memories of Ruth throwing herself upon him at the conclusion of his trial in Old Bailey crowded his brain, and muddled the process of selection.

And what was worse, he knew nothing then of the principle of universal economy . . .

PART II

CHAPTER ONE

All afternoon, the equinoctial gales whipped London with elemental violence. The wan October sun, obscured by hueless clouds, shed pallid light but little warmth. Winds screamed down avenues and alleys, while at the window-panes, a driving rain beat a merciless tattoo. It was as if all the destructive forces of Nature had foregathered, penned beasts, to howl at and threaten mankind through the protecting bars of *his* cage, civilization.

As evening drew in, the storm waned, though the wind still moaned and sobbed in the eaves like a child-ghost whimpering in a spectral schoolroom. From the Thames, great curlings of fog billowed forth, obscuring the green aits and meadows, creeping up alleys and mews, blanketing the city in an impenetrable miasma. Amber streetlamps glowed feebly in the mist-shroud like the eyes of corpses. Few foot travelers ventured out in the mud, and the only sound heard on some streets was the occasional rhythmic clip-clop and simultaneous metallic squeal of a passing Hansom.

Newman Street was deserted and smothered by the river-vapor. The mud was so thick and the appurtenances of inhabitation so difficult to discern that one might well believe a Stegosaurus could wander along its morass-like reaches. But at precisely ten past nine, a less impressive figure suddenly appeared on the empty thoroughfare: a smallish, somewhat stocky man.

His footsteps echoed down the street and he stalked along for a time before assaying a cross-street. He was inadequately dressed in a gray woolen suit with ascot tucked in at the throat. He was hatless and wore no topcoat. Though he carried an umbrella in one hand, he made no effort to use it as a shield from the steady drizzle.

Up one alley, down another, past shadowy blocks of homes, tenements, commercial establishments, the solitary pedestrian walked, his collar turned up and his head bowed. He hunched his shoulders, but the rain soaked into the material he wore on his back, ran down and squelched soddenly in his shoes, making the toes of his socks into sopping sponges. Once he stepped into a puddle deep enough to drown a cat. Shivering, he extricated his foot and forlornly tried to wring the excess moisture from his trouser-leg.

Turning into Lombard Street, he spied the lights of a distant tavern. He huddled into a covered entrance-way and fished in his pocket for his wallet. Finding it, he counted over the meager currency therein: roughly thirty-four dollars in U.S. dollars that had been generously converted to pounds sterling by his benefactor, John Wellington Wells. But would it be usable in this cosmos? And did he, in fact, reach the very place he'd been meaning to visit?

Fillmore meditated briefly, made a decision, then stepped off in the direction of the far-off inn.

After a few moments more of slogging through mud and rain, he drew near to the place. A sign suspended from an iron scrolled arm set at right angles to the bricks above the tavern-door proclaimed the name of the establishment:

THE GEORGE AND VULTURE

That disturbed him. But he wiped off his shoes on the small bracket for that purpose set next to the steps and went inside, grateful to get out of the wetness.

The tap-room was sparsely populated that evening. A trio of gamesters took turns at the dart-board, and an elderly, kindly-looking gentleman with a bit of a paunch sat at a corner table taking supper with a young, dandyish companion. The only other individual in the room when the drenched itinerant entered was the bartender.

Fillmore's bedraggled condition drew quizzical glances from the dart throwers, but they said nothing. Approaching the bar, he held out a pound-note and ascertained from the bewildered tapster that it was, indeed, acceptable tender. The newcomer then ordered a pint of ale.

"Bit of a foul night for a stroll," observed the bartender as he set the libation on the polished counter-top before his customer.

The stranger nodded, downing a quarter of the brew at one gulp. Wiping his mouth, he eyed the bartender quizzically, then motioned to him.

"I say, would you mind very much if I asked you a question?"

"Of course not."

"Even if it seems a trifle peculiar?"

The tapster grinned, placed his hands flat on the counter-top and leaned over to his customer. "If," he said in a low voice, "you think aught can surprise me after twenty-year of tavern-tending, ye've much to learn. Ask away."

"Well . . . this *is* London, isn't it?"

"George Yard, right enough."

"Well and good but—" Fillmore shrugged. "Well, what I want to know is this: what year is this?"

"Why, 'ninety-five," the other replied, a bit non-plussed in spite of his assurances.

"Yes, yes," Fillmore nodded impatiently, "But—do you mean *eighteen* ninety-five?"

The bartender swallowed, wet his lips and took a breath before trusting himself to affirm the century. Then he found a reason to busy himself at the opposite end of the tavern.

Fillmore slowly sipped his ale, oblivious to the muted buzz that rose when the tapster began to talk to the dart-players. He ignored their collective gaze, and busied himself moistening his interior and wondering how to dry off his exterior.

A tap on his shoulder. The dandyish gentleman stood by his side.

"Allow me to introduce myself. My name is Snodgrass—"

(Fillmore's ill-defined fears began to take shape.)

"I beg to be forgiven for invading your privacy but my companion and I, you see, could not help but notice your somewhat uncomfortable condition. My friend is the most compassionate of men and wishes to make your acquaintance and perhaps assist you in your putative predicament."

The stranger thanked Snodgrass and followed him back to the table at the rear of the room, where the elderly, portly gentleman in cutaway, gaiters and ruffled shirt rose to take his hand in greeting. With his other hand, he adjusted the rimless pince-nez upon the broad bridge of his nose and smiled.

"Pleased to meet a fellow scholar," he said, upon perusing Fillmore's Parker College business card. "Eh? What? Bless me, yes, quite right, you heard correctly, that *is* my name. I daresay what little reputation I may have established is not the least bit tainted with the calumnies of false report. But sit you down, sir, sit you down and dry off as you may. Won't you share some of this excellent cold beef? And allow me to refill your tankard?"

Fillmore thanked him mightily, and set to with a will, not to mention a hearty appetite. His last meal had been in prison, awaiting trial at Old Bailey. The meat and ale were so excellent that he did not permit the trifle of a possible mislocation of cosmoses to upset him.

After he'd made a clean sweep of a quarter of the beef and had his glass refilled twice, Fillmore apologized for interrupting the dinner colloquy of his host.

"Bless my soul," said the old gentleman, "this is in no way an interruption, my good sir. Mr. Snodgrass here, who is, by the way—"

"A poet," observed Fillmore.

The old man's eyebrows raised. "Goodness, does his reputation, too, precede him? How *did* you know his occupation? I had thought he'd yet to be published!"

The scholar shrugged. "Oh, it's a bit of a fey quality that I have, I fancy."

"Well, well," the other chuckled. "I am suitably impressed. But, as I say, Mr. Snodgrass here is a capital poet—"

"My blushes," the other simpered.

"Now, Augustus, modesty ill becomes a man of true

genius. You are a servant of the Muse and there is glory there! At any rate," said the host, turning to his guest, "my friend here is somewhat concerned with an affair of the heart, and I thought to give him proper advice . . . which, indeed, I did. As I completed my statement, my attention was drawn to note your extremely dampish plight. And how, if I may be so bold, do you manage to be out on such a night as this without adequate protection? I presume your umbrella must be damaged; else it should have shielded you more efficiently from the elemental deluge."

"Well," Fillmore said, somewhat reluctantly, "I do not know whether I should repay your generosity with a rehearsal of my predicament. It is so wild a tale you would doubtless judge me madder than King Lear."

The consequence of this remark was for Fillmore's host and the poet to positively entreat his adventures. So the stranger at length embarked upon his lengthy personal history, ending with his arrival on Newman Street and his subsequent trek to the George and Vulture.

When he had done at last, the others sat back, their mouths agape.

"Bless my soul," said the elderly gentleman. "That is certainly the strangest romance I have ever had the privilege to audit! No mind if it be true or no—it is an history worthy of the Arabian Nights. What do you say of it, Snodgrass?"

The poet had a dreamy look in his eyes. "I see," he sighed, "a major epic, a heroic narrative. I shall apply myself this very night while the fit is still upon me!" Suddenly leaping up, he excused himself and rushed from the room.

His companion laughed heartily, then apologized for the poet's precipitate departure. "When Inspiration

descends unto his noble rhymer's brow, it ill beseem-
eth him to let her wait admittance until he pay the
check." Still chuckling, the rotund little gentleman
rose. "No matter, though, I am better conditioned
than he, I can well afford it and had, indeed, meant
to persuade him so." He graciously waved Fillmore to
follow him.

In the lobby of the inn, he retrieved his room key,
then, turning to his guest, said, "I keep rooms in this
establishment. Pray let me loan you some fitting—ho,
ho!—apparel, for you cannot hope to go about unnoticed in your present state. No, no! I shall hear of no
polite declinings. I am very handsomely off, my good
fellow, and it shall vastly please me to make a present
of some necessaries with which you may better shield
yourself from the raging elements . . ."

An hour later, the two descended the stairs to the
lobby. Fillmore, dry and warm in slightly loose-fitting
apparel, carried an oilskin bag beneath his arm. In it
was his sopping clothing. Over his arm, the inoperable
umbrella dangled.

As they neared the front door, the scholar whispered to his host, but that person vigorously shook his
head.

"I repeat, positively not, sir! Your entertaining tale
is ample payment enow for these scraps of cloth
you've accepted. I urge you to keep your monies for a
more pressing use. Why, if your story be true, you
have but a few odd pound-notes on your person!" His
eyes twinkled as he "humored" his guest.

At the door, Fillmore asked directions to his ultimate destination, and feared it did not exist. But the
old man's answer allayed his doubts.

"Why, indeed, that street is no great ride away, but

see here, you cannot walk there on this foul night! I insist you let me fee a Hansom for your transport."

The scholar protested vigorously, but to no avail. His host, apologizing for a temporary absence of his man-servant on a family matter, himself stepped into the drizzle and smoke to hail a cab. It was no simple matter on such a night to find one, let alone flag one down in the limited visibility the fog afforded. But after much assiduous labor and much raising of the voice, the portly benefactor finally arranged for his friend's transportation.

As he entered the cab, Fillmore thanked his host repeatedly, and the other as often belittled the charity as privilege and necessary duty. Closing the cab-door, the elderly gentleman stepped around to the front of the vehicle and told the driver the proper destination. He paid him in advance.

"The address wanted," said Mr. Pickwick, "is 221 Baker Street. Just out of Marylebone Road . . ."

CHAPTER TWO

Inside the cab, J. Adrian Fillmore tried to collect his thoughts. It was not easy because of the unaccustomed joggling and jostling his bones were receiving, but he did what he could to resolve the nagging doubts as to his whereabouts.

London it was, and the year was correct, but was it the time and situation—in short, was it the *universe*—of Sherlock Holmes?

His thoughts, confused and harried by the sight of Ruth through the front door-pane of Wells' shop, rushed past in a chaotic jumble as he pressed the button to open the umbrella's hood. After that, all was a disordered kaleidoscope of colors and voids as he flew through uncomputed curvings of space. His hurried departure allowed no time to consider personal comfort. When he found himself in the middle of a dark, rainy street, Fillmore cursed the enforced celerity of his flight. "And, damn it," he muttered in the dark interior of the lurching cab, "what stupidity made me abandon my raincoat and galoshes back on the Cornwall seacoast?"

At least, Pickwick saw to it that he would be able to survive the weather until such time as he might expand his wardrobe. But the thought of the old gentleman brought fresh dismay. He was in London all right—but it appeared to be that of Charles Dickens! The benign heroes of the *Pickwick Papers* were pleasant enough, but they hardly qualified to assist Fillmore in his cerebral quest. Besides, memories of the grimmer aspects of some of the "Boz" narratives haunted him and made him most uneasy. His umbrella, ruled by cosmic quirk, would not permit him egress from this milieu until he completed a sequence of action—and Dickens' plots sometimes covered entire lifetimes. And in the meantime, what might he do inadvertently to mire himself permanently in the world of Dickens?

Was there a possibility that by some principle of universal economy, the London of Dickens was also the same world as that of Watson and Holmes? To learn the answer, the scholar was headed towards Baker Street.

"Sherlock Holmes," he mused, with a thrill of anticipation. "If anyone in the multiplicity of worlds that seem to coexist with the earth I know can analyze the umbrella, then—"

The sentiment was interrupted by the abrupt stoppage of the cab and the simultaneous hurling-forward of the passenger. He bruised his head against the edge of the opposite seat.

The driver shouted, "221 Baker." Fillmore dismounted, offering, as he did, an epithet to the cabbie in lieu of a tip.

Picking up the oilskin container of clothing, Fillmore crossed the road just as the disgruntled Hansom driver pulled away. A bit of mud spattered up from the wheels of the cab, but the scholar ignored the inconvenience in his excitement as he spied the large brass plate on the house opposite. His hopes were high as he scanned the inscription:

```
┌─────────────────────────────────┐
│              221                │
│     S. HOLMES, CONSULTANT       │
│        Apply at Suite B         │
└─────────────────────────────────┘
```

Dashing up the steps to the front door, he pushed it open and mounted one flight. The interior was cheery, just as he'd always imagined it. Green wallpaper paralleled the staircase and the flickering of gaslamps set in staggered sconces brightened the hall considerably.

He stopped in front of the B apartment and knocked. Almost immediately, a powerfully-built, mustached man in dressing-gown opened the door and invited him to enter.

Stepping inside, Fillmore asked, "You are the good doctor, I presume?"

"Why, yes," the other chuckled, "at least I hope to merit the appelation. But I imagine you have come to see Holmes, have you not?"

"I have, indeed," the scholar replied, his heart beating rapidly, like that of a school-boy who sees his first love approaching.

"Sit down, my good man," the doctor invited, meanwhile pulling on a bell-rope in the corner of the cozy sitting-room where he'd ushered his caller. "The fact is, I'm afraid Holmes is off tending to that dreadful business in Cloisterham. Chap missing, you may have read about it in the papers: Drood. But it's a close undercover game Sherrinford is playing, and my presence there would only have confused things, so—"

The doctor stopped, peering at his visitor with concern. "Pray tell me, sir, are you troubled by some indisposition?"

Fillmore, pale, could barely speak. "What," he whispered, "*what* did you call Mr. Holmes?"

"Why, Sherrinford, of course! All the world knows Sherrinford Holmes, do they not? Not the least (I fancy I may compliment myself) because of the narratives which I have penned concerning his exploits."

"And what," the scholar asked, still hoarse, "and what is *your* name?"

The doctor chuckled. "The fickleness of fortune and all that, eh? I'd thought my little publications might have added some touch of notoriety to the name of Ormond Sacker, but apparently—"

Fillmore rose in agitation and paced the room, thinking feverishly. Why were the names the doctor used so nightmarishly different from the ones he'd expected to hear? Sherrinford, not Sherlock. Ormond Sacker, instead of John H. Watson, M.D.

On the other hand, why did they also sound so *familiar?*

"Here, here, my good fellow," said Sacker worriedly, "I can see you are in considerable agitation. Pray be seated. Perhaps, in the absence of Holmes, I can shed some light on your problem. Meantime, I notice that the storm has not left you untainted. Be seated, be seated, man. I have rung for Mrs. Bardell and she will be up directly with tea and perhaps—"

Fillmore interrupted, even paler than before. "Mrs.—*whom?*"

"Why—Bardell, Mrs. Bardell, our landlady!" the doctor said, greatly amazed.

"*Not Mrs. Hudson?*"

"Hudson? I should think not. There used to be a Mrs. Warren taking care of this building, but she sold to a Mrs. Martha Bardell, and that is who . . . but see, the knob is turning now. This is the very woman."

The door opened and a plump woman entered, bearing an ornate silver tea-service in her arms. But when she saw Fillmore, the woman screamed and dropped the tray. The hot liquid splashed upon the rug.

"What the devil!" Sacker exclaimed. "Mrs. Bardell! Have you taken leave of your senses?"

"It's him," the woman wailed, "*it's him!*"

"What *are* you speaking about, madam?"

"Him!" she howled, pointing an accusatory finger at J. Adrian Fillmore.

He, in turn, stared in flabbergasted dismay at the landlady. She was dressed in a green housecoat with flounce sleeves of a lighter shade with vertical stripes. On her head she wore a white, lace-trimmed domestic's cap, tied in a bow beneath her chin. But despite the disparity of apparel, Fillmore recognized her immediately.

It was Ruth.

CHAPTER THREE

Prison. A home away from home, Fillmore mused bitterly. First, the *Pinafore* brig. Then the Fleet. Now the Fleet again. Three times incarcerated since buying the blasted umbrella. Before then, never a serious brush with the law. (He didn't count the abortive undergraduate party. At 8 P.M., no one had shown, so he glumly went out to get himself a steak sandwich. When he got back, the place was teeming with uninvited guests and a coterie of irate campus cops who, fortunately, had no idea who the host was.)

He huddled in a corner for warmth but did his best to avoid bodily contact with the lice-ridden sot next to him. In a far corner, a man with a broken nose and a piercing stare watched Fillmore every second.

At least, they'd let him keep the umbrella for the time being. After the trial, the authorities might well confiscate his property and then the scholar would be stuck here for good.

Stuck where? It was obviously Dickensian London, but it took Fillmore quite a few hours to figure out the weirdly-altered names of Holmes and Watson. When the answer came, it naturally disturbed him, but at least he began dimly to perceive the principle of universal economy.

Sherrinford Holmes. Ormond Sacker. These were

names Arthur Conan Doyle toyed with before settling on "Sherlock" and "John H. Watson." Fillmore had landed himself smack in the middle of an incomplete *draft* of *A Study in Scarlet*. An *incomplete* draft. After all, what had Sacker said Holmes was busy doing? Investigating the Edwin Drood mystery—a notoriously unfinished masterpiece . . .

"That damned Ruth," the scholar muttered, clutching his umbrella close and trying to ignore the fixed gaze of the man with the broken nose. "Must have been trying to bring charges against me for breach-of-promise."

Nothing else made sense. It was apparent he'd inherited the "sequence" from the earlier cosmos, because he was in The Fleet awaiting such a trial. Mrs. Bardell, though astonishingly similar in face and form to Ruth, was really Sacker-and-Holmes' landlady . . . the very same Mrs. Bardell who sued Mr. Samuel Pickwick and landed him in prison in *The Pickwick Papers*.

"Well, at least the old boy did me a favor, and now, it appears I'm doing him one, whether he ever learns it or no." It worried the scholar. The outrageously comic trial of Bardell vs. Pickwick is the dramatic focal point of that Dickens tome. But some bounder that resembled Fillmore apparently once jilted Mrs. B., and as a result, the hapless alien seemed to be usurping the breach-of-promise trial that ought to—

"There I go again!" Fillmore grumbled to himself. "Confusing fictional events with what takes place in these strange places I end up in. Do they follow the stories I read on 'normal earth?' Do they branch off wherever they wish? Maybe this is just an earlier trial and Pickwick's is yet to come here. *Or* maybe this is also a *draft* stage of the *Pickwick Papers* Ms. Then how do I—?"

He could not even finish the thought. It was too complicated. As hard to define as the identical looks of Mrs. Bardell and Ruth. Perhaps, he pondered, the entire cosmic system is a network of interlinking puzzle boxes, one heartwall economically doubling, tripling in alternative dimensions, and each soul, in sleep, shares identities across the gaps of space and relative times.

"Bah," he murmured. "Einstein notwithstanding. Time is a concurrency."

But his philosophic gum-chewing was disturbed by a sharp poke in the ribs. It was the shifty-eyed ferret seated by him in the corner of the cell. " 'Ere now," he whispered to Fillmore, "that's a peculiar thing ye've got there. Where'd ye fetch it?"

Fillmore tried to ignore him, but the ferret exchanged the poke for a pinch. "Ow!" the scholar yelped. "Stop that!"

"I asked ye a question," the ferret whispered. "And keep yer voice low, if ye value living!"

The scholar faced his tormentor squarely, an angry retort on his lips, but the impulse stopped when he beheld the other's expression. The ferret's face was strained, each muscle tensed to the stretching-point. His eyes rolled independent of the fixed head, and they moved in the direction of the sinister individual on the other side of the cell. The man with the broken nose.

Fillmore did not look at him. He regarded the ferret anxiously, and replied as quietly as his questioner.

"I bought my umbrella far from here. What matter is it?"

" 'im. Don't ye see how he stares at it. I never saw

one to covet something so much. Never takes 'is eyes off it."

"I thought he was staring at me."

The ferret shook his head. "Last night, when ye slumbered, 'e crept near to examine it. Mutterin' to 'isself. Thought he'd snatch it then." The ferret shrugged. "But then, where'd 'e go with it?" The beady eyes narrowed, glinting with an eager urgency. "Ye want advice, man? If he asks for it, don't argue. Sell it, or make it a gift. Don't cross 'im!"

Fillmore shook his head. "Impossible. I *can't* part with my umbrella!"

"I tell ye, man, 'e's half-mad! Don't cross 'im! They'll 'ave 'im out in a day or two and then 'e'll wait for ye, and 'e'll 'ave 'is cane."

What in all good hell is he babbling about? Fillmore wondered. The man has no cane. In fact, he walks perfectly well. Look at him—

The man with the broken nose was standing. He turned his gaze briefly on the little ferret and that person shrank away from Fillmore and cowered in a corner of the cell.

What kind of a crazy sequence is this, anyway? If this is the Bardell trial, why should I worry about strange men with umbrella fixations? Even if he is dangerous, and even if he gets out of prison and tries to wait for me, my trial will keep me here indefinitely. And then? Damn, I may *never* escape!

"Permit me to introduce myself." The tall, sinister man proffered his card.

Fillmore stood. He was startled at the meek civility of the other's mien. From a distance, he appeared *so* menacing. But now, he must rectify his mistake. A toff, doubtless, confined for some minor infraction of the peace. He was well dressed, dark suit, ruffled shirt, a thin tie which might have passed muster a century later on campus.

The card told him nothing. It bore nothing but a name, "A. I. Persano."

"I trust my reputation is not unknown to you?" he asked. His face was smiling in a way that might suggest a double meaning to the question. But Fillmore knew no one intimately in this peculiar world of confused beginnings, so he could certainly not identify the stranger by reputation.

"I have been admiring that odd instrument which you have over your arm," Persano remarked. "May I examine it more closely?"

Fillmore found it hard to deny the reasonable request, so mildly was it made, and yet, something warned him to refuse. From the corner of his eye, he saw the ferret urgently motioning him to comply. With considerable reluctance, the scholar relinquished the instrument.

The tall man minutely inspected the umbrella, turning it this way and that, pausing to push back the cloth folds and read the partially-obliterated inscription on the handle. As he did, Fillmore studied the lean, hard face. The eyes never blinked. The mouth was set in a half-grin that could easily be assessed as cruel. The nose, too, at close scrutiny, was even more disturbing than it first appeared. It was not broken after all. Rather it had been *sliced*, as if by some sharp edge. A deep lateral furrow creased the bridge, so that it resembled an ill-set fracture. But Persano was not the kind to indulge in violent roughhouse, Fillmore was sure. He was too contained, too deceptively calm. He might deal in rapier, never in bludgeon.

Persano returned the umbrella without comment.

Then, apparently satisfied, he asked what Fillmore was doing in jail. The scholar outlined the details of his case, and the other clucked in doleful sympathy.

"Who defends you?" the tall man asked.

"Myself."

"And who represents the Bardell interests?"

Fillmore shuddered. He knew who Martha Bardell's barristers *must* be. "Messrs. Dodson and Fogg, I do presume."

"What? Then you're a fool, man. You have no choice but to raise capital sufficient to fee attorneys as crooked as those pettifoggers!"

"I haven't the money," Fillmore demurred. He refused to petition Pickwick. That might be an action which would mire him in the mishmosh-world he'd stumbled into. The best course was to maintain a detached air from the circumstances afflicting him . . .

"Since you are destitute," Persano said, smiling, "I have a suggestion."

Silence.

Fillmore knew what the other was about to say.

"Sell me your umbrella. I will pay handsomely for it."

"Why?"

"It . . . amuses me."

Fillmore shook his head. To his relief, the other did not press his request. Persano merely smiled more broadly. "Very well," he murmured. "There are other ways."

The following day, A. I. Persano was released from prison.

Two days later, a warder unlocked the door of the cell.

"Fillmore." He jerked his thumb to the door. "Out."

"Is it time for my trial?"

The warder shook his head. "Won't be one. Ye're free."

"*Free?*"

The ferret clucked in warning. "I told ye."

"How. *can* I be free?" the scholar demanded, amazed, puzzled, overjoyed—and simultaneously uneasy.

"Plaintiff's counsel dropped charges. No estate worth speaking of to cover the expense."

"Estate? What are you talking about?"

The warder drew one finger across his throat in a gesture as meaningful in one world as another. "Bardell," he said. "Last night. Someone cut 'er throat."

CHAPTER FOUR

For once, he was not anxious to get out of prison. He dragged his footsteps along the last corridor before the outside gate and cudgelled his brains to make out what sort of dreadful sequence he'd landed in.

It *could* be the grimmer side of Dickens, he thought. Perhaps the only way to terminate one's existence here is to die. He shuddered.

At the front gate, he entreated the constable accompanying him to protect him, but the other merely grunted, "Oh, ye'll be noted, right enough," then turned and left Fillmore to the mercy of the streets.

What did he mean by that? the scholar wondered. Then, with a shock of dismay, he realized that he must be considered gravely suspect in the eyes of the police. "Bah!" he snapped, loud enough to be heard. "If I couldn't hire an attorney, what makes them think I could afford an assassin to murder Mrs. Bardell?"

He peered about nervously, but there was no trace of the sinister Persano anywhere. It was early, but the sickly pall of London mist obscured the sun. Few foot-passengers traversed the section of thoroughfares near The Fleet.

Fillmore walked aimlessly for a time, trying to work out the problem of the cosmic block of action he was expected to participate in. Since the breach-of-

promise trial had come to naught, he could only presume that the uncompleted sequence with Ruth in
G&S-land had finally run its course. But a new situation appears to have taken up, the scholar mused,
worriedly. A dreadful stiuation, very like.

He was just crossing Bentinck Street at the corner
of Oxford when he heard a sudden clatter of hooves
and the rumble of a large vehicle. He swerved in his
tracks and paled. A two-horse van, apparently parked
at a nearby curb, was in furious motion, bearing directly down on him. Fillmore uttered a lusty yell and
leaped a good six or seven feet onto the curb. Without
stopping, he ducked down behind a lamp-post and
did not rise until the carriage rolled into the distance
and was lost to sight and sound.

He rose, puffing mightily. The jump was the hearti-
est exercise he'd undergone since trying to run away
from Katisha weeks earlier. His heart pounded against
his rib-cage. Fillmore glanced right and left, but the
few pedestrians in view went about their business,
oblivious to the near-accident which had just occurred.

But was it an accident?

He continued his journey, but did not allow himself
the luxury of abstracted thought. Instead, Fillmore
looked right and left, backwards and forwards, fearful
of another attack. And yet the street seemed deserted.
He was practically the only pedestrian on the avenue.

His very solitariness made him even more anxious.
He was an easy target for anyone who might be following just beyond the curtain of the fog. At the next
corner, he looked down the cross street and decided to
take it, in hopes of coming to a more populous quarter
of town.

There was a constable in the middle of the block.

Fillmore breathed a sigh of relief. At least he was safe for a few steps . . .

The constable turned and regarded him. The man's face became ash-white. He stuck his whistle to his lips and blasted it, at the same time thrusting an arm directly at the professor. Fillmore, astonished, hopped back a step, and wondered whether he ought to run.

At the same instant, a huge brick smashed with tremendous impact upon the pavement directly in front of him. One more step and the brick would have crushed his skull.

Fillmore and the officer regarded each other for a second or two, too relieved to speak. Then Fillmore stepped far out into the street—looking carefully both ways—and walked over to the other, thanking him with great earnestness.

"I pride myself," said the constable, "on a quick reaction time. Fortunate for you, right enough."

"Yes . . . but who dropped that deuced brick?" Fillmore squawked.

The other's eyes widened. "Never occurred to me it wasn't an accident! Come, then! Better be brisk!"

Without another word, the constable dashed into the doorway of the large, cold tenement house from which the missile had apparently been impelled. Fillmore accompanied him, preferring to be in the company of the law at that moment than to be left waiting defenseless in the street.

They climbed dark, interminable stairs, redolent of cabbage and other less tolerable reeks. At length they found the skylight, which was reachable only by means of an iron ladder stapled with great brackets against the wall. It was a sheer vertical climb and Fillmore did not relish it.

At last they stood upon the roof, a good four or five

stories above the street (Fillmore lost count of how many flights they'd taken in the ascent). There was a large chimney-stack off to one side, and the remnants of a clothesline, evidently blown down by a gust of wind. By the street edge of the roof lay a pile of shingles, slate and brick, the flotsam of some antique building venture.

"There's your accident," the officer said, jerking his head towards the pile of construction leavings. "Wind must've worked one loose. Bit of a hazard, I'd best move 'em."

Fillmore, after thanking the policeman once more, left him laboring on the roof. He doubted it was an accident, and if it was not, then he was in danger from the assailant who must still be in the neighborhood. He wanted to cling to the protection of the law, but his conscience would not permit him to endanger the officer who saved his life—and proximity to J. Adrian (what a beastly name!) Fillmore might do just that.

On the stairwell, he tried the catch of the umbrella, but it would not open. The sequence was far from finished.

Just as he was turning the corner of the last landing leading to the street level and the doorway out, he thought he heard a slight noise below, in the corner of the corridor alongside the first approach of the stairwell. He peered down the side of the bannister but it was dark and he could see nothing.

He paused, unsure of what to do, whether to go back or forward. To rejoin the policeman would only prolong the danger. With a sudden burst of nerve, Fillmore leaped the railing and, umbrella pointed downward, dropped to the floor below.

A thud and a moan. A burly body broke his fall. He

lugged the lurker into the moted dustlight and saw a feral visage, rich in scars and whiskers. A life-preserver—the British equivalent of a blackjack—was still clutched in the assailant's hand, but the man was unconscious.

Fillmore slumped against the wall, almost nauseous with fear. In the past half-hour, his life had been attempted three times, and, what may have been worse, he'd met the dangers with expedition and a physical courage all unsuspected in his makeup. It worried him as much as the danger.

Maybe *that's* what's got me stuck in this damned place! Fillmore shook his head to clear it of the vertigo that the fall brought about. No time for cosmic trepidations. Probably more danger, any moment, any second . . .

He quickly turned out the pockets of the man on the floor, but found nothing incriminating or enlightening. The life-preserver he stuck into his own back-pocket.

Slowly, fearfully, Fillmore cracked open the front door. The street was no longer sparse of population. A knot of people milled about, shouting, giving unobeyed orders; one person was busily engaged in retching on the sidewalk.

The professor hurried down the front steps and peered through the press of people. There was a body smeared along the street, a bloody rag of flesh and dislocated bone.

It was the policeman. Someone must have shoved him from the roof, Fillmore realized, horrified.

"The chimney! The bastard must have been behind it!"

Angry for the first time since the game of stalk-and-attack started, Fillmore wanted to punish the killer who destroyed a man who'd saved his own life. He trotted to the middle of the street, shielding his eyes from the glare of hidden sun shining through blanched clouds. Was there someone still on the roof? Could he take him, too, like the thug in the stairwell?

For answer, a fierce face suddenly appeared at the edge of the building-top. An odd weapon quickly swiveled into position and pointed straight at the scholar.

He ran zigzag, hoping to evade the inevitable shot. But the other was a crack marksman. Even with the difficulty of hitting a moving target, the villain managed to lodge one shot in Fillmore's shoulder.

The professor staggered. What did that character say in the Fredric Brown novel? "If you are killed here, you will be dead . . . in every world." Fillmore stumbled to his feet. The strange weapon—which made no noise—was already in position for another shot.

My God! It's an air rifle!

The horrible universe suddenly fell into place. Terror overcame Fillmore and gave him the strength of mad desperation. He shot out across the street, waving the umbrella in huge, confusing arcs, changing direction every few seconds. He headed for the juncture of streets again, and as he did, shouted and screamed for help. Some of the denizens of the neighborhood huddled about the constable's body stared at the crazy fellow and decided instantly that it was he who must have murdered the officer. No one advanced to Fillmore's aid.

Oddly enough, there was no second bullet. Fillmore reached the intersection safely. He saw a Hansom slowly rumbling down the middle of the avenue. "I must look a fearful sight," he thought, "shoulder bleeding, weird umbrella waving about like a Floradora girl's prop . . ."

Fillmore took no chances. He ran straight into the path of the Hansom, shouting for it to stop. At the last instant, remembering the dreadful attempt of the two-horse van to run him down, he experienced an awful qualm. But the cab pulled to a stop.

"Baker Street," Fillmore gasped, jumping in and slamming the door. "Number 221."

The cab rattled off slowly. The scholar gasped for sufficient breath, then pounded the sides and shouted for the driver to make haste, but to no avail. The Hansom lumbered sluggishly along, neither creeping nor hurrying. Fillmore stuck his head out of the window and surveyed the street behind. There were no vehicles in pursuit.

He leaned back against the wall of the cab and panted. "Safe for a time, at least," he murmured. "I just hope that Sherringford—"

Before he could even complete the thought, the cab lurched to a stop. Fillmore stuck his head out the window. "Here, what is this? This isn't Baker Street!"

"No, sir," the cabbie said, dismounting. He walked to Fillmore's door and stood by it, preventing it from opening. "Taking on another passenger, we are, sir."

Fillmore regarded him blankly. Then he swung around in his seat, hoping to get out the other way. But that door was already opening.

The new passenger rested his cane against the seat and closed the door behind himself. He settled comfortably into the place opposite Fillmore.

"You've caused us a deal of trouble this morning," A. I. Persano remarked mildly.

CHAPTER FIVE

The cabbie whipped the horse to a froth. The Hansom rattled along at breakneck speed. Fillmore braced himself to keep from bouncing straight through the flimsy ceiling. He gritted his teeth at the ache in his shoulder.

Persano, riding as skillfully as if mounted on a thoroughbred, was quite amiable. He regarded the other's persecution as a tiresome necessity, to be managed with swift expedition, but utterly without malice. *Not* to be discussed in polite company. The Code, by all means!

"Had you been reasonable," he stated mildly, "all this pother might have been eclipsed."

"Meaning I should have given you the umbrella?"

Persano gravely inclined his head.

"Rubbish!" Fillmore said with great asperity. "You are in a frenzy to get this instrument. Therefore, you must know its function. It follows, then, that you know I couldn't part with it at any price."

Persano clucked disapprovingly. "I could tell the authorities that the umbrella was stolen from my employer."

"You are blathering nonsense! Anyone with a shred of sense must deduce your employer has no desire to see this instrument's astonishing properties made public. You could have reported it stolen in prison. Instead, two people are dead because of it, and I have a bullet in my shoulder."

"An unfortunately staged episode," Persano agreed, stifling a yawn. "The Colonel has no idea of how to achieve maximum effect with minimal effort. His aggression grows in inverse proportion to his waning manhood."

Suddenly, the puzzle, nearly solved, all clicked into place. The ferocious Colonel Sebastian Moran! ("The second most dangerous man in London, Watson!") And the kindly sorcerer, John Wellington Wells, admitted to spying on *a master mathematician,* from whom he stole the umbrella. The instrument must be the brainchild of the brilliantly evil kingpin of London crime, Professor Moriarty! And then, another thought: Holmes once spoke of two especially dangerous members of the Moriarty gang. One was Moran. Persano must be the other.

Fillmore, shuddering, commented on Persano's remark. "You are, of course, referring to Colonel Moran."

For a split-second, the mask of indifference dropped, and the other subjected Fillmore to a deadly scrutiny. Then his eyes clouded over again and Persano propped his cane by his chin and chuckled.

"Cards on the table, eh?" He nodded approvingly. "Very well, then, an end to games-playing: you, sir, are either an agent or a fool."

"What do you mean?" Fillmore stanched the wound in his throbbing shoulder with a handkerchief.

"It cannot be that you are with the Yard," Persano mused. "A *provocateur* would not allow a fellow-constable to blindly face an unseen foe without ample warning. Nor, for that matter, would Sherrinford

Holmes stick someone else's neck on the chopping-block. No. You did not lure me into an imminent trap. You are engaged in a lone game against the greatest organization of its type in the world. You are, there-fore, a colossal fool."

"In a word, you refer to Professor Moriarty's organi-zation."

"*Who?*" Persano asked, pretending perplexity.

There was a lengthy silence.

"I do *not* know to whom you refer," Persano said, "but I might amend what I said before. I called you a fool. I suspect you are worse: a veritable lunatic. But the tense soon shall alter . . ."

Fillmore clutched the umbrella tight, his thoughts racing. His life was in great danger. In whichever world he blundered, he ended up a victim. In this clime, he might well end his sequence *permanently*.

"This needs no further discussion, I think," Fillmore said airily, attempting an ease of manner which he hoped might match his opponent's. He shifted in the uncomfortable carriage seat. "You will steal the um-brella and there's an end of it."

Persano shook his head, an earnest expression on his face. "Really, that is not possible. Don't you see? You, an independent agent, are somehow privy to details that my employer would not like bruited about. You are able to set my face and name to several recent incidents of dubious merit. You carry a pellet in you from an air-gun and there are many unsolved crimes connected with such a weapon. What is worse, you know the Colonel's last name. No, no, it's quite impos-sible, surely you see my position?"

His eyebrows raised quizzically. He really seemed concerned lest Fillmore fail to comprehend and sanc-tion the deplorable step that must be taken.

It did not fool Fillmore. Persano had never taken pains to cover his involvement in the "incidents." What was worse, he freely volunteered information about Moran's association with other atrocities. Persano evidently never at all intended to let the scholar survive.

"Look," he blurted, "I have a different suggestion. Come with me someplace else so that I am no longer in this world. I'll go back to my own cosmos! Then you can take the damned umbrella and return here!"

Persano shook his head again. "I can't do that. How do I know how long it will take before that thing decides to work again? If it could work now, you wouldn't be here at this moment. But even if you could waft us elsewhere immediately, you know I could not use the umbrella for long afterwards, and I have no time to wait."

"Why couldn't you use it?" Fillmore asked.

Persano eyed him curiously. "I think you actually don't know."

"Know *what?*" His shoulder still hurt. The carriage decelerated to a more bearable rate, but he still was unable to sit comfortably.

Persano reached over and took the umbrella. Fillmore tried to hold tight, but the other easily plucked it from his grasp. Persano pushed aside the hood-folds and put his thumb on the catch.

"Observe." He pushed the button.

Nothing happened.

"It is imprinted with your brain-pattern. It will take it a long time to readjust. Unless . . ."

He let the thought dangle in the air, drumming his fingertips on the central pole of the bumbershoot.

A long while passed. They stared at one another without speaking.

Then the horse slowed to a walk.

"We are almost there," Persano said in a low voice.

"Where?"

"A warehouse. Prepare to disembark."

Persano looked out the window. As he did, Fillmore suddenly realized why he was having so much trouble sitting comfortably. There was something in his back-pocket—

The life-preserver!

Carefully, carefully, he reached his hand around to get the sapping tool. His fingers crept. Persano stared out the window.

Good! Teeth clenched, a cold perspiration bespangling his brow, the pedant strained for the ersatz blackjack. *Another quarter-inch . . .*

It snagged in a fold of his pocket, and he could not yank it free. Fillmore tugged, but his arm was in an awkward position and he hadn't ample leverage to twist out the thing cleanly.

The carriage shuddered to a stop.

"End of the line," Persano announced, turning. His eyes narrowed. "What *are* you doing?" he asked, his tone suggesting the indulgent displeasure of a kindly schoolteacher towards a wayward urchin.

Fillmore frantically pulled at the cosh. The whole back-pocket of his pants ripped off. At last, he had it in his hand!

But the quick movement triggered Persano. Swiftly, soundlessly, he shot forward and clutched Fillmore's throat in a steel grip. He was not angry, only methodical. Whatever Fillmore was trying to do, Persano immediately recognized it as a last-ditch effort and knew he must bring it to nought. Though the business was clearly beneath him—throttling was the preserve of brutal underlings—he squeezed Fillmore's windpipe quite efficiently, nonetheless.

The scholar once read that it only takes a professional killer seven seconds to choke someone to death. Already the lights of life danced dimly and dwindled. He knew he only had strength in his arm for a single assault—

He cracked the preserver against the base of Persano's neck. (Gesture derived from countless spy and war films.) Persano slumped for a second, only a second; the quick mind analyzed the extent of damage with incredible celerity and marshaled strength for a new attack.

But Fillmore only needed the one respite. He heaved Persano off and simultaneously raked one hand upwards over the other's face from jaw to nose (a trick out of *Shane*) while the other hand slammed the life-preserver into the throat thus presented for the blow (*Bad Day at Black Rock*).

Persano gagged and doubled up.

Dropping the cosh, Fillmore wrested free the umbrella and jumped out the opposite side of the carriage from whence he'd entered. Just then, the driver pulled the other door open; seeing he was gone, he cursed at Fillmore, slammed the door and started after him. Fillmore threw his weight against the Hansom, hoping to tip it over onto the driver, but the effort drew fresh pain from his shoulder-wound and only earned him a good jarring butt.

He saw the feet of the driver rounding the carriage, so he started the other way. An idea struck him and he vaulted onto the driver's seat. ("Thanks to Gene Autry!") and slapped the reins.

The horse ambled forward two inches and stopped.

"Damn! It always looks so *easy!*"

The driver came up on him. A sinewy, saturnine thug he was, with a dagger in his hand. He hauled himself onto the seat, slashing at Fillmore, but the professor administered a stunning blow to the chest with the whip-handle ("courtesy Lash LaRue") and the rascal landed on his back in the street, roaring.

The horse, mistaking the bellow for an order, reared up.

"*Whoa!*" Fillmore yelled. The animal, unfamiliar with the western idiom, interpreted the word as a seconding motion and immediately adopted the measure by dashing forth. The cab careened to one side, righted itself and lurched behind the crazed beast.

The jolt pitched Fillmore backwards. He nearly lost his grip on the umbrella, but clutched frantically, regained his hold, and simultaneously squirmed onto his face so he could embrace the cab-roof with arms spread wide.

The horse stormed down the cobbled thoroughfare, which was a road that directly paralleled the river. Warehouses sped past; a confusion of disappearing drydocks. Cursing dockwallopers sprang out of the path of the runaway.

Fillmore hugged the roof, too winded and frightened to move. But suddenly, the blade of a sword swiftly emerged from the roof one-sixteenth of an inch in front of his nose. He decided to budge after all.

While the blade was withdrawing for another thrust, he scrambled into the driver's seat and fished for the reins. No use; they hung over the lip and jounced in the roadbed; he strained but could not reach them. Next thing he knew, the furious pitch of the ride bumped his teeth together so he bit his tongue and shoved him straight back against the cab housing. He instantly pushed forward, narrowly avoiding the sword-point which emerged at the place where his body made impact.

He ran his hand down the umbrella and tried to snap it open. *No go!* Then he saw a new danger up ahead. About two blocks in the distance, the street curved sharply; where it turned, the embankment terminated and there was a sheer unprotected drop into the river.

Two thoughts, born of desperation and an acquaintanceship with Hopalong Cassidy and screen versions of *The Three Musketeers*, popped into his head. He peered ahead—*yes!* Just before the turn there was a custom-house with empty flagpole jutting from the second-story . . .

He sprang forward onto the traces and grabbed the link-pin with the handle of the umbrella. Fillmore seized the shaft of the bumbershoot and hauled up until the pin was almost free. He stood up, balancing wobbily, squinting to gauge the correct angle and distance, waiting for the vital precise second.

"*Now!*"

Jumping as high as he could, he latched onto the flagpole with one hand, at the same time tugging on the umbrella so the link-pin disengaged. The carriage-top smartly smacked his ankle and, with a tremendous effort, Fillmore hooked the umbrella over his other arm and got a second purchase on the pole with his left hand. The carriage rumbled past beneath him. A bolt of pain struck his shoulder, but he endured it, watching with grim approval the event happening in the street below.

The cab lost speed and the steed, no longer shackled to it, pulled on ahead. It negotiated the bend,

but the carriage lumbered straight to the edge, tee-
tered for a fraction of a second, then plummeted into
the icy Thames with a colossal splash.

"And that," Fillmore observed with satisfaction, "is
the last anyone will see of Mr. A. I. Persano!"

His pleasure was short-lived. Now that the immediate danger was over, it occurred to him that he hadn't
the foggiest idea of how to get down from the flagpole without breaking his neck. (He'd never caught
up with any Harold Lloyd films.) But it didn't take
him long to devise a course of action.

"*Help!*" Fillmore shouted. "*Get me the hell off of
here!*"

CHAPTER SIX

Sacker shook his head incredulously. "That is the strangest story I have ever heard, sir. Either you are up to something nefarious, or you are mad."

"I tell you that I am not lying!" Fillmore protested. "Would I mention Professor Moriarty if I were part of his gang?"

The argument had been going on for several minutes, and the professor was beginning to despair of ever convincing the good doctor that he was anything but a raving lunatic. Had it not been for his shoulder wound, Sacker probably would not have permitted him entry into Sherrinford Holmes' flat, half convinced as he was that Fillmore was indirectly responsible for Mrs. Bardell's murder.

The doctor shook his head slowly. "You come to me with wild tales about dimensional transfers—whatever that means—and worlds where I only exist in an unpublished manuscript and Holmes is not Holmes! The least marvelous portion of your romance is that which you claim happened this morning: runaway Hansoms, customs-clerks hauling you off flagpoles, brickbats and dead policemen! Surely, sir, you do not find it marvelous that I have some difficulty swallowing all this?"

Fillmore nodded wearily. It had been a most exhausting day, and his bandaged shoulder still throbbed dully. The night was drawing on and he wanted nothing more dramatic than sleep. But duty was duty, in whatever world he inhabited. If the Moriarty gang were so bent on attaining the umbrella, it could only follow that the infamous professor had some awful scheme in mind.

But Sacker was adamant. "Holmes only mentioned this pedagogue of yours once, and that recently. Whatever he did, I do not know. For Holmes only alluded to him on that one occasion at the time of his disappearance."

"*His disappearance?!*"

Sacker nodded. "Yes. I *do* recall Holmes' relief. *And* his perplexity. One day, he said, Moriarty was in London, the next he was nowhere on the face of the earth. 'And good riddance, Sacker!' he remarked, and there was an end of the conversation. I never heard Moriarty's name again until you brought it up tonight."

"Well, well," Fillmore said impatiently, "whatever may be the status of the professor, he has a strong and wicked organization which still carries on his works. It must be quashed. And since its lieutenants know about my umbrella, it is imperative that I speak to Sherrinford Holmes immediately!"

"Well, as for that," Sacker suggested, "I suppose you could come along with me tonight. Holmes has communicated from Cloisterham, where that business is all but wrapped up. He needs some final service pertaining to one Mr. Sapsea, and I am to perform it." Sacker chuckled. "Holmes rarely asks me to tackle anything histrionic. It must be a goose, indeed, to whom I must play the poker!"

Fillmore's brows knit. It sounded familiar . . . ah, yes, the "Sapsea" fragment found in Dickens' study after his death, an enigmatic portion of the *Edwin Drood* manuscript that remained unpublished for many years. The rough-draft aspect of the present world still held. It occurred to the scholar that in a place comprised of unfinished or half-polished literary concepts, it might not be *possible* to complete a sequence and get free. He nervously tapped his finger against the curved grip of the umbrella and tried to follow the thought, but Sacker spoke again.

"I must ask you not to interfere with the progress of the case, or attempt to communicate with Holmes until he gives me leave to bring you forward. If you can agree to that, then you may accompany me on the 10:40 out of Charing Cross."

"Very well," Fillmore replied reluctantly. "But perhaps I might be able to give you a note to pass on to Holmes when we arrive. Time *may* be of the essence!"

The doctor nodded. "And now, since we can do nothing until it is time to entrain, I suggest we follow my friend's habit of tabling all talk of hypothetical crises until we have detabled. I will send round for an amiable Bordeaux and ask Mrs. Raddle, our new landlady, to set out supper. Does that seem agreeable?"

"Oh, of course," Fillmore concurred, dimly wondering where he'd heard of Mrs. Raddle before. "I take it you have decided not to regard me as an imminent threat."

"Well, sir," Sacker chuckled, "I must admit that is an odd angle for a man to shoot himself as a piece of corroborative evidence. I still cannot accept the wild history you related, but if you are mad, sir, at least it is an engaging malady. Besides, I detect a man of learning in you, and a scholar is by no means the worst of dinner companions."

Fillmore thanked the doctor for his courtesy and

mentally noted that Sacker/Watson certainly matched the old Holmesian observation (was it first made by Christopher Morley?) that a man might be honored to meet the Great Detective, but it would be Watson with whom a wintry evening, a cold supper and brandy would be most enjoyed.

While the good physician stepped downstairs to talk to Mrs. Raddle (she's in *Pickwick Papers*, too, isn't she?), Fillmore busied himself looking about the drawingroom/library. It was easy to tell which portion of the bookshelves belonged to Holmes and which to Sacker. One half, or better, was cramful of standard references and albums of clippings of criminous activity. The other side of the room was devoted to a broad assortment of escape literature—tales of early English battles, ghost stories, high romance on the seas, an occasional sampler of sentimental poetry and (perhaps in deference to Holmes' profession) a tattered copy of the lurid *Newgate Calendar*, a volume destined for ignominy in another world.

Sacker had one book open on a table by his easychair and the professor walked over to inspect what it was. "Ah! A man of similar tastes in fantasy," he murmured. "Benson's *The Room in the Tower* and other ghastly tales." He turned the book around and flipped through it, holding Sacker's place. The doctor evidently had just begun reading a short story, "Caterpillars." Fillmore remembered it with a shudder.

The doctor reentered the room and made a courteous remark concerning escapist literature, the likes of which Fillmore held in his hand. "Yes, yes, the Bensons *are* rather a dynasty," Sacker agreed. "I have another one, by Edward's brother, Robert Hugh. *The Mirror of Shallot*. Odd. Excellent."

Fillmore checked himself. He had been about to

comment on the finding of the identical volume years later on the day he purchased the umbrella, but it occurred to him that the doctor would regard the assertion as further evidence that his wits weren't all in working order.

Supper was sumptuous, if simple fare. A roast beef, rare and huge. A brace of game. Trifle, coffee and brandy. The only disappointment was the Bordeaux, which was temporarily out of stock. In apology, Mrs. Raddle sent up a cherished tawny port, which Sacker set aside for post-dessert, if the professor so desired. The doctor clearly had no enthusiasm for the stuff. Fillmore, however, had not dined well since sharing supper with Mr. Pickwick, and he availed himself of all there was to be had, including the landlady's prize port, the effect of which was to lull him into a much-needed sleep.

He awoke with a start. It was dark in the room, and there wasn't a sound. He reached out, encountered a night-stand with a box of matches on it. He fumbled for one, lit it, noted the box to be one of those cheap cardboard pillboxes into which matches had been crammed. Perhaps it belonged to Holmes; it sounded like his brand of freeform adaptation, persian slippers used to hold shag tobacco, knives stuck to the mantel to fix correspondence in place . . .

There was a lamp nearby. Fillmore lit it and turned up the key so he could better determine what surroundings he had. It was a small bed-chamber, plain, with a wardrobe and a low table with mirror behind it where Holmes assuredly put on his disguises. There was a piece of paper affixed to the mirror in a place where Fillmore could not help but notice. He rose and took the lamp with him so he could read what was written thereon.

"My dear Fillmore," it said, "I had no idea your injury so exhausted you. It was impossible to rouse you, and considering this as a physician, I am not so sure it will be wise for you to spend the better part of the night on a drafty railway train. Your resistance is low and you may do yourself an injury by coming, susceptible as you may be to sundry ills and fevers. I have put you in Holmes' bed, mine being uncharacteristically untidy and his having had the benefits of Mrs. Raddle's ministrations, and am off to catch the 10:40. If you do not sleep the night, you may wish to read; I will leave the drawing-room lights on for you. You are, of course, welcome to whatever fare you can find, and you may also use my toilet articles, shaving brush, etc. We shall return in a few days. If you feel the urgent need to see Holmes as soon as possible, you may, of course, join us in Cloisterham. The decision is yours. But, pertaining to the dangers you rehearsed, I must say, on your behalf, that a hasty perusal of Holmes' files shows that there is indeed in London one "Is. Persano," an athlete, duellist and singlestick competitor of awesome accomplishment. His card is checked in red ink, which Holmes employs for particularly dangerous criminals. If this is the same individual whom you claim to have dogged you, it may be wisest to stay at Baker Street and do not set foot out-of-doors until we get back. But I must not miss the train.

Farewell. O.S."

Fillmore was too drowsy to clear his head and recall the reference that was bumping about in the back of his brain. He still felt logy. Rubbing his eyes, yawning, he walked to the door connecting with the drawingroom/library. At least sleep had refreshed his memory on the matter of Mrs. Raddle. She was Bob Sawyer's landlady in Dickens, and a contributory vexation to Mr. Pickwick. A low, spiteful shrew who might do anything for money.

Roused from sleep, Fillmore's appetite had also returned. He wondered whether any of the beef was still left, or if it was all put away.

And what about the umbrella?

Certainly Sacker would have left it behind, yet Fillmore experienced a few qualms until he opened the door and saw the instrument propped in the same corner where he'd left it. That was reassuring; even more so was the sight of the unconsumed food still waiting, covered, on the table.

"The benevolent Dr. Sacker-alias-Watson," Fillmore beamed, stepping forward to lift the cover on the plate of beef. And then his warm sense of well-being plummeted and died.

There was a man seated in the doctor's easy chair by the fireside, a book on his lap; he was reading intently.

"By all means, sit and eat," Persano invited. "I have a few pages yet to go."

The man with the sliced nose did not even deign to look at Fillmore. He seemed possessed by the Benson volume in his hands.

Fillmore dashed over to the umbrella, and got a grip on it. He pushed aside the drapery that encloaked the left front window. The street outside was empty.

Should I smash through the glass, make a bit of a vault into the street? But a thought occurred to him concerning air-guns. He peered at the dark edifice directly opposite. A sudden glint of reflected light shone and was instantly gone, but it was enough to inform Fillmore that someone lurked behind one of the windows of Camden House, which must be the empty home across Baker Street from #221. (It was in Camden House that Colonel Moran lurked when he attempted to assassinate Sherlock in "The Adventure of the Empty House.")

There was no point in trying a dash for it. Unless there was a back way, Fillmore was trapped with Persano.

"In case you are in a gymnastic mood," Persano remarked, "allow me to advise you that the house is entirely surrounded. Now pray wait a moment longer. I have but a single page to complete."

Fillmore stood rooted to the spot, his appetite gone, waiting for the villainous Persano to come to the end of the tale in which he was engrossed.

Persano perceptibly shuddered as he closed the book. "That was indeed a horror!" he remarked. "I have always been a devotee of the fantastic. Are you familar with the genre?"

Fillmore said nothing.

"Oh, come," said the other, "the mere matter of the umbrella and your inevitable demise can surely wait. There is nothing more soothing in this world than to contemplate something truly dreadful, such as Benson's 'Caterpillars,' and then come safely back to this mundane world where the only atrocities are the humdrum stuff of daily business. The tale is not up to 'The Room in the Tower,' but then, what is? Still, the idea of ghastly crab-like caterpillars, giant ghostly creatures and their miniature daylight counterparts that scuttle about with their excrescent bodies and infect those that they bite with cancer—such is no ordinary *cauchemar*. It almost makes the idea of ordinary death-by-violence drab and comfortable."

Persano flashed his mirthless smile at Fillmore. Then, in a leisurely fashion, he extracted a thin cigar, bit off the end, spat it and requested a light from the scholar. Numbly, Fillmore tossed the pillbox to the other, who caught it, took out a match, struck it and lit the cigar.

Persano regarded the matchbox momentarily. "A box like this figures in the tale. Do you know it? An artist captures a miniature crab-like caterpillar and keeps it in the box until he changes his mind and treads on the insect, which seals his doom." His shoulders went up and he shivered in fear. "I believe if I found such a creature in this box, my mind would snap. I have seen the ravages of the disease." He regarded his cigar with melancholy dissatisfaction. "That is the curse of all earthly endeavor, is it not? We bargain and bully and bludgeon for our own ends, but in no wise can we crush the microbes that infest us from within. I should *hope* I should go mad and do terminal injury to myself rather than undergo such a horror as I once witnessed and have just read about." He regarded the professor darkly, then his wicked smile reappeared. "But I wax melancholy. Shall we proceed to brighter matters?"

"How did you get in?" Fillmore asked hoarsely.

"Ah, that's the spirit! Ask questions, buy time, my friend. Since you ask, The Raddle's holdings were recently purchased by our interests and we set her up here after the death of Mrs. Bardell. She was instructed to inform us if anyone of your description and peculiar appurtenances—(he indicated the umbrella)—should appear to Dr. Sacker. I presume that you are an agent of Holmes, after all, in which case the dear boy is grown uncommon careless."

"I thought you'd drowned," Fillmore accused sullenly.

"Sorry for the disappointment. But be assured, sir, I hold no grudge for your maneuver. It was cleverly executed. But I am no mean swimmer. And as for tracking you down again, our system of surveillance is so thorough that you would have been found out in any event within a mere matter of hours. I confess, though, I did suspect this is where you would probably go. The only thing that at all bothered me was the possibility that the umbrella might function once more. But it does not appear to be in any hurry to remove you from this unlucky world, does it?"

"One must finish a sequence," Fillmore grumbled.

"I beg your pardon?"

The scholar briefly explained the necessity of participating in some basic block of action correspondent to the base literary form of the cosmos in which one was deposited by the parasol.

Persano nodded. "I see. That explains why the Professor has not yet returned. But what a deuced unpleasant condition! Imagine, for instance, ending up in Stoker's Hungaria and having no other way out but to combat Count Dracula. A horror, this umbrella, if one were carried by it into a world of night."

"Yes," Fillmore observed, stalling for time, "but no one who knows how it works would deliberately choose such a place."

"Well, no matter," Persano said, extinguishing his cigar, "the time has come to terminate this disagreeable matter. You will give me the umbrella."

"I will not!"

Weariness etched lines on Persano's face as he contemplated a struggle. "Come, come, man, bow to the inevitable. You cannot escape, and you know it perfectly well. Moran has a bead drawn on the front of the house and there are thugs in front and back." He consulted a pocket-watch. "It lacks two or three minutes of midnight. My men have been told to wait until twelve. If I haven't returned by then with the umbrella, they are to forcibly enter and destroy you on sight. I'm afraid they would be rather messy about it."

Persano rose, picked up his cane, which had been resting on the floor, and withdrew the sword from its innermost depths. "Permit me to dispatch you swiftly and mercifully, while there is still time. It is the least I can do for so innovative and tenacious an opponent."

"*Have at you, then!*" Fillmore shouted, suddenly lofting the umbrella. Swinging it in both hands, he swept it at Presano in the manner of an antique broad-sword.

Persano appeared rather disappointed in Fillmore as he dodged the blow. "As a gentleman, I waited until you woke. Perhaps, after all, I should have slain you in your sleep." He parried an umbrella-swash with a neat turn of the wrist. "Didn't you read Sacker's message? I am expert at this. Your form is barely passable academy, and rusty at that."

Fillmore, not wasting energy replying, panted and puffed as he tried to hack Persano to pieces. But the other met each attack with easy indifference, not deigning to attempt to get under Fillmore's guard with his own stroke.

When, at last, the scholar collapsed, breathless, back against the wall, Persano clucked dolefully. "You expend precious time needlessly. There is but a scant

minute ere the clock chimes twelve, and then there will be tedious butchery. For the love of order, sir, I entreat you to accept an easy death!"

Fillmore lowered the umbrella. "Well, then," he gasped, still winded, "I suppose I must recognize the inevitability of my mortality. But it's hard." He nodded for the stroke that would end his life.

Persano reached across the table and, seizing the tawny port, poured a measure into a wine-glass. He approached Fillmore, sword in one hand, the glass in the other. He held out the wine for the professor to take. "Drink this. It contains a potent sleeping-draught. When the doctor called for Bordeaux, The Raddle, following my instructions, brought this instead. It works quickly. I will withhold the *coup de grâce* until you slumber."

Fillmore took the wine. The clock began to chime midnight as he raised the glass to his lips . . .

No!

The instinct for survival was too strong. He tried to dash the liquor into Persano's eyes, but the villain, half-expecting the gesture, ducked; the wine spattered his shirt. Persano's hand shot out. He grabbed the umbrella and wrenched it around, but Fillmore desperately resisted.

The two struggled fiercely, silently. But the exertions of the day were too much for Fillmore and he finally collapsed beneath the weight and superior strength of the other. Persano, pulled off balance, toppled onto his opponent, but even as he did, he jammed his elbow against Fillmore's throat.

"Yo *do* believe in last-minute heroics! You can't say I didn't try to bring you a painless death."

He stood up, planting a foot hard against Fillmore's chest, pinioning him. A pounding noise at the street door. The landlady shot the bolt. Coarse voices, the sound of many feet pounding up the stairs.

"My men," said Persano, mildly regretful. "Farewell." He poised the sword in the air, ready to plunge it into Fillmore's throat.

The scholar braced himself. A wave of hatred for Persano supplanted what fear he might have felt. He clutched the umbrella, wishing he could wield it one more time. His thumb brushed against the release-catch.

The tip of the sword started down for Fillmore's jugular. But as it did, something unexpected happened.

The umbrella snapped open with a click.

CHAPTER SEVEN

There were dark, rolling clouds overhead, and in the air the heavy, oppressive sense of thunder. Slowly the darkness fell, and as it did, Fillmore felt a strange chill overtake him, and a lonely feeling.

Of Persano, there was no trace. He'd fallen off somewhere during the flight of the umbrella, his sword flailing wildly as he fell, screaming, to whichever earth Fillmore's distracted imagination dictated.

A dog began to howl in a farmhouse somewhere far down the road—a long, agonized wailing, as if from fear. The sound was taken up by another dog, and then another and another, till, borne on the wind which sighed along the dark and lonely mountain road, a cacophony of howling tormented his ears. In the sound, too, there was a deeper chuckling menace—that of wolves.

An arch of trees hemmed in the road, which became a kind of tunnel leading somewhere that he dreaded to contemplate. But there was no use trying to avoid a sequence, that was one fact he'd finally learned. The professor trudged on in the darkness, shivering at the icy air of the heights. The trees were soon replaced by great frowning rocks on both sides; the rising wind moaned and whistled through them and it grew colder and colder still. Fine powdery snow began to fall, driving against his pinched face, settling in his eyebrows and on the rims of his ears.

The baying of the wolves sounded nearer and nearer. Off a ways to the left, Fillmore thought he could discern faint flickering blue flames, ghost-lights that beckoned to him, but he fearfully ignored them.

How long he trod the awful lightless road, he could not tell. The rolling clouds obscured the moon and he could not read the crystal of his watch, nor could he strike a match. Persano had never returned them.

The path kept ascending, with occasional short downward respites. Suddenly the road emerged from the rock-tunnel and led across a broad, high expanse into the courtyard of a vast ruined castle, from whose tall black casements no light shone. Against the moon-lit sky, Fillmore studied the jagged line of broken battlements and knew instinctively where he was.

A bit worse than Persano, he mused, approaching the great main door, old and studded with large iron nails, set in a projecting arch of massive stone. There was no bell or knocker, but he had no doubt that soon the tenant would sense his presence and admit him.

Perhaps it would be better to flee. But he did not relish the thought of another minute on the freezing road with the wolves constantly drawing nearer. True, he'd heard them to be much maligned animals, gentle and shy, but somehow he found it hard to believe at that moment.

The occupant of the castle was fiercer than wolves, but Fillmore guessed it was his destiny to meet him, and if so, it would be better to do so face to face rather than hide and wait for *him* to seek Fillmore out.

The matter was settled when he heard a heavy step approaching behind the door. A gleam of light appeared through the chinks. Chains rattled, huge bolts clanged back, a key turned in a seldom-used lock and the rusty metal noisily protested. But at last, the portal swung wide.

An old man stood there, clean shaven but for a white mustache, dressed in black from head to toe. He held an old silver lamp in his hand; it threw flickering shadows everywhere. He spoke in excellent English, tinged, however, with the dark coloration of a middle-European accent.

"I bid you welcome. Enter freely and of your own will." He did not move. But neither did Fillmore. A frown creased the old man's brow. He spoke again. "Welcome to my house. Come freely. Go safely; and leave something of the happiness you bring!"

A bit better, Fillmore thought, stepping across the threshold. As he did, the host grasped his hand in a cold grip strong enough to make him wince.

Fillmore started to speak, but the tall nobleman held up his hand for silence until the howling of the wolves died away.

"Listen to them," he beamed. "Children of the night! What music they make!"

Damn Persano! Fillmore swore to himself. *I'm right! He* would *have to put such a notion into my head just before the umbrella opened!*

He followed his host upstairs. En route, he had to tear a passage through a gigantic spider-web.

The tall man smiled, and Fillmore knew what he was about to say. "The spider—" he began, but the professor finished it for him.

"—spinning his web for the unwary fly. For the blood is the life, eh?"

The Count frowned. "How did you know what was in my mind?"

Fillmore shrugged. "Bit of a fey quality, I fancy."

Some five hundred miles distant from the castle is a town, Sestri di Levante, situated on the Italian Riviera. Near it stands the Villa Cascana on a high promontory overlooking the iridescent blue of the Ligurian Sea.

It was the latter part of a glorious afternoon in spring. The sun sparkled on the water, dazzling the eye so the place where the chestnut forest above the villa gave way to pines could not easily be discerned.

A *loggia* ran about the pleasant house, and outside a gravel path threaded past a fountain of Cupid through a riot of magnolias and roses. In the middle of the garden there suddenly appeared a stranger, walking with a cane. He seemed bewildered.

"I've lost him temporarily," Persano murmured. "But he must be in this world, and if he is, I'll find him and finish him at last. Then I'll take the umbrella and go home. Meantime, there are far less pleasant places where I might have ended up."

He gazed about, noting with pleasure the marble fountain playing merrily nearby. He drank in the salty freshness of the sea-wind and decided it would be a good place to sit and devise a scheme of action. Persano strolled the gravel-path and stopped at a bench near the Cupid fountain. He sat down and lit a cigar with the last match remaining in the pillbox he'd secured from Fillmore. He tossed away the empty box. It arced high and landed in the fountain.

Overhead, a bird twitted in the chestnuts. Someone seated in the villa—spying Persano and wondering who he was—hailed the stranger, but the shouted greeting received no answer. Persano was staring at the pillbox bobbing on the surface of the water. An awful presentiment overtook him, and the blood drained from his face.

Slowly, reluctantly, step by step, he dragged himself to the fountain and stared, horrified, at the floating pillbox, which had landed open, like a miniature boat braving the crests of the fountain freshet.

A small caterpillar crawled into the cardboard box and scuttled this way and that. It was most unusual in color and loathsome in appearance: gray-yellow with lumps and excrescences on its rings, and an opening on one end that aspirated like a mouth. Its feet resembled the claws of a crab.

Persano's eyes bulged as the creature, sensing his presence, began to wriggle out of the box and swim in his direction . . .

"I admit you are an unusual visitor," said Dracula. "An interesting fellow, if that is the slang these days. Try some of this wine. It is very old."

"No, thank you," Fillmore demurred, having had his fill of soporifics-in-disguise. "I must say that you are an excellent host. The chicken was excellent, if thirsty."

"Perhaps you would prefer beer?" the vampire asked, anxious to please.

"If I can open the bottle myself."

Dracula shook his head. "You do me wrong. There are ancient customs which no host may defy, even if he be—how do the peasants call it?—*nosferatu!*"

"Yes, but I seem to recall the case of one Jonathan Harker—"

"Harker?" Dracula echoed surprised. "How do you

know him?" He is at this moment on the way from England to conduct some business for me."

"And you have no intention of letting him leave here *not* undead," Fillmore accused Dracula.

"You wrong me, young sir. When the formula I repeated below is stated by a host and a nobleman, it dare not be violated. *I* will do nothing to prevent Harker's departure."

"Except lock the doors and ring the castle with wolves," Fillmore countered sarcastically.

The vampire shrugged. "If I did not lock the doors, the wolves might get in . . ."

"Well, at any rate, you can see why I do not trust your wine."

"Yes," Dracula nodded, "you seem totally cognizant of my identity, nature and intentions. But knowing all this, why would you enter here of your own free will?"

"Well, it's a long story."

Dracula smiled icily. "I have until sun-up."

So Fillmore told the story of the umbrella yet again, omitting only the references to Mrs. Bardell's cut throat and the near-skewering of his own jugular by Presano . . . details that he was afraid might disagreeably excite the Count.

"Hah! Can such things be?" the vampire mused once the tale was done. His piercing eyes shone with an unholy crimson light. "Long ago, what arcane researches I carried on, seeking things beyond the mundane world in which I felt trapped. And the things I discovered only proved a far worse incarceration for me. But this—this umbrella—what opportunity lies within its mystic compass!"

Fillmore began to grow uneasy. He'd spun out the

history till close to daybreak, figuring that the coming
dawn would enable him to escape while Dracula
slept. Even more to the point, he mentally punned, he
might be able to rid the place of the vampire with a
stroke of the point of his umbrella and, in such wise,
complete the sequence and get out of this world of
horror into which his fight with Persano unluckily
plunged him.

It escaped him until that moment that Dracula
might look on the parasol as a far greater tool for
spreading the brood of the devil than the original plan
he'd devised to purchase Carfax Abbey from John
Harker and move to England and its teeming millions.
But how could London compare with the available
necks of countless billions in worlds without number?

Fillmore stole a nervous glance towards the case-
ment, hoping that dawn might shine through it soon.
By no means could he allow the umbrella to fall into
Dracula's hands!

"The night is nearly ended," the caped nobleman
said, rising. His eyes fixed Fillmore's in an hypnotic
stare. "I must sleep the day. Let me show you your
room."

"The octagonal one, I know. Never mind, I'll find
it." Fillmore strode across the large chamber and
opened the door to his bed-chamber. It was just
where Stoker said it would be. At the door, he paused
and fixed the vampire with a stern gaze that he hoped
would command respect.

"I depend on you, Count, to be as good as your
word. A vampire may lie—but a nobleman, never."

"We understand each other perfectly well," Dracula
smiled, bowing his head gravely. "I have given my
word, and I will repeat it. No harm to you shall come
from *me*."

And he strode from the room, slamming the door shut behind him. Fillmore hurried to the portal and tried it, but it was securely locked.

The professor was worried. Dracula could not be trusted, and yet he had given his word as a patrician. Could he go against it, evil though he was? Fillmore did not think so.

He walked back to his room and stretched out on the bed, exhausted from the perils of the umbrella's flight and the terrible walk through the Carpathian forest. He began to sink into a delicious lassitude.

No, no, no, no, no, no! his mind repeated over and over, a still, small voice protesting a fact out of joint, a snag in logic, an unforeseen menace . . .

"I have given my word, and I will repeat it. No harm to you shall come from me."

Dracula did not say Fillmore would be unharmed. He said *he* would not *personally* hurt him.

Fillmore tried to get up, but his limbs were leaden. Above him, not far away, a dancing swirl of dust-motes pirouetted in a beam of moonlight. In the middle of the mist shone two mocking golden eyes, like those of an animal.

He tried to groan, but no sound emerged. He had forgotten Dracula's three undead mistresses who lived (?) with him in the vaults beneath the castle.

The fairest and most favored of the three was in the coffin-shaped room with Fillmore, baring her teeth for the inevitable bite.

He fell into a merciful swoon.

CHAPTER EIGHT

Some days, it is nigh onto impossible to get out of bed. The body, filled with a not altogether unpleasant lassitude, refuses to function. Too weak to protest, the mind feebly struggles to rouse the limbs, but to no avail, so weak is the will, so sapped the corporeal being. Easier to capitulate, to drift in that half-state between slumber and waking.

And so Fillmore remained in a condition of wan enthrallment for the greater part of the day. Only as the autumnal gloom began to draw in, signaling the approach of evening, did his torpid brain make an effort to gather in those wandering fantasies which possessed it and pack them away. Very deep within, clawing at the prison-door of consciousness, a voice urged him to wake.

He pushed himself up unwillingly and sat on the edge of the soft bed, head dangling, trying to recollect where he was.

A wolf greeted the oncoming sunset.

With a start, he sat bolt upright, remembering everything. He peered across the room with nervous dread, but to his surprise, the umbrella was still there. Getting to his feet, swaying from unexpected weakness, he lurched over to it and tried pressing the catch, but, as he anticipated, it did not open. He turned this way and that, seeking a mirror, finally recalling that Dracula did not keep any such reminders of his vampiric status about the house.

When Fillmore put a hand to his neck, he knew he needed no glass to confirm what his fingers felt. He winced at the two tender spots, the tiny punctures that still felt tacky.

Luckily, according to Bram Stoker, vampires rarely finish off a victim in one night. But Fillmore felt so enervated that he very much doubted whether he could survive a second attack.

And the sun was going down.

He ran to the large casement in the dining-room and stared out. The castle was built on a rocky precipice. The valley, spread out far below and threaded with raging torrents, was such a great distance straight down that if he fell, only a parachute could save him.

But how did Harker escape in *Dracula?* He emulated the Count, creeping from rugged stone to stone, crawling down the side of the castle like a great lizard to the courtyard underneath. But the drop was sheer, with no apparent footholds or niches for the hands to grasp. Nor was there a courtyard; only cruel and jagged rocks . . .

He ran to his room and pushed open the narrow aperture. The same vista—exit was impossible from either window!

Then how did Harker scale the walls? He beat his fists against his temples, thinking, thinking. He remembered that, in the novel, the solicitor walked out the dining-room door into the corridor and explored the vast pile. Somewhere on the castle's south side must be the window that permitted access to the lower floors and the courtyard.

But the door to the corridor was locked.

Fillmore tore about like a madman, trying the door at the end opposite the octagonal room, but it, too, was locked. He set his back to the main door and bumped it, but the only thing that gave was his back.

Darting to the window a second time, he watched in fascinated horror as the sun dipped beneath the ridges and crests of the mountains. Only a thin slice of the golden rim remained on the horizon.

Figure another five or six minutes worth of sunlight, and perhaps an equal time of after-light. Another minute for the vampires to rouse themselves and come up here. Then, at the most generous estimate, I have an unlucky thirteen minutes to—

"Well, say it!" he snapped at himself, aloud. "To save myself from a fate worse than death. Literally."

The teacher sat upon the edge of his bed and applied his mind to his predicament. Panic would accomplish nothing, he realized, so he might as well employ the residue of time in seeing whether there were any way out at all.

A chorus of wolves shivered on the rising wind.

He shuddered.

"There's enough of that, damn it!" he told himself. "It's about time I stopped behaving like a victim everywhere I fly to. Let's see now: can't get out the doors, windows are too high up, no way to safely climb down the wall. I'd probably dash my brains out, anyway, even if I tried it."

And then a new and startling notion flashed into his mind. He jumped to his feet and nervously paced the room.

"No time to follow it all up," he declaimed aloud like the actor he once aspired to be, "but some of it *must* be scanned! Is there an alternative reason? Quick—work out a chain of logic!"

He ticked off propositions on his fingertips. "*One:* a sequence has to be completed wherever one goes with the umbrella. *Two:* I am no longer in the Holmesian rough-draft world. *Hence:* I completed the sequence there. But how? Some of the literary works on which that place is based were unfinished in *my* original earth. Could it be that my adventure with Persano stopped just because it isn't over?!"

Fillmore shook his head. "Too many paradoxes. *The Pickwick Papers* was completed by Dickens, and that was—is—a part of Persano's world. So events cannot be dictated by literature that I know, at least not entirely. Which is confusing, but forget philosophy for now; ask Holmes, if I live to meet him!" He put the issue behind him with a flourish of one hand, a gesture he often used when confronting an adamantly incorrect student. "The vital question now is—*why did the umbrella open?*"

Only one answer fit. When Persano aimed his sword at Fillmore's throat, the scholar's life in that world was, for all practical purposes, terminated. Therefore, the sequence had to be at an end, and the umbrella finally worked.

Therefore, in a world of horror, where there are victims galore, all one must do to escape is . . . die.

He certainly hoped he was right.

Picking up the umbrella, Fillmore strode purposefully to the window and tried opening it. But the rusty latch would not budge. He spied an immense pewter candelabra, seized it and hurled the thing forcibly. It bumped the glass and clattered to the floor.

"*Hell!*" Exasperated, he stuck his face against the

window and saw that it was doubly thick. He also perceived that the last sliver of sun was gone and the after-light was fading swiftly.

Then, from far below in the very bowels of the castle, he heard a metallic grating noise, followed by an iron thunderous clang, like a great door slammed open. Desperately he wrestled with one of the Count's chairs. It was incredibly heavy, and took a tremendous effort of the will for him to loft it at all, let alone swing it. But swing it he did, and the window shattered most gratifyingly. The massive piece of furniture tumbled after the raining shards down, down into the depths of the valley.

Fillmore scrambled onto the window-seat, umbrella in hand, thumb on the catch. Gazing out at the panoramic vista, he felt queasy. Heights terrified him. If he were wrong, and the umbrella did not open, he would be crushed on the rocks and then—since he had been bitten by the vampire-woman—he might have to join the legions of the undead.

There was the sound of a heavy tread in the corridor outside. Screwing up his courage, Fillmore forced himself to look out at the landscape and conquer his fear of falling. He saw the valley cloaked in shadow, and very far off, the glint of rushing water, a distant cataract.

The cataract strong then—

"NO!" he admonished himself. "No other literature this time, just Sherlock Holmes!"

—cataract strong then plunges along—

"Sherlock Holmes!"

—striking and raging as if a war waging—

"Sherlock Holmes, Sherlock Holmes, Sherlock Holmes!"

—its caverns and rocks among—

"SHERLOCK HOLMES!" Fillmore shouted, jumping out the window.

Behind him, in the room, the doors flung wide. The blond fiend raced to the window, snarling.

"Gone!" she howled, turning to accuse her mate. "How did you dare permit this? You might have taken the umbrella while he slept!"

The Count, entering with a swirl of his cape, coldly replied, "I pledged my word I would not harm him. I may be a vampire, but I am a Nobleman first, and a *boyar* does not break his word." In truth, Dracula had realized that transporting fifty boxes of native soil across the dimensions would be a grueling project. London was quite good enough . . .

The woman told him precisely what she thought of his aristocratic airs. "Your precious blue blood," she snapped spitefully, "is tainted with the plasma of the lowest village peasants."

"And yours isn't?" he sneered, staring haughtily down his long aquiline nose at her.

"The least you could have done would have been to hide the thing so I could have supped again!"

"As for that," said Dracula, waving his hand with grand disdain, "you are already more plump than is seemly."

"*Plump?!*" she screamed. "You told me that's the way you like me best!"

The matter proceeded through a great many more exchanges and retorts, but it is perhaps indelicate to dwell at length on the secrets of patrician domestic life, and so it were good to draw the present chapter to a close.

CHAPTER NINE

Fillmore wanted to throw up, but he was too terrified to move. Below, the ferocious cataract raged. A needle-spritz of foam slashed up through the curtain of mist created by the falls, occasionally spattering droplets on his face. The long sweep of green water whirled and clamoured, producing a kind of half-human shout which boomed out of the abyss with the spray.

"Miserable damned umbrella!" he grumbled. "I said 'Sherlock Holmes' time and again—NOT *The Cataract of Lodore!*"

The shelf on which the umbrella deposited him was barely big enough for his posterior. Fortunately, it (the shelf) was cut high and deep enough so he could arch his back against the black stone. There was just enough space to stand the umbrella upright next to him along the vertical axis of the niche, but otherwise there was no room to move or turn. Eventually, he supposed, he would either fall into the chasm or else figure a way to get down safely.

His feet dangled precariously over the edge. Below them, the cliff bellied out so he could not see straight down. But to the right, he spied a footpath that looked as if it ought to pass directly beneath his perch. Yet to the left there was a sheer drop into the torrent, so he could not be certain that the path extended all the way to the point just south of where he sat. If it did, he might be able to slide down the cliff-side and land on the narrow walkway. It looked about a yard wide, surely large enough to break the momentum of his fall.

But what if the path stopped before it got to where he was sitting? Then he'd plummet right down the mountain.

Well, sooner or later I'll have to risk it. Unless—.

Unless the umbrella had whisked him back to his own world, where Southey's cataract was situated. Sequence-rules did not seem to apply to one's home cosmos (or else the bumbershoot could not have operated in the first place, or so Fillmore reasoned).

He pushed the button half-heartedly. Nothing happened. He was still stuck on the meager rocky mantel.

He glanced above him and saw, too far to reach, a bigger niche, covered with soft green moss. He looked down and was seized by vertigo. He shut his eyes and shoved his back against the eroded cliff-wall, wishing he could sink inside it.

"Get hold of yourself! If you have to drop, you'd better be in full control of your muscles!" he told himself, wishing that he could somehow find a way to shut off the sound of the cascading flood—a strange, melancholy noise like lost souls lamenting in the deep recess of the pool into which the churning streams poured.

He tried to reestablish his equilibrium by turning his attention to the expanse of blue sky above him. The weather was mild and there was a pleasant breeze that he wished, all the same, would stop tugging and flapping his sleeve like insistent child-fingers begging him to come play in the rapids below.

There were few clouds and none obscured the sun which shone high and bright.

Gazing nervously into the heavens, squinting to minimize the glare, Fillmore suddenly opened his eyes wide in surprise. A fact popped into his head, something he'd read in the rubric to *The Cataract of Lodore* in the textbook he used to teach English Romantic Fiction.

"Tourists who make special jaunts to view the site which inspired Southey's famous exercise in onomatopoeia are generally disappointed because—"

Because why? How did the rest of the rubric read?

Before the thought could be brought to mind, Fillmore was distracted by the sound of approaching footsteps . . . a rapid, yet heavy tread.

He sighed with relief. *Maybe it'll be someone who can help me get down from here!*

The footsteps neared. Fillmore stared down at the footpath curving around the mountainside to his right. A long moment passed, during which the footfalls grew louder, but slowed to a walk. And then a man rounded the bend and emerged into the professor's angle of vision.

The newcomer was extremely tall and thin. Clean-shaven, with a great dome of forehead and eyes sunk deep in his skull, the stranger was pale and ascetic in cast. Chalk-dust clung to his sleeves; his shoulders were rounded and his head protruded forward as if he had spent too much time in closet study of abstruse intellectual problems.

Stopping in the middle of the narrow path, he peered with puckered, angry eyes at a place some steps in front of him. He spoke in an ironical tone of voice.

"Well, sir," he said, "as you are wont to quote, 'Journeys end in lovers meeting.'"

For a brief, disoriented second, Fillmore thought he himself was being addressed. Then there was a murmur from a spot directly beneath the ledge where he was dizzily balanced, and he realized that someone had been waiting all the while right under him, hidden by the bellying rock-swell that the mountainside described just below his feet.

"I warned you I would never stand in the dock," the tall man said in a dry, reprimanding voice. "Yet you have persevered in your attempts to bring justice upon my head."

The unseen man murmured a laconic reply.

"In truth," the other continued, "I doubted that you could so effectively quash the network of crime it took me so long to build up. But you have outstripped your potential, and I underestimated you, to my cost." As he spoke, his head was never still, but moved in a slow, oscillating pattern from side to side, like some cold-blooded reptile. "However," he went on, "you have also underestimated me. I said if you were clever enough to bring destruction on me, I would do the same for you. I do not make idle threats."

Another murmur Fillmore could not hear—more protracted this time—and then the tall one grimly nodded. "Yes, I will wait that long. He who stands on the brink of world's-end rarely objects to the delay of a second or two before time stops."

Crossing his arms patiently, he waited silently, staring fixedly at the person Fillmore could not see.

But by then, of course, the teacher knew the identity of both antagonists, seen and unseen. With the knowledge came the recollection of the forgotten detail pertaining to the cataract of Lodore.

"Tourists who make special jaunts to view the site which inspired Southey's famous exercise in onomatopoeia," said the rubric, "are generally disappointed because the falls dry up by the time they visit in summer. The Lodore falls are best seen in colder weather."

The sky and sun and the breeze told Fillmore it must be late spring. Therefore, the cascading waters below could not be Lodore.

It had to be Reichenbach Falls, instead.

Reichenbach Falls . . . scene of the dramatic final meeting between Sherlock Holmes and his archenemy, Professor Moriarty . . . perfectly logical, considering that Fillmore simultaneously thought of Holmes and a waterfall. The umbrella took him precisely where it had been told.

All the same, he mused grumpily, *it might have picked a less disagreeable ringside seat!*

And yet, for all his fearful giddiness, Fillmore felt a bit like an Olympian looking down on the petty squabbling of puny mortals. The analogy was furthered by the fact that he knew both what was taking place and that which was about to happen.

Right now, he thought, *Holmes is writing a farewell message to Watson. When he finishes it, he'll put it on top of a boulder close by and anchor the paper by placing his silver cigarette-case upon it.*

Fillmore had read "The Final Problem" several times. It was a bitter tale, the one in which Arthur Conan Doyle tried to kill off his famous detective; Fillmore often wondered what it must have been like to read it when it first appeared in print, not knowing that Holmes would be resurrected ten years later in "The Adventure of the Empty House." (Fillmore grinned to himself, thinking of the heresy his mind had just committed: referring to Conan Doyle as the author of the Holmes tales. "Are ye mad, man?" his pals at the local branch of the Baker Street Irregulars would say. "Watson wrote those *factual* accounts. Doyle was just the good Doctor's literary agent!")

Fillmore finally knew what he was going to do: simply wait until the adventure ran its course. Holmes would finish the message, rise and walk to the edge of the footpath. Moriarty, disdaining weaponry, would fling himself upon his enemy and the pair would struggle and tussle on the very edge of the falls. At the last, Holmes' superior knowledge of baritsu ("the Japanese system of wrestling, which has more than once been very useful to me") would win the day and Moriarty would take the horrible, fatal plunge alone. Then Fillmore could hail Holmes, who would surely help him to get down.

After that, I'll warn him that Colonel Moran is skulking about here someplace and—

And?

There was no point in making any other plans just yet. If Holmes were unable to rescue him from the awful ledge, there would be no future for J. Adrian (Blah!) Fillmore!

At that moment, Moriarty unfolded his arms.

"If the message is done, sir," he said, "then I presume we may proceed with this matter?"

A murmur and then footsteps.

He's walking to the end of the path. Now Moriarty will follow him and suddenly try to push Holmes off balance.

Moriarty did not move. A mirthless trace of humor tilted up the corner of his mouth.

Fillmore was suddenly seized by the chill premonition that something extremely unpleasant was about to take place.

"You surprise me at the last," the evil Professor remarked. "Had you expected some gentleman's Code of Honor, sir? My foolish lieutenant Persano might subscribe to such nonsense, but then again, he would be better suited physically to grapple with a man thoroughly skilled in singlestick. *And* baritsu."

"What!" It was the first time Fillmore heard the crisp voice beneath him.

"Come, come," said Moriarty, drawing a revolver out of his coat, "I keep files on my enemies, too, you know."

No! This is wrong! Fillmore was stunned. *This isn't how the story turns out!*

"I am vexed," Moriarty stated. "You have twice underestimated me, sir." He raised the pistol and aimed.

Fillmore had no time to wonder whether direct interference might change the texture of the world he was in—it was *already* different. He did not concern himself, either, with the dangers of subsumption or, for that matter, the more immediate risk that he might break his neck.

Transferring the umbrella to his right hand, he shoved himself off the perch with a yell to warn the detective below. As he descended, he flailed the umbrella in Moriarty's direction.

The Professor immediately raised his arm and snapped off a shot at Fillmore, but he was aiming at a moving target and the bullet ricocheted harmlessly off a boulder. Before he could fire a second time, Holmes grasped his arm in an iron grip and instantly afterwards, Fillmore landed on the path in a heap.

The arch-antagonists struggled violently scant

inches from the end of the walkway. Fillmore did his best to get out from underfoot, but elbows poked his ribs and feet trod his toes. He was an integral part of the *mêlée*.

The detective grunted. The criminal cursed. They swayed on the very lip of the precipice. Then Holmes unexpectedly and slickly slipped out of Moriarty's grip. The movement set the Professor off balance. With a cry of fear, he flailed, both hands clawing the air. One touched the grip of the umbrella and, instinctively, Moriarty clutched at it, wrenching it from Fillmore's grasp.

Forgetting all danger, Fillmore lurched forward and tried to get the umbrella back, but Moriarty, uttering one long terrified scream, pitched over backwards into the abyss.

Fillmore scrambled on his hands and knees to the edge and, with Holmes, watched the Napoleon of Crime falling, falling, the umbrella wildly waving. He vanished from view in the scintillating curtain of spray.

For a long while they watched, but they could not discern any movement in the maelstrom. Fillmore thought he could hear Moriarty's cry of terror eternally intermingled with the half-human roar of the falls.

Rousing themselves, they walked down the path a ways. Then the tall, thin man with the well-remembered face addressed Fillmore good-humoredly.

"In the past," he chuckled, "I have been skeptical of the workings of Providence, but nevermore shall I doubt the efficacy of a *deus ex machina,* no matter what guise it descends in!"

Fillmore would have replied but they were all at once interrupted by a barrage of rocks from above.

"That would be Colonel Moran," Fillmore remarked. "He's just about on schedule."

Holmes looked at him curiously but decided to forestall all questions until after they escaped from the assiduous administrations of Moriarty's sole surviving lieutenant.

CHAPTER TEN

Late that evening, two men sat drinking ale in a pothouse in Rosenlaui. For a long while, only one of them spoke, but at last, he ended his narrative.

"That is certainly the most singular history I have ever heard," said the other, taller one, signaling to the waiter for more brew. "It is more surprising to me than that awful business at Baskerville and, at least to you, quite as harrowing."

"And now," said Fillmore, "I suppose you are going to suggest I consult a specialist in obscure nervous diseases?"

"Not at all, old chap," the lean detective grinned. "There is an internal cohesion that I should be prompted to trust in, to begin with. But knowing all that I do about the late Professor Moriarty, your tale makes considerable sense."

"It *does?*"

"Moriarty himself prefigured the possibility of a dimensional-transfer engine in his brilliant paper on *The Dynamics of an Asteroid*. Not in so many words, you understand, but the concept was buried within if one had the comprehension and the philosophical tools to prize it forth. The Professor certainly foresaw the ramifications of his theory, at least in this interesting—and rather distressing—side-channel of his research. I shudder to think what might have happened had he manufactured enough of them to arm his entire army of villains! Criminal justice in England (perhaps in the entire cosmos, eventually) would be totally unworkable." Holmes tapped his fingers against the frosted stein which the waiter set down before him. "Of course, I suppose it would have then been up to me to devise a similar engine and make it available to society at large." He shook his head, smiling ruefully. "I wish you could have held onto it. I should have been most interested in examining it."

"I'm extremely disappointed myself," Fillmore said. "I came here specifically to ask you about the umbrella, and now it's gone!"

"You wanted to find out how it worked?"

"No," he replied, shaking his head. "I wanted to learn *why* it works so strangely."

Holmes laughed. "Oh, you are referring, I suppose, to the business of its taking you to so-called 'literary' dimensions?"

Fillmore nodded. He had a sudden inkling of what Holmes was about to say.

"That, my dear Fillmore, is quite elementary! The physics and mathematics of space strongly imply the co-existence of many worlds in other dimensions. What are these places like? Surely, space is so infinite that there must be an objective reality to planets of every conceivable kind, variances and patterns mundane and fantastic."

"Yes, yes, but why *literary* permutations?"

"You have been going about the problem backwards," said Holmes. "These places do not exist because people on your earth dreamed them up. I should say rather the reverse was more likely."

"Meaning?"

"Meaning the 'fiction' of your prosaic earth must be borrowed, in greater or lesser degree, from notions and conceptions that occur across the barriers of the dimensions. Have you not heard writers (though surely not Watson) protest that they do not know from what heaven their inspirations descend? Even my good friend the doctor's agent, Conan Doyle, has sometimes told me that he invents characters in his historical romances that 'write themselves.' Does this not suggest that these artists may be unwittingly tapping the logical premises of other parallel worlds?"

"Then, in my case—" Fillmore began, but Holmes already knew.

"Of course! You are an instructor in literature and drama. Your mind is evidently psychically attuned to the alternative earths which the literature of your world has told you of—and succeeded in captivating your imagination with."

Fillmore nodded and sipped his ale. They sat in silence for a few moments before he spoke again.

"Your theory makes a great deal of sense, and yet—"

"And yet?"

"It does not totally explain why it has been necessary for me to complete a sequence of action in each world I visit."

Holmes nodded. "That, I should say, is a three-pipe problem. But it will have to be left for a time when we can breathe more freely. Colonel Moran will surely pick up our trail before the night is over. We must proceed swiftly, and you must stay close by. Since he may have observed your role in the death of his chief, you may well be marked for extermination."

"I don't mind at all sticking with you," Fillmore admitted as they rose from the table, "especially since I have no recourse now but to be subsumed."

"I am not positive that subsumption is an inevitable function of the umbrella," said Holmes, insisting on taking the check, "but you are right to the extent that the instrument is now out of reach of our human resources."

They walked out of the tavern and inhaled the clear, cold air of evening.

"I suppose you do not intend to get in touch with Watson, under the circumstances?"

"No," Holmes shook his head, "it would involve him in too great a risk. The dear boy is an innocent when it comes to dissembling. Moran will reason my path lies homeward, but if I do go to London, there will be danger for all and sundry. Moran might kidnap Watson to flush me out. No, I must stay away from England for a time."

"And therefore you will change your name to Sigerson and—"

"How the devil did you know that?!" Holmes snapped, his brows beetling. Then his face cleared and he nodded merrily. "Of course! You have a contemporaneous awareness of certain likely events in this world. But I pray, sir, if we are to travel companions, please refrain from casting yourself too often in the role of a Nostradamus. There is a piquancy to quotidian unawareness of one's Fate."

Fillmore agreed and they walked on for a time in silence. Then Holmes suggested that the professor ought to consider what role he might want to assume in the present world.

"Why, no one knows me here," the other said in some amazement. "Why should I need to be anyone but myself?"

"Because you will bring us into rather risky focus during our travels abroad if you insist on remaining a man without a background and point of origin. First thing we must do is purchase a good set of false papers. You will need a well-worked-out history—"

"And a new name!" Fillmore said, suddenly and decisively.

"What on earth for? What's wrong with the one you have?"

"I thoroughly detest it!"

"Yes, yes, but you are apt to slip up if you stray too far from your original nomenclature. If you *must* pick a new name, choose one close enough to the present one so it won't take long to get used to it."

"Very well," Fillmore agreed, lapsing into thoughtful silence.

I'll get rid of that hateful middle name and call myself by my original first one, the one my aunt didn't like because it belonged to my father. A bitter memory crossed his mind, and he determined to be done entirely with the painful past. *The hell with the surname, too! I'll go back to the old spelling.*

They stumped along for another quarter-hour and at last Holmes suggested they take shelter in the barn he saw upon the rise and stay there until the morning came. Fillmore agreed.

A few minutes later, they stretched out in straw and prepared to slumber. A peculiar idea occurred to the scholar at that moment, and he smiled.

"Something amusing?" Holmes asked.

Fillmore nodded. "It just crossed my mind . . . if your theory is correct and artists in my world really do unwittingly borrow from the events of alternative earths, then it is possible that I am already figuring in some work of literature back where I came from!"

Holmes chuckled. "I do not think I am going to

dwell on that thought just now. My poor tired brain has had enough of metaphysics for one day!'

With that, the Great Detective said good night and went to sleep.

His companion lay there for a long time, thinking about the morrow when he would take on his new name and identity and start a new and exciting life. The professor gazed into the darkness and pondered the perilous perplexities of the stars.

In his cozy Victorian study, the doctor gazed down on the new manuscript. The thing was more fun, he thought, if he could think of the perfect name.

There was already evidence that his readers enjoyed the wry device of Watson's "stories-yet-to-be-told." It was a clever method of injecting humor into the often grim tales: tease the readers with promises of outlandish-sounding stories not yet written up by Watson.

For instance, there was the adventure of the Grice-Pattersons in the Isle of Uffa (wherever that was!) or the Repulsive Tale of the Red Leech, or—among the most outrageous—"the strange case of Isadora Persano, the well-known duellist, who was found stark staring mad with a matchbox in front of him which contained a remarkable worm said to be unknown to science . . ."

But this name now: J. Adrian Fillmore. It didn't have quite the properly quaint tone he was seeking. It was a trifle stuffy and stolid. Perhaps it was the middle name . . . try eliminating it. And what might the initial stand for? John? James? (He chortled as he thought of the printer's error that caused Watson's wife to call him James by mistake. What a tizzy of pseudo-scholastic comment that had provoked!)

James it would be then, he decided finally. And perhaps an older and quainter spelling of the surname . . .

And Arthur Conan Doyle wrote:

". . . the incredible mystery of Mr. James Phillimore, who, stepping back into his own house to get his umbrella, was never more seen in this world . . ."

PART III

CHAPTER ONE

Mr. James Phillimore sat in an overstuffed chair at 221B Baker Street and grumbled to himself about the hyperbolized attractions of High Romance.

"Odd," he groused, "to be bored to death thirty-seven years before one's birth."

Watson's ship's-clock ticked away the tedium. The scholar was alone. In one hand he held a strong whisky-and-soda. His other hand smoothed the latest copy of a London daily across his knees.

He was looking for a job.

"Damn and double-damn! They all want references!"

Without capital, Doyle's London was no great delight. Holmes was away, Watson didn't know he existed, and Mrs. Hudson had a great plenty of prattle with little admixture of matter therein. Phillimore was bored and broke. So long as he stayed at 221B, he was welcome to share the landlady's larder, since Mycroft Holmes kept up his brother's rent at Sherlock's own devisement. However, a protracted stay at Holmes' digs was decidedly inadvisable, the professor knew.

Everything had gone awry. Originally, Phillimore was to purchase false papers and fashion a new identity, but Holmes, never the most organized of men when he wasn't on a case, kept forgetting to make the

necessary arrangements. Then the grand plan to accompany the detective on his Tibetan perambulations
was scotched in an odd manner.

It seems that Holmes' cousin, Professor George Edward Challenger, was about to sail to South America
to search for traces of sentient prehistoric life on that
continent. Holmes was asked to come along. Delighted at the prospect, he was yet afraid to let it be
known he was still alive for fear the Moriarty survi-
vors would wreak vengeance on the entire expedition.
So instead of assuming the false identity of Sigerson,
Holmes made special arrangements to impersonate a
genuine world explorer, Lord John Roxton, an individual whose presence in the Challenger team would
hardly excite suspicion.*

The detective extended an invitation to Phillimore
to come along as well, but the scholar, having read
Doyle's *The Lost World,* decided he would prefer esti-
vating in London to possibly furnishing himself as an
hors d' oeuvre for a teratosaurus. Against Holmes' better judgment, Phillimore remained behind.

"But do not tarry long in Baker Street," the detective
said before starting out. "Moran saw you upon the
Reichenbach ledge. He won't forget you. I have
sources which tell me he is temporarily out of London, but I also have ascertained he will return by the
end of the month."

This allowed the scholar a scant week to assidu-
ously search the dailies for employment opportunities . . . but to no avail. He had no past, therefore
there was no way to satisfy the strict scruples of the
Victorian educational system.

---

* Further details are available in Chapter Five of the author's
The Histrionic Holmes (Luther Norris, 1971).

Time was running out. So was his money. Without his umbrella, he felt trapped.

A low tap sounded at the door. Phillimore bade the tapper enter. The gray-haired landlady walked in bearing a silver tray on which rested an envelope embossed with an official-looking crest.

"It was brought a moment ago," she said, proffering the tray. Silently marveling at the London postal system which guaranteed upwards of ten deliveries a day, the professor picked up the envelope and saw his name neatly inscribed on it.

"Strange," he murmured. "Who else knows of my existence?"

The landlady shrugged, unable to advance a viable theory.

He withdrew a single folded sheet of cream-colored paper, smoothed it out and read the terse message thereupon . . .

IT IS IMPERATIVE THAT WE DISCUSS THE UMBRELLA. PLEASE CALL AT MY CLUB THIS EVENING.

M.H.

The address was inked beneath the initials.

"Hmm," Phillimore mused, "perhaps the game's afoot . . ."

CHAPTER TWO

As he stepped out upon Baker Street, the professor debated whether to walk or hail a Hansom. Since it was a warm, pleasant evening, he decided to apply shank's-mare toward Pall Mall.

As he strode briskly along, Phillimore mused on the import of the note. What was there to discuss? The umbrella was gone for good, borne off by the death grip of Moriarty, lying at the base of the Reichenbach torrent.

"Well, as Holmes would say, it's foolish to speculate with insufficient data. When I reach the club, I'll find out." The opportunity was too good to miss, in any event: a meeting with the one person even more brilliant than Sherlock Holmes.

Approaching his destination from the St. James' end, he stopped at a door some little distance from the Carlton. Upon stepping through the portal, Phillimore entered a club that was reputed to be the oddest in London. He followed a short hall to a glass panel through which he observed a large, luxurious chamber in which a great many men sat reading periodicals, determinedly preserving an elaborate communal silence.

A melancholy retainer accepted his card and bade the teacher wait in the visitors' room, just off the hall.

It was a carpeted chamber with the suffused light of a fireplace to offset the gloom. Phillimore sank into a comfortable overstuffed chair and awaited his summoner.

That individual was not tardy in coming. Before very long, a heavy footfall announced the arrival of a large, florid newcomer. The man was positively obese, but his face, though massive, still reflected keen intelligence. Yet the peculiarly watery-gray eyes held a far-off look, the expression of a dreamer.

He extended a broad flipper and shook Phillimore's hand, saying, "I am pleased to meet you, sir. Sherlock has related your incredible adventures to me."

"And I take it that you are able to countenance the possibility of an engine which transfers the user to other dimensions?"

"Oh, I should say so," the large man wheezed. "I have bethought myself of such a device for quite some time. However, I am the most indolent individual in England, and I never bothered to follow the notion to its practical conclusion. It should have meant wearisome computations, hypotheses, trails and trials, mistrials and counter-trials. But had I inherited Sherlock's penchant for induction, I would have postulated the likelihood of Moriarty conceiving and following through the identical concept."

The melancholy retainer reappeared and accepted their preferences in libation. After he left, Phillimore placed his fingers against one another, steeple-fashion, and spoke.

"I take it then that you are capable of explaining precisely how the umbrella works. It appears to modulate to the brain-pattern of each user, that much I have understood."

"Well, I haven't examined the Moriarty model, but I

doubt it could vary greatly. The engine draws on cosmic power sources through the attuning of the individual's mental patterns. When a destination is decided on, the thoughts affix the frequency the device must seek out."

Phillimore held up his hand. "But if it is completely governed by the operator's mental patterns, why have I not been taken precisely where I wish every time I use it? And why must I finish a sequence? And how could it allow me to become subsumed in—"

"Now, now," the other rumbled, "*festina lente*, my good man: one point at a time. In order to fully control the umbrella, you must first totally manage your own thoughts. Self-control is a rare commodity, sir; can you truly profess that you were in charge of your faculties when the engine whisked you to that place you label a 'draft-world'? Were you not distracted by the imminence of the over-amorous Ruth?"

"Indeed I was."

"You see, then? You feared you would not escape her and, at the same time, you pressed the umbrella-catch, hoping to visit the world of Sherlock Holmes and myself. The umbrella, by a sort of law of universal economy, always aims to consume the least quantity of energy possible. When it sensed your muddled thoughts, it interpreted them by a destination which must have drawn on less energy than *this* world. The result: you were taken to a place on which reside analogous individuals to Ruth and Sherlock."

"And I had a devil of a time getting off again."

"That," the large man said, waving a flipper, "is another matter. There is no reason why a sequence, as you call it, must be completed. True, the engine is unlikely to work after usage until certain energy sources are redistributed and equalized, but within a day or two, at most, I should think—"

"No, I tell you I tried it repeatedly! The umbrella only operated for me in that draft-world when it seemed my life was over there, not before . . ."

A moment of silence. The big man sat and pondered, his lips working in and out. Then his eyebrows raised and he uttered a surprised, "Ahh!"

Before Phillimore could divine his host's latter thought, the retainer reappeared with a whisky-and-soda for him and a decanter of Tokay for the large man. They pledged one another's health and sipped in silence.

At length, the big man rumbled, "Your Achilles' heel would seem to be your sense of structure."

"I don't follow your meaning."

"You are a literary professor, a scholar of artificial worlds. Where but in fiction may one find an ordering of events such as pale existence cannot hope to imitate?"

"You are saying that my artistic sense dictated my adventures?"

"Precisely! The recharged umbrella read your inner thoughts and saw you were attuned to 'completing a sequence.' My dear Phillimore, this is totally consistent with the device's adaptation to the user's mental patterns."

The professor stroked his chin thoughtfully. "Subsumption, therefore, would appear to be similarly explicable."

"Indeed so. You could have traveled by umbrella any time you wished, if you had been aware of these factors. But self-ordering is no simple business, you see."

Nodding, Phillimore downed his drink and gestured to the passing retainer for a refill. "What a shame," he sighed, "to learn all this when it is of no practical use. The umbrella is gone for good."

"*I have my doubts.*"

Phillimore glanced up sharply. "What do you mean?"

"I ask you to cast your mind back to the struggle upon the ledge. Describe for me, the precise physical attitude of Moriarty as he plunged into the torrent."

Mystified, Phillimore complied, sketching the verbal picture as best he could recall: the flailing limbs, the scream of terror, Moriarty toppling backwards into the boiling cascade, snatching desperately at the umbrella . . .

"*Oh, no!*"

"I fear the same, sir! If Moriarty invented the umbrella, is it not probable that he would have activated it to save his life?"

"Then somewhere, on some outpost world, he may, even now, be constructing his evil schemes."

"It is quite conceivable," the large man agreed. "Who knows what alien powers he may be marshalling preparatory to reinvading his native London?"

"Dreadful," Phillimore shuddered. "But what may we do about it?"

"Sherlock was too exhilarated over the demise of his arch-foe to consider any alternative possibilities. Thus he is not in England and I fear it shall be some time before he returns. So it is up to us. But my girth ill suits me for strenuous physical activity . . . so it devolves upon you to execute a plan of my devisement."

"Which is?"

"To pursue Moriarty and reclaim your umbrella."

The professor sputtered. "That's impossible."

The large man ignored him. "At the very least, loss of the umbrella will delay Moriarty, hopefully until Sherlock can take a hand in this. At best, he might be on some unyielding world where a paucity of certain natural resources would render it impossible for him to build a new umbrella-engine."

Phillimore was on his feet, glass in hand. "But see here, your theories are fine, but how the deuce may they be acted upon? First of all, I have no umbrella. Secondly, if I did, how would I have any idea where to seek in a multiplicity of cosmoses?"

Setting his glass on a tray, the large man sat back and cradled his paunch in clasped hands. His lips worked in and out for a few seconds, then he fixed Phillimore with a keen gaze. "I will address your first point: the absence of an umbrella. Observe my hands." He stretched them out so they were side by side, palms upward. "Let us consider my left hand to be *this* world, the one of the original Moriarty and Sherlock Holmes. Let us also conceive my right hand to be the so-called 'draft-world' you visited, a place where you found that villainous Persano and heard of one Sherrinford Holmes. On this 'draft-world' "—here he waggled his right hand for emphasis—"there also lived a Professor Moriarty, according to Persano's report. Call him the Ür-Moriarty, if you will. Now it appears as if the umbrella you lost was originally stolen from the Ür-Moriarty. If such is true . . ."

"Of course!" Phillimore exclaimed. "Then *our* Moriarty, the one who went over Reichenbach, is likely to have his own umbrella!"

"Precisely! If by good fortune he had not yet invented one, then he is, in truth, a corpse at the base of the torrent. But if he did create a dimensional transfer-engine, then it is likely to be hidden in his now-vacant headquarters. Seek it there, Phillimore, by all means, seek it there!"

The scholar quaffed the last of his whisky-and-soda, then set the glass down. "I suppose there is no harm in doing that much at least. It would be reassuring to possess a means of egress from this particular island earth. But as to seeking Moriarty elsewhere . . . I still do not see how it is possible. I suppose I could affix my thoughts on the evil professor, but that might merely fetch me to some place where the Ür-Moriarty has gone. For that matter, there could be dozens of Moriartys on a myriad of quasi-earths!"

The large man rose and put one broad paw around Phillimore's shoulders. "Have no doubts upon this latter consideration. I have an excellent theory as to how you may determine the 'real' Moriarty's. whereabouts . . ."

The time would come when Phillimore recalled these words of assurance with some little pique.

CHAPTER THREE

Far off, a clock tolled midnight. The pale moon, partially obscured by black clouds, shed a sickly glare that glimmered on the surface of the nearby Thames.

Creeping around the side of the gloomy mansion, Phillimore stepped carefully, wishing he could have found a dark-lantern amongst the clutter of Holmes' untidy catchall closet of implementa, old files and disguise components. He yearned for the familiarity of a compact, comprehensible flashlight; instead he was saddled with a battered, rusty lantern with broken shuttering. Because of the latter liability, he did not dare employ the thing till he was inside Moriarty's lair.

Rounding a corner, he walked toward the rear entrance, testing each window along the way. But everything was shut up tight.

It was a vast, ugly pile without concession to aesthetic ornamentation. At the squat, solid-looking back door, Phillimore removed certain tools and began worrying at the lock. Before setting out, he'd studied one of Holmes' myriad monographs, a slim manuscript concerned with the intricacies of lock-picking. This knowledge, bolstered by the teacher's rusty conjuring lore, enabled him to make reasonably short work of the back portal. He was a bit surprised how relatively easy the job was, but Moriarty probably never expected anyone to be so foolhardy as to burglarize his unsanctuary.

Having achieved ingress, Phillimore lit the lantern and looked around. The interior contradicted the baleful aspect of the outside: the flickering light hinted at expensive furnishings, thick carpeting, paintings, tapestries and armorial artifacts. Luxuriance everywhere, even to the point of decadence.

He listened intently. Nothing. Not a sound. The big house was chilly and still. The only noise was the suspiration of his rapid breathing which he could not control.

The size of Moriarty's mansion daunted him. Where in all its shadowy eyries was he to seek out another umbrella, whose existence, anyway, was purely hypothetical?

On the latter point, he soon was to be reassured, but for the moment he confined himself to trying to locate the library.

His conspirator had reasoned thus: as Phillimore's own dimensional adventures depended on the literature with which he was most familiar, it was conceivable that when Moriarty plunged over the falls, he chose a place to fly via umbrella that derived from his own leisure reading. Theoretically, then, Phillimore might trace the evil professor just by studying his bookshelves.

He stepped forward, a few inches at a time, playing the light across the floor to see where it was safe to put his feet, occasionally lofting the lantern to study the direction in which he was headed. Soon, his perambulations brought him to a wide, peaked archway through which he spied a globe so enormous he could not hope to encircle its girth with outstretched arms.

Reasoning a globe would be kept in a study/library, he entered, shining the lantern about the chamber. He saw tables butted against the walls, surfaces strewn with charts and sheets of jottings. The walls themselves held graphs and maps, some of the latter depicting London, with black stickpins thrust through at various locations. At the far side of the room stood a polished teak desk that bore a neat array of papers, ledgers, writing instruments and miscellaneous calculatory paraphernalia. An ample decantered sideboard completed the roll-call of movable furniture. Behind it, set into the wall, rose a tall, moderately wide bookshelf.

Phillimore stepped across the room, rested the lantern atop the sideboard and scanned the volumes jamming the shelves.

"Hmmph. As I expected . . . mainly scientific works. Some philosophy. Nietzsche—no small testament to Moriarty's percipience, few enough sold in the original German editions.. *Tertium. Organum.* Kant. Schopenhauer. Paracelsus. *De Rerum Natura.* Kepler. Albertus Magnus. *Principia Mathematica.* Alhazred. *The Discoverie of—*"

The murmured soliloquy ceased. His eye backtracked to the Russell-Whitehead tomes. "Just a moment! *Principia Mathematica* . . . they didn't see that in print till about 1910, and even then it was only the initial volume!"

It was clearly an anachronism. Suddenly, Phillimore no longer regarded the notion as remote that Moriarty might have an umbrella stashed somewhere in the house. He scanned the books with renewed fervor: Rimbaud, Baudelaire, Villon in French jostled for space with great piles of political tracts and mouldering esoterica on every subject from thaumaturgy, kheft and culling . . .

There! On a shelf just above eye-level he found a scant collection of fiction. The fat Burton translation of *The Arabian Nights* stood beside and dwarfed Abbott's amusing tale of life in a two-dimensional universe, *Flatland.* Here were both 1818 and 1831 editions of *Frankenstein,* as well as the endless, lurid *Newgate Calendar,* appropriately accompanied by *The Beggar's Opera* libretto and Fielding's exercise in sustained irony, *Jonathan Wild.* The only other thing on the shelf was a thick pile of sheets laboriously handwritten in German. On the top page, Phillimore noticed a vaguely familiar place name, the Rue d'Auseil. But it was no time for idle browsing.

"Must jot down the titles," he said to himself, rummaging through his pockets for paper and—

"May I be of assistance?"

He whirled, stunned. A shadowy figure, nearly six feet tall, stood in the doorway.

It was bad enough to be surprised in a master criminal's home at midnight during an act of burglary, but the fact that he recognized the newcomer made it all quite a bit worse. There was no mistaking the hard, lean jawline; the unblinking eyes, the mouth set in a grin that might easily be assessed as cruel. Lofting the lantern, he saw, sure enough, the deep lateral slice that creased the bridge of the man's nose.

"Perhaps you might like to tell me what you are doing here," suggested A. I. Persano mildly.

The scholar's thoughts raced. *Enough light to see, but he doesn't recognize me, I'm sure of it! Why not?*

The answer immediately struck him. He'd met Persano, Moriarty's lieutenant, in the "draft-world" and left him in a world of horror from which there could be no escape. *Then that must have been an Ur-Persano, and this one is the genuine article!*

"It is, you must admit, a peculiar hour to pay a social call, let alone browse through a library." Like the other Persano, the dangerous gentleman spoke politely, never flaunting his puissance in vulgar display.

Phillimore cleared his throat. *Think fast!* "I trust you are Mr. Persano?"

The other's eyes narrowed. "Perhaps. Why do you ask?"

"Well, the—ah, the fact is—"

"One of our ablest dramatists," Persano interrupted, "has stated that the phrase, 'the fact is—,' invariably signifies the imminent commission of a spectacular lie. However, do not let me stay your story."

Phillimore resolved to fabricate a history not totally removed from the truth. "Professor Moriarty told me to seek you out."

"In the middle of the night?"

"He suggested you would be able to bring me his special umbrella."

Persano smiled. "It must be quite special to do him any good at the base of Reichenbach."

"He did not fall to his death. By a strange rent in the fabric of time, he was propelled to the world which I have been inhabiting until recently. There he had me create another umbrella and sent me here to bring the original, which he says is a far superior model."

"An interesting story," Persano remarked. "Why did he not return for it himself?"

Phillimore silently cudgeled his brains. *The story's full of holes. What do I tell him?*

"You see," he improvised, "when I met him, he was in prison; I was just about to be released. He dictated the plans for making an umbrella; I made one and arrived just outside the house. But it was a flimsy affair; it didn't survive the trip. I threw it in the Thames." *There! Fast and fancy!*

Persano nodded sagely. "Ah, yes, I see . . . very plausible." He smiled pleasantly. "You wait right here, I'll fetch the Professor's original umbrella." Before Phillimore could say another word, Persano retreated through the archway, closing the double doors and locking them.

"Damn! He doesn't believe me," the teacher said to himself, casting about for some means of escape. But the study was an interior chamber lacking windows. His mind clicked off alternatives, saw only one possibility. "I've got to get hold of the umbrella, press its button and quit this world. But where should I go?"

He spun around to the bookshelf and desperately studied the choices. "Where would Moriarty be likely to choose? *Let's see* . . ."

Persano's footsteps sounded overhead. Evidently the need for silence no longer concerned him, a fact which subtly disconcerted Phillimore. He studied the book titles intently, weighing possibilities.

"Surely Moriarty would go someplace that offered the opportunity for criminous expansion. In which case—"

The footsteps started downstairs as he flipped through the pages of *The Newgate Calendar*, found what he wanted and replaced the tome. "Yes. He even has the chapter heading underlined: 'Jonathan Wild, The Prince of Robbers.' Doyle drew the obvious analogy; Wild was a sixteenth-century Moriarty. He banded all burglars and highwaymen under a common government, his own . . ."

The lock clicked.

"But would Moriarty choose to horn in on Wild or would he hit upon one of the fictional characters based on Wild? What advantage would there be in each?"

He terminated his mutterings as the doors opened and Persano stepped through carrying two objects, a large black umbrella devoid of decorative device and an ebony cane which dismayed Phillimore.

Setting the umbrella against the wall, Persano asked if it was what the other had come to obtain.

"Indeed it is." Though he tried to sound casual, Phillimore stepped too hastily toward the umbrella. Immediately, Presano interposed himself between object and subject, simultaneously grasping his cane with both hands. A long metallic *whoosh*—and the weapon in the ebony sheath pointed naked at Phillimore's breast.

Persano did not appear the least bit ruffled or perturbed. In his customary even, well-modulated voice, he suggested that Phillimore might do well to offer some plausible explanation as to what he was doing in Moriarty's house.

"But I told you everything. Put that dreadful thing away!"

The other clucked disapprovingly. "I preceive a mere exhortation that you practice candor is of no weight. Very well; let me simply note that, according to your tale, you just arrived here from an alien world."

"That's what I said."

"Then it seems a trifle unlikely that you would be aware that the river which flows nearby is named the Thames."

Phillimore winced. *Reconcile it quickly, or—*

"I beg you spare me the fruits of hurried mental

revision of your original tale. I have spoken ere this with Colonel Moran, and he told me of a chap who fits your description showing up out of nowhere on the ledge at Reichenbach. He also said you had an umbrella which the Professor bore away with him.

"It has occurred to me and the Colonel that if that umbrella were of similar design to the one here beside me, our chief may have activated it. Your presence tonight tends to confirm that supposition."

Phillimore's resolve plummeted. Casting about for some desperate mode of aid, he returned to the sideboard where the lantern still flickered its lurid glare over walls and furnishings. "Well, I suppose I must admit you have me at a disadvantage. What next?"

"Kindly keep away from that lantern," Persano sharply warned, making a tiny circle in the air in its direction with the tip of his sword. "Eschew heroics and hear me. We may be of use to one another."

"Impossible!"

"Tut, gratuitous rudeness suggests ill breeding. There is a clear advantage for both of us to grasp."

Phillimore shrugged. "I fail to see it."

"You can help me bring the Professor back, I don't doubt."

"How do you deduce that?"

"Just before I heard you thumping around down here, I was upstairs mulling over the problem of locating him. It suddenly occurred to me the key might be in that bookshelf. When I walked in, you were inspecting it, an action that confirmed my belief."

"I still don't see what benefit that provides me," Phillimore argued.

"Simple. You tell me your deductions. In exchange, I tender you your life." It was beneath Persano to make the alternative explicit, but the still-lofted sword was eloquent enough.

Phillimore mulled over his predicament. In no way did he trust Persano to keep his word. The only hope he had to twist the situation in his favor was to get hold of the umbrella.

"I appear to have no choice but to accept your proposition."

Persano shrugged. "I certainly see no other way."

"Well, as a matter of fact," Phillimore lied, "I had just conclusively ascertained where Professor Moriarty went when you walked in."

"And where is that?"

The scholar waggled his finger in the fashion of a pedagogue admonishing the class wag. "No, no, I should be a veritable dunce to inform you of my secret. Give me the umbrella and I'll prove I'm right by going on and fetching him back to this world."

Persano chuckled. "All collective bargaining begins, does it not, with impossible demands which neither party expects to obtain, *n'est-ce pas?* Now that we have both insulted one another's intelligences, let us come up with a reasonable compromise. You work the umbrella so that it takes you where you have in mind, thus keeping your secret. I will make the flight with you."

"And skewer me, I suppose, upon arrival!"

With one palm upward in a gesture of bonhomie, Persano demurred. "My word as a gentleman to the contrary. If we cannot trust one another, we shall never get on with this." As a token of his earnest, the villain replaced his sword within its scabbard. Picking up the umbrella, he bade Phillimore take hold of it.

Well, might as well try what may. The question was

which source to select—the *Newgate Calendar*, Fielding or John Gay's *The Beggar's Opera*. Fielding, he decided instantly, was incorrect; in that book, Jonathan Wild was little better than a cutpurse highwayman. Surely Moriarty would be more eager to consort with a criminal who organized London's greatest network of crime during the early 1700s. On the other hand, there might be practical value to dealing with Gay's Peachum, a character modeled on Wild. Peachum might easily rid Phillimore of the dangerous Persano; a word in his ear and the pious double-dealer would "peach" on Persano to the authorities and—

"Come, come!" Persano snapped. "Enough woolgathering! Activate this thing instantly, or I shall think twice about our arrangement."

Phillimore sighed. Just once he wished he might take his time and work the umbrella properly. *However* . . .

He pushed the button, which was in practically the same spot as the one on his own model.

The universe reversed itself and did its giddy tarantella. Phillimore, who was somewhat used to umbrella-flight by that time, did his best to joggle Persano loose, but the other merely clutched his cane tighter and paid no attention.

The flight was brief. The umbrella, automatically closing itself, deposited them on a hard floor. The air was close, cold, clammy.

They were in total darkness.

Thrashing about with his free hand, Phillimore tried to locate something solid, a wall, anything. He did not succeed. The blackness was absolute.

"Where in hell have you taken us?" Persano demanded.

At the sound of his speech, there came a sudden

chorus of raucous voices. A tinder scratched, a torch flared. Snarls and imprecations. Then sudden laying-on of hands. Phillimore flailed in terror; Persano began to withdraw his sword.

Two bright objects flashed and fell, and the pair, groaning, sank to the stone floor, unconscious.

CHAPTER FOUR

As it is necessary that all great and surprising events, the designs of which are laid, conducted, and brought to perfection by the utmost force of human invention and art, should be elucidated to the satisfaction of the startled peruser of this modest history, it is therefore essential to explain that the hapless Phillimore and his nemesis, Persano, were brought by the device of Moriarty's umbrella to the very stronghold-cellar of that same Jonathan Wild who kept the minions of crime in London, circa 1716, under his ruthless guidance and instruction by the simple system of turning all obstreperous objectors directly over to the governmental authorities, a method which ironically caused the common press to greatly value the public services of the same Mr. Wild. But irony was one of Wild's favorite devices, and he was frequently wont to state in moments of well-concealed candor that he should far prefer to stand upon the summit of a dunghill in Hell than at the bottom of a mountain in Paradise.

Irony, indeed, presided over the appearance of our protagonist in Mr. Wild's cellar that particular evening. For some time, the duplicitous Wild was troubled by the unruly exploits of a young burglar by name of Jack Sheppard, a gentleman whose derring-do excited the honest London citizenry as much as his bravura attitude towards the Prince of Robbers awoke unexpressed sympathy amongst Wild's necessarily loyal underlings. If the reader will permit yet another anachronism, Sheppard was a veritable eighteenth-century Houdini, having escaped repeatedly from confinement. When informed he must contribute a percentage of his criminous gains to the Wild organization, Sheppard sneered that "the fat rogue may seethe in his own gallows-grease ere that come to pass!" Whereupon, the same being reported to Wild, he bespoke himself to a certain corrupt official, and shortly thereafter, Sheppard was apprehended and remanded to prison. The next morning, the bird was flown the coop and word circulated amongst the tapsters of the underworld that Sheppard vowed to avenge himself upon Wild by burglarizing his very establishment within a fortnight.

When Phillimore and Persano awoke, they found themselves bound with stout rope and secured to great iron rings high above the cellar floor so that they must perforce dangle, feet scant inches from the stone surface below. The ache was intolerable in their limbs, but the spectacle presented to their dismayed view took their minds a little off their physical discomfort.

It was a large cellar, stacked with wine-casks, arched here and there with portals to further recesses where all manner of rich costumery and pelf lay in tagged orderliness, the merchandise which Wild was wont to take in trade from his henchmen, thence to be "sought out amongst the lower classes and returned, sans questions," to the anxious original owners, though never for a fee other than what the good hearts of the grateful victims served by Wild might choose to dis-

burse upon his "poor honest efforts on their be-
halves."

A small company of unwholesome-looking brigands
stood in a band, observing Persano and Phillimore.
One particularly nasty giant (whose oft-scarred countenance was distinguished by skin tinged an unheal-
thy blue tint) held Persano's sword-cane, the weapon
partially withdrawn; the ghoulish villain leered with
pleasure upon the thing, which he evidently considered to be his own fairly-gained property. Phillimore
glanced anxiously about, saw the black umbrella neg-
ligently laid in a corner, an object apparently of no
worth to his captors.

The group of thieves and murderers, for so they
were, parted to allow their chief to descend to the
middle of the cellar. This illustrious personage, none
other than Mr. Jonathan Wild himself, was tall and
uncommonly portly; his complexion, though fair, was
mottled and pocked, and his lips protruded in a par-
ody of a judge's opprobrious pout. His raiment was of
the finest cut, but the topknot which adorned his skull
might have been better for a washing. He carried his
hands behind his figured waistcoat and clasped them
in the mode of a stern headmaster; his head turned
constantly in a curiously reptilian motion as if he were
seeking out the pranks of a mischievous urchin who
only chose to dally when his principal's back was
turned. Wild, as he passed the rogue with the blue
skin, paused to observe the fine woodwork of the
ebony sword-cane.

"What doth this signify, rascal?" he growled. "I flat-
ter myself this is booty justly earned for the betterment of the establishment at large, of which you and
all your fellows are pleased to benefit! Restore it at
once!"

He held his hand out expectantly, and there was some hesitation on Blueskin's part before he set the stick in Wild's hand. "Take it, if tha's a mind," the henchman grumbled, "but take care it do not turn about and do ye damage."

Wild glowered at the man. A more perceptive observer than his underlings would have fairly heard the fatal computation clicking in his skull to do over Blueskin to the authorities come next quarter. Having silently damned the luckless scoundrel, Wild turned and regarded the two hanging captives. Setting his weight pompously upon Presano's cane, he swaggered to a place a few feet before them, far enough back so neither could aim a kick at him.

"Well, lads," he chuckled oilily, "Sheppard fee'd ye to a bitter purpose. I wondered how he dared to brag of this venture and hope to 'scape incarceration."

"Let us down," Persano demanded. "We know nothing of this Sheppard. Free us and we will satisfy you of the strange, but innocent reason for our appearing thus."

"By addressing you," Wild admonished, "I did not mean to instance you toward debate. You will maintain silence, base fellow! It is unseemly such unprincipled rascals, garbed like lunatics, should befoul the ears of an honest citizen with the foul billingsgate to which you are accustomed in your element." He turned to one of his gang. "Fetch Mr. Brown hither with his men and deliver over these rogues to justice." Wild again studied his captives, this time with an air of perplexity. "How you managed to enter without disturbing the locks, I cannot hope to perceive, yet your master, Sheppard, has witch-power with the instruments of security, and I venture to suppose he has played for his immortal part when he spirited the pair of you within mine honest walls!"

Shaking his head, Wild continued his discourse in song, much to Persano's amazement. The villains by the stairs crooned softly in harmony, and Phillimore winced and murmured, "Not again!"

AIR to the tune of *An old woman clothed in grey*

WILD.   Through all the employment of life,
                Each neighbour abuses his brother;
          Jack Sheppard, persistent in strife,
                Doth cause me interminable pother!
          The thief calls the robber a cheat,
                While poor honest Jonathan Wild
          Is slandered, although I'm as sweet
                As an unsullied innocent child!

The song ended, he observed, "A lawyer is as honest as I. We both act in double capacity, against rogues and for 'em! And so, gentlemen—" he winked wickedly at the dangling duo—"and so, good-night!" Turning, Wild ascended the stairs, followed by his ghastly crew.

The sound of a heavy door clanging shut resounded through the cellar; immediately ensuing was the noise of bolts being shoved into place. All the torches having been borne away, Phillimore and Persano again found themselves in the dark.

"You wretched fool!" Persano grumbled. "In what nonsensical world have you enmired us?"

Phillimore, by now a veteran of abortive umbrella-flights, hung relatively unperturbed. "It is obvious what went wrong. Had you not hurried my choice, we would have fetched the world of Jonathan Wild. But because of your precipitancy, I would venture to guess we are on a bastard earth composed of equal elements of the *Newgate Calendar*, Henry Fielding and assuredly John Gay."

"How do you make that out?"

"Wild is pretty much as history paints him, yet he speaks in a florid style suggestive of Fielding—"

"And the song obviously reflects *The Beggar's Opera?*"

"Precisely."

"But why," Persano raged, "would you pick *any* of those places?"

"Because I postulate that Wild's iron-fisted grip on the London underworld would appeal to Professor Moriarty. Here would be a network of crime ready to hand . . . all he need do is arrange some compromise in exchange for his unique talents. Or perhaps, he might choose to wrest power away from Wild and—"

"And stuff and abominable nonsense! My leader would not be fool enough to attempt to bargain with the most unprincipled rogue in the annals of illegality. And as for taking over, why run the dreadful risk? It would be as foolhardy as Wild attempting to oust the Professor: there are too many loyal lieutenants who would carry the intelligence to the proper source and work to quash him. No, no, he *never* would have come here, or anyplace like it!" Persano glowered at Phillimore, but it was dark and the expression served no purpose. "And you told me you knew precisely where he'd gone . . ."

Phillimore said nothing. As usual, Persano lived by the code of proper conduct. One might slit a throat or two in the course of everyday business, but deliberate prevarication was rather ungentlemanly, ergo, shocking.

"Well," the scholar sighed, "never mind where we are. The question is, how do we get away?"

"As for that," Persano grunted, "I have been swinging my feet in hopes of clamping hold of the umbrella. They . . . left it . . . within reach. Except—"

"Except what?"

"I can only approximately recall its position. This blasted darkness . . . !"

"Well, you might as well spare the effort. It won't do us much good; the thing needs to be recharged, and it takes quite some time."

"Not this model. It's quite efficient. Half-an-hour is all it requires to rebuild its energy, and we have surely been here close to that, perhaps longer, it's hard to say how long we were unconscious . . . There! . . . No, not quite . . . but now I know where it is . . . and . . ."

Phillimore heard Persano grunt. There was the sound of his feet striking the stone wall; a clatter followed, then Persano cursed.

"What happened?"

"I'm afraid I knocked the umbrella out of reach. And I thought—"

"*SHHH!*"

Persano, always lightning-rapid in his reactions, immediately hushed, no questions asked.

The two hung, arms aching, breaths stilled. In the darkness, they heard the stealthy rasp of metal against metal. The most subtle of scrapings repeated twice . . . thrice . . . and then a muffled *click*.

A cold breeze suddenly flooded the cellar. The gloom dispelled slightly; Phillimore was able to see the glimmer of his own scuffed black shoes, though nothing else.

A lengthy silence, then to their strained ears came

the gentlest sussuration, an all-but-inaudible scuffle which indicated that someone stealthily trod the stone flagging of Wild's basement.

After an interminable period, during which no other sound was heard, the newcomer, apparently satisfied the place was temporarily safe and secure, lit a small flambeaux. Phillimore strained his neck to one side to perceive the aspect of the person who stood, unbidden, in the cellar of the Prince of Thieves.

It was a young man, scarcely past his teens, he judged. A handsome, regularly-featured face contained black, glinting eyes and was surmounted by a shock of pitch-black glossy hair. The mouth had broad, generous lips that surely were no stranger to mirth.

The intruder shone his torch around the cellar. Suddenly spying the two suspended occupants thereof, he emitted a startled hiss, immediately quelling it as he assessed their helpless situation. Laying a finger perpendicular to his mouth to caution them not to say anything, the youth approached Phillimore, the nearer of the two, and brought his lips as close to the captive's ears as the awkward updrawn position would permit.

"I daresay ye've run aground of that foul and fearsome bloodsucker, Wild," he whispered.

"Aye," Phillimore confirmed. "Can ye cut us loose?" He would have feared to adopt the accent of the place, save for those assurances he had been given at the Diogenes Club as to the purely subjective nature of subsumption. Phillimore knew perfectly well this newcomer must be Jack Sheppard arrived to make good his boast, but for once kept his seerish knowledge to himself, lest the other grow suspicious."

"Any man who is enemy to Wild is my friend," the young man said, withdrawing a knife to sever the

bonds. "I do not know who ye may be, attired in ludicrous gallimaufry as you are, but I will number ye
evermore my fast friend, so ye do likewise. But do ye
ken thy benefactor?"

"Oh, ay, right enough," Phillimore replied. "Only
Jack Sheppard himself could work such wizardry with
that devil Wild's locks!" As he spoke, the rope parted
and he slumped to the floor with a stifled groan, rubbing his chafed wrists.

Sheppard, flattered at his renown, bowed, grinned
a crooked grin, then, *sotto voce*, began to sing. Phillimore sighed; he knew from Gilbert-and-Sullivan-land
that the etiquette of place dictated waiting the
damned verses out.

AIR to the tune of *A soldier and a sailor*

SHEPP.   A fox may steal your hens, Sir,
    A scrivener all your pens, Sir,
    But all the rest you own, Sir,
    With Sheppard's surely flown, Sir,
      No bar is lock or gate!
    For every stay I'm picking;
    And omnes: pens, hens, chickling,
    Shall ever be my fee, Sir,
    And if I do but see, Sir,
      I'll also—

"Will you have done with that untimely caterwaul-
ing?!" Persano interrupted in as loud a snarl as he
deemed advisable.

Stopping the song at once, Sheppard turned an affronted countenance upon his aural intruder.

"Who is that ill-mannered bumpkin?" he demanded.
"Never in this short life have I met one so confound-

edly low-bred as to cut in on one's musical peroration! That goes beyond every runagate knave, even Mr. Wild!"

Persano, stung by the aspersions cast on his breeding, haughtily demanded that he be cut free upon the instant.

"The devil I will!" Sheppard snapped. "If your companion finds aught to pleasure him in such surly company, let him set ye at liberty, for I'll have none of it!"

Phillimore looked sharply at Persano, expecting him to speak. But that quick mind instantly assessed his personal predicament and knew better than to petition aid from the one quarter where he was certain it would not come.

Suddenly, from above: a babble of voices. The three cast apprehensive glances in the direction of the stair.

"Hurry," Phillimore whispered. "Wild has sent for the authorities to take us to prison. Mr. Sheppard, you must quit this place on the instant, otherwise you will be in great danger!"

The other pressed the scholar's arm reassuringly, cast about for some valuable to spirit away, found a large, ornate pearl-inlaid jewel-box. He gave Phillimore a broad wink. "The fat jackanapes will miss this right enough!" Then, without another word he sped from the cellar into the night.

Phillimore cursed his own stupidity. Sheppard, having taken his flambeaux, left him no light to find the umbrella. Dropping on his hands and knees, he fumbled frantically about the cold, grimy floor. Above, the voices neared.

"To my left," Persano whispered. "Judge the spot from my voice!"

Phillimore practically threw himself into the indicated corner, scrabbling every which way, arms flailing. His sleeves brushed something. He slapped his hands palm-flat upon the flagging and located the umbrella.

"I've got it!"

"I'm delighted to hear it," Persano said unenthusiastically.

Phillimore bit his lip. His conscience could not accept the responsibility of leaving Persano—arch-villain though he was—to the savage ministrations of eighteenth-century British justice.

"Well, I *would* get you down if I could, but Sheppard took away his dagger."

"I have one strapped to the inside of my left leg."

Shuddering at Persano's resourcefulness, Phillimore felt for the weapon, a six-inch blade honed to razor-keenness. Withdrawing it, he slashed at Persano's bindings. The voices upstairs approached the cellar door.

"May I remind you," Phillimore grunted, sawing at the thick rope, "it was your impatience that served to keep you in this predicament."

"As for that," the other rejoined, "it was you who first chose this wretchedly inauspicious world."

Phillimore heard Wild's rumbling voice above. The keys began to turn in the lock as someone shot back the bolts. Just then the long dagger severed the rope. Persano, though his limbs must have ached bitterly, landed on his feet. He instantly snatched at the dagger, but Phillimore leapt backwards even as he grasped the umbrella securely. He tossed the dagger into a far corner so it was too distant for Persano to risk fetching in the scant time available.

"Now—*where* should we go?" Phillimore demanded, placing his thumb on the umbrella.

"I'll do that!" Persano argued, quickly grabbing at the instrument with both hands. "Don't you see, the Professor would choose a world where some important resource indigenous solely to it would be at hand. Think what a formidable tool he might fashion if he could but commandeer the—"

"Magic!" Phillimore exclaimed, cutting off the other.

"No! I was *going* to say—"

The cellar door flew open with a bang, interrupting Persano a second time. Torches flared, feet clattered downstairs. Wild, at the rear of the group, spied the unshackled unprisoners and roared in anger and dismay.

"Apprehend them! They are surely devils!"

"QUICK!" Persano shouted. "Move your hand!"

He and Phillimore simultaneously scrabbled to press the button of the umbrella. Both forefingers hit it at once.

Just before the first of the thugs threw their arms about the two of them, the umbrella sprang open and the quarry quickly faded from view.

"By God," Blueskin whispered, horrified, "Sheppard is indeed in league with Satan!"

"That's as may be," Wild growled, "but what is more to the point, the fiends hath swiped my second-best jewel-box!"

CHAPTER FIVE

Dimensional riptides battered them. Phillimore's stomach flip-flopped; he clutched the leather curved handpiece with a strength born of colossal panic. Cosmic cross-winds shrieked, buffeting the umbrella so ferociously that the fabric fluctuated with a violent flapping that the scholar feared would soon tear the material to shreds.

"Persano, tune out!" he screamed. "It isn't made to receive two frequencies of thought at once!"

The other did not hear him in the wild cacophony of universal protestation. Persano clung desperately to the metal shaft, though it was growing uncomfortably hot.

What if it uses too much energy? Phillimore worried. *Can't let it burn out!*

There was only one thing to do. Phillimore silently commanded it to compromise with the other signal. *Hope it can figure out what I mean!*

The umbrella emitted a high-pitched whine. Persano howled in pain. The shaft glowed red.

Compromise, damn it! Compromise!

In response, the umbrella suddenly nosed downwards, yanking Phillimore head-under-heels into a star-shot darkness. Below, though the teacher could not see, Persano had to let loose of the fiery pole; he snatched desperately at the cloth-folds. All Phillimore knew was that there was a sudden lightening of the drag. Before he could sort out his thoughts, the umbrella swerved the other way, and he came rightside-up, feet glancingly scraping ground.

A wind of demoniac fury . . . peals of thunder . . . an awful yell . . .

Another weight depended downward from the umbrella, but the pull was enormous, easily three times that of Persano's. The umbrella soared straight up, and the renewed velocity, even with its heavier burden, swiftly cooled the shaft. In the midst of all the brouhaha and wrenching alteration of motion, Phillimore fancied hearing a half-human snarl close by, while, in the distance, Persano's dismayed wail dwindled to nothingness.

The flight was surer now, swifter. Phillimore was so giddy he had to shut his eyes against the cartoon constellations gyrating in his head. He squeezed the leather handpiece, afraid that in his faintness he might lose his grip and fall.

Abruptly, all sense of motion ceased. The noise of flight dwindled to the hushed whisper of breakers on a nameless beach; the stars winked out and left him in pitch darkness. His feet touched down on the soft-hard shifting surface that was a great stretch of sand.

Nearby he thought he heard the dull plop of some ponderous weight sprawling flat. He was too weary to think about it.

Phillimore's numb fingers released the now-shut umbrella. He pitched headfirst onto the sand, sighed thankfully for the cool breeze soothing his face and sank into an exhausted slumber.

CHAPTER SIX

He woke when the first gentle plash of incoming tide slid a clamshell under his nose. Sputtering at the salt-taste wetting his lips, Phillimore sat up and blinked at the bright morning sun glimmering on the cresting ocean. The dissonant cries of a flock of circling sea-birds filled the air, and a mild breeze fluttered the umbrella where it lay, but there were no other sounds or signs of animation.

A second incursion of the surf hurried him to his feet and back a few steps to dry sand.

Facing inland, umbrella in hand, Phillimore studied the coastline. The broad sweep of beach curved gently and steadily backwards about a mile on either side, suggesting he might be on an island. Following the contour of the seafront at a distance of fifty or sixty feet was a thick tangle of palm, coconut, and less familiar trees and brush. Further inland, the tops of lofty rockfaces were just barely discernible. Some distance away to the left, a narrow gap broke the barrier of greenery; through it flowed a thin sparkling twist of fresh water, a small stream seeking the sea.

He turned right and saw the footprints.

They began alongside a great irregular indentation in the sand close to the spot where he lay all night.

They stretched in a crooked line to the trees and disappeared there.

Phillimore approached the prints, noted their size and felt vaguely uneasy. He walked beside them to their terminus at the jungle's edge. At that point, he spied a twisted, trampled alley through the brake that something must have torn open in its passage.

The scholar felt thirsty, anyway, so he saw no reason to enter the thick woods just there. Turning, he stepped along the beach in the direction of the stream, nervously darting glances into the trees as he strode the skirts of the sand.

"At least I've lost Persano. Wonder if I got where I wanted to go? How in hell am I to find out?"

At the streamside, Phillimore slaked his thirst. He opened his collar and removed his jacket, for the morning sun already felt bake-oven hot. As he pondered the best course of action to embark on, a curious sound drew his attention to the jungle. He could not be certain, but it seemed as if someone was sobbing.

Taking a final gulp of water, Phillimore put down his jacket, shifted his umbrella so he might, if necessary, employ it as a club, and stepped off in the direction of the whimpering. He followed the creek-bank into the shelter of the trees.

The shade of leaves far above his head made the heat more bearable; he filled his lungs with air heavied by the sour-sweet odor of decaying matter. Carefully, Phillimore walked along the bend of stream that, like a crooked finger, beckoned him toward the source of the misery.

A few yards further and the trees parted to reveal a small, lush glade. In its middle, seated on a low, flat stone, a small man of advanced years huddled with

his head in his hands. His shoulders heaved with elaborately melodramatic sighs and eloquent sobs. Phillimore noted with satisfaction the man's outlandish garb: red balloon-leg pantaloons cinched by a broad yellow silken cummerbund; blue sandals with uppointed toes and a matching turban blotched with sweat, tattered from years of neglect. The barechested stranger was short, portly and white-bearded. When he lowered his hands from his puffy jowls and wrinkled brow, he displayed a pair of woe-filled eyes that flowed copious streams of sorrow.

"Almighty Allah!" he wailed, hands stretched above his head. "Is the unspeakable sin of Abu Hassan never to be forgotten? Must I endure the whips of public opprobrium even here where I had thought to shun the scornful faces of my fellow-men forever? Is not my name sufficiently blackened? Cannot the divine mercy of Blessed Allah expunge from memory the loathsome crime of Abu Hassan?" He beat his breast and plucked out a patch of chest-hair in wild grief.

"Here, here," Phillimore exclaimed, taking pity at such protracted and deep-seated suffering. Entering the glade, he asked, "Is there anything, poor fellow, that can be done to relieve you?"

Abu Hassan turned a mournful countenance upon the newcomer. "Sir, leave me to my remorse and do not mock me. Must I be shamed even here on this deserted isle where I betook myself in voluntary exile in order that I might never more see the leering eyes and pointing fingers of those who judge and condemn me? Is there no balm in Gilead? No nepenthe of my griefs?"

"But look here, I don't know what you're talking about! I never heard of you before. I only thought I might be able to help somehow."

Abu Hassan stared for a long time at Phillimore, an expression of mingled wonder and joy flitting coquettishly about the edges of his hangdog face. Rising from his rock, the tubby little penitent took a tottering step toward the scholar, then paused fearfully. "Stranger," he said pleadingly, "do not be crueler than mine own conscience! Is it possible that never to your ears came the report of Abu Hassan's dreadful and nameless deed? Can there be a single soul who has not listened maliciously to the shame and fall of one of the most opulent merchants of the City Kaukaban of Al-Yaman?"

"I tell you, I don't know anything about it. I shall not despise you for what is long past and gone." In truth, Phillimore was beginning to recollect some vague detail of the tale of Abu Hassan, but its principal essence still escaped definition. But the important thing was he recalled it was a story from *The Arabian Nights*, and that proved the umbrella had eventually listened to him. He reasoned that Moriarty, who owned the Burton translation of the famous anthology of Oriental anecdota, might well decide to fly to a world where magic was an operant part of the underlying plan. *Think what a tool he might make from Aladdin's Lamp!* Phillimore mused, unconsciously paraphrasing Persano as he last saw him in Jonathan Wild's cellar.

Meanwhile, Abu Hassan still harangued the teacher for assurance that he was indeed a perfect stranger and might embrace his company without shame.

"Believe me, I do not know you," Phillimore asserted, only partly lying. *But I'd better pretend total ignorance if I'm to get anything out of the old windbag!*

It took many minutes to satisfy the distrustful Abu

Hassan, but at length Phillimore succeeded in turning the conversation to other topics.

"You said we are on an isle. But on what part of the globe are we quartered?" That was the trouble with the umbrella: it had no especial discrimination in the places it chose to deposit the user. If Moriarty were somewhere about, it might be thousands of miles from where Phillimore landed. *How to find him?*

"This is an uncharted isle," Abu Hassan stated, "somewhere in the southern tropics to the west of the Sea of Indus."

"And are we the only living things upon it?"

The other broke into a delighted grin, the first truly light-hearted expression he had been able to don since the arrival of Phillimore. "Ah, no, sir! You are indeed fortunate to make the acquaintance of Abu Hassan at this propitious time! For one of the most wondrous spectacles in the entire vastness of this world is about to take place upon the crags of yonder peak! Ah! how grateful I am at the limitless compassion of Mighty Allah that at length my prayers are answered . . . for lo! these many years have I, in my most secret heart, forlornly (so I thought) yearned for a companion ignorant of my foul transgression. For such a one, I vowed, would I ope the scintillant spectacle of this magical clime. The isle is full of noises, good friend, ay, and sights beyond dream! And but this time of year, for a little while only, the fabled great creatures of the air woo the earth and bring forth their young!"

Phillimore wearily expressed polite interest. It was apparent that Abu Hassan would be no ready font of data, at least not without enduring a mighty spate of tedium intermixed. With resignation, he suggested that the other bring him to witness the marvelous thing he hinted of.

"Hush then, stranger!" cautioned Abu Hassan. "Hush, and follow me, for we must go some little distance and the journey is not without peril." With that, he turned and began to pick his way through the underbrush, signaling Phillimore to follow.

Peril? A cold prickle hopskipped up and down his spine as some of the less pleasant details of the stories of Scheherazade occurred to him. There was magic in *The Arabian Nights*, sure enough, but also fabulous monsters and frights.

He followed reluctantly, realizing he had no choice if he wanted to question Abu Hassan on possible modes of escape from the island. Phillimore's stomach rumbled hungrily. Abu Hassan turned and motioned for utter silence; whether his expression denoted fear or simple disapproval Phillimore could not tell.

Their path lay steadily, inexorably uphill. As the hike grew increasingly strenuous, Phillimore paused ever more often, winded. The climb was difficult enough, but he was also encumbered by the awkward size and considerable weight of the black umbrella.

The greenery grew sparser the higher they mounted. They scrambled over steep expanses treacherous with small stones underfoot. One such place, the scholar's foot slipped; he sprawled on his face to save himself from pitching down the slope. This action precipitated a small hailstorm of pebbles clattering down the rockside. Abu Hassan, whirling, hissed for quiet, his face white with fear rather than anger.

"There is now great danger," he whispered, pointing across to a ledge many feet higher and to the right. "The purple troll's lair!"

He insisted on remaining perfectly still for some minutes. While they waited, he strained to hear anything which portended menace.

"I thought you said there were no living things save us and the birds on the isle," Phillimore murmured directly in Abu Hassan's ear.

"That is Allah's own truth, sire," the other replied softly. "There are no other *living* things . . ."

Phillimore swallowed with considerable difficulty.

After a long motionless time, during which neither breathed more than necessity required, a subtle *whirr*, low and distant, came to Phillimore's ears. As he listened, the sound drew nearer, greatly increasing in pitch and volume. A moment more and he identified it as a colossal clamour of bird-cry and wing-flapping, louder, more terrible than any such mundane noises had any right to be. The tops of the trees beneath them began to sway and bend in the wind and they felt a sudden draft, fetid and powerful as a hurricane. The sky grew dark.

"Quickly!" Abu Hassan exclaimed in the deafening din. "This flight covers our movements!" He sprang up and scuttled diagonally across the slanted plane of rock, moving away from the direction of the troll's eyrie. Phillimore hastened to follow.

It was long past midday. The sun's burning-rays beat fiercely upon them. Phillimore was so thirsty he temporarily forgot his hunger. Up and up they climbed, the wind propelling them with double speed. They had to fight to keep from being swept off the precipice as they worm-inched around a sharp spine that divided the different-facing mountainsides. Phillimore clung to the umbrella with difficulty, averting his eyes from the Cineramic riot of island, forest and sea below.

On the other side of the spine, the cliff mercifully leveled out somewhat; their feet found relatively horizontal terrain to tread upon. The wind died down, and in the sudden disquieting hush, Phillimore heard the sound of the great birds more clearly than before. The noise proceeded from a point not far above.

The slope was gentle now. Abu Hassan swiftly made his way up till he gained the apex of the slanted path. Attaining it, he waved his hand warningly at Phillimore, then, lying flat on his stomach, cautiously beckoned the professor to come and join him.

Phillimore crept up the final distance and, emulating his guide, stretched out prone. Carefully he raised his head till his eyes saw beyond the latter extremity of the path.

What he beheld was a wide mesa far below the overhanging lip of rock which comprised the latter end of the slope they'd climbed. Devoid of vegetation, the vast plateau was cupped by the ridges and shelves of the confining precipice. In the middle of the tableland was a spectacle that bulged his eyes.

A stupendous white dome shone in the dwindling rays of the sun; next to it lay the rubble of an identical globe: two gargantuan hemispheres seamed, splintered and fragmented by some colossal force. Phillimore had no doubt concerning the source of the dome's demolition since, next to it, there stood a black-feathered bird as big as a brownstone in College Heights. The avian monstrosity calmly balanced first on one mammoth foot, then the other. It lifted its head up expectantly.

"It's just hatched," Abu Hassan whispered. "It's only a baby."

"I presume it's a roc?"

"Yes. See . . . the mother came to see if it was hatched. Now it's gone again to get junior some food."

They waited while the baby announced its hunger in periodic cries so loud Phillimore had to stick his fingers in his ears. After seven or eight minutes, the rapid approach of the mother-bird was prefigured by the same raucous whirr of wings heard before, as well as similar wind and the inevitable blotting-out of the sun.

GRAAK!!

The baby bird signaled its joy at its mother's return in a cry so mighty it nearly knocked Phillimore off the cliff. Abu Hassan pointed up at the mother roc, a bird bigger than Mallin Hall at Parker College. A creature far surpassing the hyperbole of nightmare, the roc carried an elephant in its bill, a tidbit which it delivered to its baby.

"And now," Abu Hassan chortled wits suppressed glee, "you shall hear a thing that even a Caliph could not command for his pleasure!"

The pachyderm being disposed of, a mere high-tea snack, the baby roc waddled to its mother, nestled in her wings and started to croon as softly as an express train late for dinner. The mother bird joined in, and the combined nerve-shattering sound made the mountain quiver.

Phillimore, fingers in ears, was about to suggest a rapid return journey when Abu Hassan nudged him to look across the plateau to a ledge some seventy or eighty yards distant.

On it squatted a purple quasi-human thing with protrusive toad-eyes, pimpled hairy tongue and thin arms terminating in sabre-curved talons. The entity mildly contemplated the cooing birds below for several seconds, then, opening its fang-filled mouth wide, began to howl and squawk in a manner calculated to bring bad dreams unto the sleeping dead. Phillimore felt the hair rise on his forearms as multitudes of goose-bumps declared their presence.

"Every year," Abu Hassan confided to him *sotto voce*, "when the newborn chicks hatch out, the purple troll blends its voice with the bird-song. A rich thing, I declare, that so fell a beast can be thus moved by the beauty of nature's birthing music!"

"Yes, yes," Phillimore agreed wearily, shuddering at the aspect of the purple troll, "but see here, I'm ready to climb down. If I don't eat something soon, I won't have the strength to descend."

"But nay!" Abu Hassan protested. "It is too soon to return. This opportunity doth come but once a year, and it is my habit to hear all the melody that they care to produce."

"In that case," the scholar groaned, "you'll excuse me. I'm going."

He started down the slope. Behind him, Abu Hassan sadly shook his head, convinced that his new companion was a tone-deaf lout. Yet in defense of our protagonist it must be declared that the very opposite was true: Phillimore's ears were too sophisticated for the grating primal musicale taking place on the mountain. For, after all, a man whose ears are accustomed to the subtly chiseled harmonies of a Dowland or Purcell, a man who revels in the ascetic tonal architecture of a Bach can hardly be expected to stay still and tolerate the primitive dynamic crudities of a roc and troll concert.

CHAPTER SEVEN

By the time he reached the jungle floor, it was nearly
dark. Exhausted, ravenously hungry, Phillimore also
was hopelessly lost. He had no idea in which direction
lay the stream.

"Well, one thing at a time," he chided himself. "Better look for something nourishing before all the light
is gone."

Not adept at natural science, Phillimore dimly
guessed he was more likely to turn up edible seafood
at dawn than dusk, and anyway, he didn't want to
waste the twilight wandering aimlessly through the
woods. Aware of his shortcomings as a botanical expert, he avoided berries he did not recognize and settled for a handful of nuts and a pair of coconuts recently fallen to the ground. These latter proved an
immense problem to open, and he only did so by desperate measures which most him most of the milk
within one of the nuts.

Choosing an adjacent glade to consume his meager
fare, he sat down and rested his back against a palm
tree. Supper was soon over. Phillimore made a feeble
effort to rise, but his stiff, aching limbs protested and
he did not budge.

"Ought to look for Abu Hassan," he mumbled thick-
ly, as he fell asleep.

Phillimore slumbered for hours. A pale crescent moon rose and in the forest, night-things snuffled and rooted for forage. A sea-breeze stole into the jungle, eradicating the noontide heat. He shivered, partly from the chill air, partly because of the malevolent creatures romping through his over-stimulated subconscious.

Shortly past midnight, the breeze died down. Phillimore woke abruptly, vaguely aware that something was horribly wrong. Still tired, he could not immediately single out the disturbing circumstance, but at length he gathered his wits sufficiently to isolate the thing that made him rouse from troubled sleep.

It was too quiet. The dell lay in an unnatural silence that was curiously ominous, impending. He heard nothing of the myriad sounds that small animals produce among the thick maze of boles and bramble that constitute a forest; no sound, not even the stridulation of a lone insect.

A black cloud concealed the moon. He could barely see two feet in front of his nose. And yet—

By the foot of the mountain, etched hazily against the slightly less gloomy background of the night sky, a great bulky shape loomed. Motionless it stood, possibly nothing more sinister than a slanting stand of fern. Yet Phillimore conceived the nasty notion that the thing was watching him.

Thinking over his predicament, he decided the first thing on the agenda was to get hold of the umbrella, though he was uncertain whether to use it as a weapon or as a mode of escape. Still, if he should decide the most prudent course was to indulge in a nocturnal run, he would have to take it with him, anyway . . . so . . . slowly, very slowly, he edged his fingers

through the moist grass toward the place where he remembered laying the instrument.

But no sooner did he commence to move his hand,
snail-slow, than the menacing patch detached itself
from the surrounding murk and headed in his direction. Suddenly, the hush was shattered by a diabolic
snarl/shriek that turned his blood to frost.

As the thing hurtled at him, Phillimore rolled over,
grabbed the umbrella, whirled and shot to his feet,
thrusting forth the up-pointed umbrella so its tip was
aimed in the general direction of the onslaught. The
fiendish howl rose in pitch as it neared . . . and then
he felt a bone-jarring impact that almost made him
sit down again. He staggered backward from the blow
and the umbrella instantly was wrenched from his
grip.

Just then, the cloud sailed past and let the moon
shine upon the glade once more, bleeding a wan light
that revealed dimly Phillimore's awful adversary.

It was the purple troll. Close up, the dead thing was
even worse than he'd imagined possible. Well over six
feet, it stank with the odor of rotted blood. Glowing
amber eyes shone malevolently down on him; he was
sure the thing could see perfectly in the darkness. Protruding from its middle was Moriarty's umbrella, half
of its great length puncturing the vile creature. And
yet, though it was deeply impaled, the troll showed no
sign of discomfort, or even of *noticing*.

Rooted with fear, Phillimore nearly succumbed to
the hypnotic glare of the beast's eyes. But as the
wicked talons whooshed towards his neck, self-
preservation surged and he jumped aside with a
frightened yelp, almost braining himself against the
palm tree. The troll pivoted, reared back and bared its
lethal claws for a second try.

At the last possible instant, Phillimore ducked behind the tree. The troll slammed smack into the trunk, driving the umbrella further within its innards. Slavering horrendously, it slashed out at Phillimore around the curve of the bole, but only succeeded in sinking its long claws into the bark. It yanked, but they would not come out.

Panting from exertion and terror, the frightened mortal backed away and watched, ready at any moment to run if the troll showed a sign of freeing itself. But after a full minute of growling and gnashing of its teeth, it still was stuck. Phillimore approached with trepidation, knees knocking, teeth chattering, heart pounding.

But he knew he had to pull out the umbrella.

First he tried to stretch forth his hand and grab the curved grip, but the troll snapped at him so ferociously that he almost lost a finger. He leaped back five feet before timorously resolving to try again.

This time, he crouched low so its fangs couldn't reach. Ignoring the noisome breath as best he could as it ranted, he carefully stretched up his hand, grabbed the shaft and yanked. It gave slightly, then stopped. Kneeling on both knees, he leaned as close as he dared, grasped the umbrella-handle with both hands and extracted another inch of the oversized parasol, but then it was impossible to budge it further.

One at a time, he wiped his sweating hands against his trousers and tried a new purchase on the grip. The troll howled with frustrated fury, and vainly tugged to free its sharp nails from the bark of the tree.

Phillimore gained another inch of umbrella from the troll's bloodless innards, and then a remarkable thing occurred. The beast suddenly stopped howling and champing its jaws. The professor, startled by the

dramatic silence, looked up to see the creature gawk-
ing at something behind and above Phillimore. The
troll's saucer eyes goggled so wide the scholar thought
they would pop out. All at once, the purple troll began to thrash and shake with renewed vigor, mewling
and whimpering as it did. Phillimore, glued to the umbrella, was knocked this way and that, but with each
toss, more of the shaft came loose.

At last, with a supreme effort and a bloodcurdling
ululation, the troll twisted its wrists so hard that its
hands snapped off and remained nail-embedded in
the tree-trunk. Not even pausing to notice the latter
inconvenience, it clambered off the way it came,
dragging Phillimore with it. The professor doggedly
hung on, though the blundering flight bounced and
jounced his posterior cruelly. But at length the umbrella twisted free and he and it tumbled once, twice,
three times before sprawling in a heap at the base of a
coconut-palm.

Unencumbered now, the troll lumbered swiftly off
through the underbrush, burbling and gibbering.
Reaching the cliffside, it scrambled its way upward
toward the safety of its own lair.

Below, Phillimore lay too winded to move, a mass
of bruises. Panting for breath, he had enough of his
senses left to comprehend that somewhere close by
lurked a hobgoblin so terrible that it even frightened
away the sufficiently ghoulish purple troll.

His curiosity did not have long to wait for satisfaction. Heavy footsteps smashed through the jungle.
The ground trembled with the coming. Wincing, Phillimore rose to his feet to see what new surprise ironic
fate had up its sleeve.

He beheld the figure of an enormous being, fully
seven feet tall, glowering down upon him in the twi-

light. The stranger's hair was a lustrous black and its teeth shone white in the feeble rays of the moon, but these luxuriances only formed a more horrid contrast with its watery, disdainful eyes, its shriveled complexion and straight black lips. The creature's unearthly ugliness rendered it almost too loathsome for human eyes to behold.

"Devil!" it exclaimed. "Vile insect! how didst thou dare wrest me from mine creator's island upon the very eve of the day when I was to be joined forever with my mate? I thought to see thee perish at the shore of this accursed isle, but behold! thou hast survived that I may wreak vengeance on your treachery—which, I have some little fear, was engineered by He from whose hands I ought to have expected and deserved the most!" Here the monster gnashed its teeth and wrung its hands, wailing hideously. It was a frightful spectacle, and yet some doit of pity stirred in Phillimore's breast.

Everything came clear to him in an instant. This was the great weight that was exchanged for Persano's when Phillimore willed the umbrella to compromise with its two passengers' orders. Thus he arrived in the world of *The Arabian Nights* in the company of the "tool" that Persano thought Moriarty might be eager to commandeer.

Frankenstein's monster.

CHAPTER EIGHT

Fortunately, Phillimore had once written a term paper about Mary Shelley's bizarre tragedy and therefore was quite familiar with the lineaments of its plot. More to the point, in that minithesis he maintained that the true villain of the tale was not the monster, but rather Frankenstein himself: spoiled, selfish, unable to love or even pity his innocent creation. Thus the monster's latter cruelties were but the logical consequences of a child denied its parent's affection.

Like many perfectly sound closet theories, it was difficult to derive courage from it in actuality, especially with the creature hulking over him with murder in its mind. But Phillimore resolved to put aside his natural aversion to the fearful aspect of the monster, and try to deal with it humanely.

"See here," he said in a voice he hoped was steady, "you've got it all wrong! I didn't come to kidnap you, but rather to rescue you. I have your best interest at heart, which is more than I can say for the wretch who infused life into your limbs!"

The monster growled. "Speak no ill of mine illustrious father!"

Oh, damn! Family loyalty in monsters?

"But see here," Phillimore demurred, "I grant you that Victor Frankenstein is a scientist of extraordinary capacity, but what did he ever do for you besides bring you into existence? He abandoned you immediately thereafter!"

The monster moaned. "Yet he promised to make me a bride that I might go elsewhere and fill out mine days in mildness and peace."

"Rubbish! He never meant to keep his word. At the end of the experiment, he tore your intended to shreds."

The creature glowered so malignantly that Phillimore began to nervously finger the umbrella-catch. But then a puzzled expression crossed its face and it sat down on the grass and eyed Phillimore oddly.

"See here," it demanded, "how is it that you know so intimately the secrets of my past and future?"

It was no time for casual flippancy. He needed a colossal lie. "Well, the—uh—the fact is, I am something of a scientist myself: Or you might call me a magician."

"Magic?" the monster beamed. "I love magic! Do me a trick!"

"Later," Phillimore promised, realizing the monster indeed possessed a great child-brain.

"Now! Now!" the other grunted, clapping its big hands eagerly.

Oh, Good Gad! "All right, all right, calm down!" Phillimore proceeded to pretend to remove his thumb, stretch his middle finger and clap his hands without taking them apart, much to the delight of the monster.

"Teach me how to do that!" it growled delightedly.

"Only if you promise to behave and be good!"

It vigorously nodded its head, so Phillimore went through the arcane secrets of his digital conjurations. At last, when he'd regained the creature's attention with some little difficulty, he explained he chose to

spirit him away from Victor Frankenstein in order to
bestow eventual happiness upon him.

"How?" it demanded. "And shall I call thee master?"

How, indeed? "That won't be necessary," Phillimore
replied, blushing. "When my mission is done, I will
take you to a world where people won't shun you, a
place where you may live happily ever after." The
scholar kept his fingers crossed. *But there just might
be such a place, after all. Perhaps—*

The thought was choked off, along with his breath,
by the sudden seizing of the scholar by the Frankenstein monster. His first terrified thought was that the
fiendish being doubted Phillimore's campaign-promise,
but then he realized the bruising embrace was a thing
of sheer gratitude.

"O unexpected angel!" the monster proclaimed joy-
ously, hugging him with bone-crushing enthusiasm.
"How beneficent thou art! To think I shall be delivered from the affrighted malice of the small men who
would not comprehend the love I have within mine
nature, could it but be unleashed! O, grant me this
and I shall follow you faithfully, doing your every
bidding!"

"For starters," Phillimore gasped, "how about letting me go?"

"You have but to command!"

The professor coughed and wheezed for several
minutes, ruefully fingering his aching ribs and tender
neck. But it occurred to him he could do worse than
confront Professor Moriarty with the monster in tow.

"I suppose," he said at length, "that if we are to
work together, you ought to have a name. Mine, by
the way, is Phillimore."

"Mighty Phillimore, I greet thee. Though my crea-

tor failed to christen me, I am proud to take the family name of Him who endowed me with life. Call me Frankenstein."

Phillimore nodded. *Might as well, that's how most people refer to the monster, anyway.* He suggested that he might want to use "Frank" for short, but the monster thought this a sign of disrespect to his father.

"Since you, Mighty Phillimore, hath adopted me, it is meet that you select a first name for me to carry."

"Very well." The only name that came to his mind was Boris. Fortunately, the monster liked it immensely.

"It begins with the same letter as 'beautiful,'" he crowed happily.

"And now, Boris, let us return to the subject of my mission."

The monster nodded its head eagerly. "Tell me the story, Mighty Phillimore, O tell me!"

So Phillimore spun out the history of his adventures, translating certain parts for more ready accessibility to Boris' frame of reference. Thus Moriarty was transformed into a powerful evil magician, and his umbrella became a stolen magic wand.

"Now, Boris, the question is how do we get off this miserable island? And once off it, where do we seek for the nefarious Moriarty?"

"As for that," Boris said, "I should think the powers of Mighty Phillimore would be sufficient to effect both ends."

"Unfortunately, I don't seem to possess the kind of magic tool necessary. An umbrella-wand is all very well and good, but it's no Aladdin's—!" Phillimore broke off, leaped to his feet. "Of course! Aladdin's Lamp! That's what we need!"

Boris had a vague recollection of such a story when

he taught himself to read by browsing through a set of books in another forest of another world. "Was not this lamp the property of a great wizard who dwelled in the land of China?"

"Yes! Now all we need is a ship to take us off this island and—" He paused, wondering why the monster suddenly got to its feet and stretched its hands above its head.

"What in hell are you doing?"

"Look at the sky!" Boris crooned raucously. "So beautiful, the sky above the island, the sky . . ."

A thought started to surface in Phillimore's mind, an important thought, but he couldn't quite catch hold. Looking up to see what thrilled the monster, he beheld the pale tints of morning streaking the night sky.

Sky! Hold onto that word! Sky! What else? The sky above the island . . .

SKY ISLAND!

"*I have it!*"

"Have what?" Boris asked.

"The way to get off this island! The way to go wherever we want to go . . . at least I *think* so."

The monster shrugged. "I did not doubt that Mighty Phillimore could work the spell, if he so chose."

"Thanks for the vote of confidence," the scholar replied, wishing he could get Boris to stop calling him Mighty Phillimore. But perhaps there was wisdom in letting the other adulate him . . .

"Something you said," Phillimore explained, "reminded me of a book I read a long time ago: *Sky Island.* It's all about this boy who travels all the way from Philadelphia to the Pacific Ocean just by finding a magic *umbrella.*"

"And so?" In truth, the monster had no idea what the other was talking about, never having heard of Philadelphia. Yet, Watson-like, he sensed that what Mighty Phillimore needed was a sounding-board, so he urged his putative benefactor to continue.

"You see, Boris, up to now I've only used umbrellas for interdimensional travel. But if it really responds to the coordinates dictated by the user, why shouldn't it be capable of a simple overland hop in the same world?"

Boris gestured, palms-up, in a what-can-I-tell-you? fashion. He didn't know what to tell Phillimore.

But the scholar needed no further prompting. His mind made up, he immediately set their plans in motion. First of all, they went to the beach where he retrieved his jacket and scooped up fresh clams. The two sat and breakfasted off shellfish and coconuts. Boris experienced no difficulty opening the latter, though the clams were something of a trial.

Slaking their thirst at the stream, Phillimore instructed Boris to wait while he went to get Abu Hassan. (He thought the little man would do better being told about the monster before setting eyes on Boris.) But Abu Hassan refused to come with Phillimore.

"If you have decided to leave the isle as mysteriously as you came, that is your business, sire. Abu Hassan remains exiled in his eternal shame. I ask only that you do not tell a soul of my whereabouts. Let my memory die when I am perishèd!"

Promising he would keep his secret, Phillimore bade Abu Hassan farewell and walked away, still wondering what heinous deed the little stinker once committed.

Back at the beach, he instructed Boris to grab hold of the umbrella-shaft. "If you keep your mind blank, I

don't think it will heat up." Actually, he had no idea
what the thing would do, but the worst that could
happen, he told himself, was that Boris would fall off,
and Phillimore was still undecided whether the monster's presence was an asset or a liability . . .

"All right, Boris, you ready?"

"Yes, O Mighty Phillimore!"

"Then here we go!"

Affixing the idea in his mind of Aladdin's Lamp
and, secondarily, the general direction of China, Phillimore brushed the catch with his thumb and pressed
down.

Instantly the umbrella rose in the air. Boris
whooped with delight, but Phillimore squinted his
eyes shut at the dizzy panorama of surf that suddenly
yawned beneath him.

Up, up they went, higher than the clouds. *Easy! A
little lower!* Phillimore ordered in panic, gasping for
breath. The umbrella gently descended until he was
able to adequately fill his lungs. *That's fine. Now—
let's go!*

And it did. They zipped across the sky at a speed
that terrified the professor, though the monster
thought it all great fun. After several minutes of dare-
devil flying, Phillimore ventured to open one eye,
only to shut it immediately when he beheld the ocean
far beneath his dangling feet.

He had no idea how long they flew; it seemed an
eternity. But eventually, Phillimore sensed the umbrella both decelerating and losing altitude. Daring to
look down once more, he beheld a picturesque landscape not so very far below. Close by and coming up
fast was a tall, intricately-sculpted pavilion with
peaked spires and rosy-tinted minarets.

The umbrella floated closer, closer to the pavilion

that shone gold in the setting sun. Leveling with one of the upper windows, a glassless casement that revealed within a mandarin-red bedchamber, the umbrella hovered undecided for an instant, then swooped through and set the adventurers gently onto the thickly-carpeted floor. The hood closed automatically and the flight-button popped back out with a click.

The monster sucked in a sharp, startled breath, let it out again in a deep, contented sigh.

"O Mighty Phillimore!" Boris breathed. "O benevolent master! *O, wow!*"

CHAPTER NINE

Billowing in the honey-laden breeze, the scarlet tapestries shyly hid from view the maiden secrets of nook and niche and ceiling. The floor—clad in costly rugs blazoned with dragons and sailing vessels worked in gold wire—bore but two articles of furniture. The first was a lofty wooden cabinet hand-carved with a riot of heroes, handmaidens and holy men; its top was festooned with garlands of sun-bright blossoms in crystal bowls, jade-girdled hookahs, decanters of strange-colored liqueurs made from violet and hibiscus. The other furnishing was the great bed itself, a downy field of luxurious pillowing held by a sturdy frame of gold inlaid with silver, studded with star sapphires, opals, rubies, opulent amethyst, giant pearls, chrysoberyl and bloodstone. The gleaming corner posts supported an ornate canopy of cinnabar from which depended gossamer veneers of silk tied back by gold-rope that, released, would whisper into place the diaphanous stuff so it might shield from untutored eyes those arcane rites practiced by the initiates of that alluring inner sanctum.

Expensive joint, thought Phillimore, *but over-decorated. Rather tacky.*

Jasmine scent heavied the air. From someplace far below, the reedy piping of a seductive melismatic melody wafted upward. Taken altogether, the richly-appointed chamber, the perfumed breeze, the distant sinuous music combined to create a delicious redolence that lulled the senses and hinted at ecstasies bordering on dreams.

But what of that she who dwelled therein? For surely it was none of the rare pleasantries of the place that so transported the newly-arrived monster, but rather the incomparably alluring inhabitant of the vermilion bedchamber who introduced within Boris' innocent breast the unfamiliar condition of transcendent rapture.

It was a damsel slender of form and dazzlingly beautiful, as she were the effulgent sun itself. Clad in translucent veils of delicate pastels, she languished upon the yielding textures of the bed and there recalled the words of the poet Oubralz:

She shines forth in the night and all our thoughts
    arise
To seek the nutless meat of her swell almond eyes;
And all men yearn to spread their honey-praise so
    sweet
Upon the well-bred turn of her well-bathed feet;
When she unveils and all her hidden charms
    appear,
I shall not crave aught else, unless it be a beer.

Oping her doe-like eyes upon espying the two strangers alight upon the thick pile of carpeting near her bedside, the ineffably lovely damsel parted the curved grace of her coral lips and spake unto them thus: "Suffering Sinbad, who in the howling hot halls of Eblis are *you?*"

Boris began to speak, but Phillimore cut him off.

"We're sorry to—uh—drop in unexpectedly, but we're looking for Aladdin's magic lamp."

"Ooh, that bum!" she exclaimed, slipping out of bed so she could stamp her tiny foot upon the floor in petulance. "That's all he cares about, is it? I'll give him from lamps!"

"Who are you talking about?" Phillimore asked, confused.

"Aladdin, that's who! That bum, that no-good, I should only get my hands on him! Sending somebody else to pick up the lamp, he couldn't come in person! Me, I should have my head examined; I must have a hole where the brains used to be. Husbands! Did my mother tell me to wait, don't grab the first klutz that comes along? But no, I think I'm so smart! So I get a real jerk, some prize my hubby is . . . without that damned lamp, he'd still be the son of a peasant and maybe I'd be married to a Prince instead of a bum!"

The tirade continued in a similar vein and Phillimore waited impatiently for it to run down. He was uneasy, suspecting that he and Boris had landed in the latter portion of the Aladdin tale, the part in which an evil magician gained possession of the lamp and bade the genie carry the pavilion and its inhabitants to a remote clime where he, the mage, might at leisure enjoy the uses of the lamp, the palace and also the Princess.

Which means the wizard must be close by . . .

The Princess finally stopped vilifying Aladdin long enough for Phillimore to explain that he and Boris had nothing to do with her husband, though it wouldn't be long before Aladdin saved her from the loathsome advances of the sorcerer.

"Actually, if he'd wash his turban once in a while,

he wouldn't be so bad," the Princess yawned. "What'd you say your cute friend's name was?"

He introduced her to Boris, but oddly enough, the creature's ardor for the Princess had noticeably cooled. Inscrutably peculiar are the ways of monsters.

"And now," Phillimore insisted, "do you think I might have the loan of your husband's lamp?"

She shrugged disgustedly. "You imagine that if I could get at it, I'd still be here? That old smelly-headed clown of a wizard has it locked up."

"Where?"

"Right there." She waved her hand off-handedly at the carven cabinet. "It's inside."

"All right," said the teacher. "Boris—*fetch.*"

"Yes, O Mighty Phillimore!"

The monster lurched over to the cabinet, flung his arms about its midpoint and hoisted it into the air until he was able to shift the balance and raise it over his head.

"Watch out!" Phillimore warned as Boris dashed the cabinet onto the floor. He and the Princess skipped back a few steps while Boris hefted it a second time and again pounded it against the carpeting. On the third try, its doors sprang open.

"I'm afraid the noise will summon the sorcerer!" the Princess exclaimed, dashing forward to scrabble amongst the splinters for the lamp. "Hurry up and help me find it!"

Phillimore joined her. The cabinet was filled with bolts of costly cloth, jeweled bowls, goblets and less-recognizable ornamentalia, but nowhere could either of them see a lamp.

"Look, master!" said the monster, pointing across the floor to a drawer which must have flown out of the cabinet during one of the impacts. Phillimore and the Princess scrambled over and peered within. The drawer contained a single smooth box, polished and painted to depict a Shinto temple by a placid lagoon. It had no crack or keyhole, but when the Princess shook it, something inside rattled.

"The lamp!" she exclaimed. "Quick! Open it!"

"I'm *trying* to!" the professor grunted, running his fingers around the corners and edges, seeking a panel to push. "Must be a puzzle box. I used to have one . . ."

"Hurry!" the Princess nagged. "Before the wizard arrives!"

Someone chuckled. *"Too late. I am here."*

The unctuously menacing voice sent shivery pizzicati down Phillimore's vertebrae. Turning, he saw, looming gaunt and terrible in the doorway, a cadaverous old man with knife-edge features, tangled beard and rock-hard vulpine eyes. The mage wore a winered robe embroidered with cabalistic hieroglyphs; on his head there was a wrapped white turban so dingy as to verily cry for an ammonia bath. In one gnarled hand the sorcerer carried a long ebony stick tipped with silver that glowed with an unnatural light.

Phillimore, for once, was at a loss for words. An excuse that he merely wanted to borrow the lamp, though strictly accurate, would seem barely plausible in the face of the destruction which had been wrought upon the locked cabinet. His thoughts raced, but to no purpose, while simultaneously his fingers skittered frantically back and forth along the edge of the box, trying to find a section to jog or shift or slide.

"Foolish intruder," the magician gloated, "thou hast displayed uncommon courage and a great want of wit coming here to take possession of mine most valuable treasure. But didst thou truly imagine I would be such a dullard as to flaunt yon puissant artifact wholly un-fettered? Bah!"

Saying so, he waved his wand and the wooden box slid out of Phillimore's grip and began to flop end over end towards the wizard. The Princess threw herself upon it to stop its progress, but the wizard just laughed and waggled his wand. The box responded by shooting up into the air; he aimed the wand higher, higher, until the object hovered just beneath the silken-sheathed ceiling.

Now this maneuver was the undoing of the miracle-worker. Standing in the doorway, he could not see the corner of the room where Boris stood. The monster, in turn, had not yet set eyes on the magician, but he commanded a perfect view of the middle of the chamber. Thus the animation of the box riveted him with boundless wonder, and when the thing soared high in the air, Boris could no longer contain his enthusiasm.

"MAGIC! MAGIC!" he crowed, hopping up and down in his excitement and clapping his huge hands. "I LOVE MAGIC!"

The room shook with the monster's jouncing de-light. The startled sorcerer took an uncertain step into the room, then turned to discover the cause of the ruckus.

His jaw flapped south. The towering fiend outdid in ugliness the most malevolent afreet that had ever gibbered at him during his most dire evil spells. With a great effort of will, the magician forced his para-lyzed vocal cords to work overtime at a scream.

Boris' feelings were deeply hurt. Pounding his hands together in a fit of anguish, he howled, "Curses! Scorned again!" and as he did, his watery eyes rolled in his head and his black lips twisted wide, displaying his great white teeth.

The spectacle was too much for the magico. His knees buckled and sagged and he slumped onto the carpet in a dead faint. The magic wand slipped from his numb fingers and nestled in the deep pile of the scarlet rug.

As soon as the wand left the wizard's grip, the puzzle box smashed straight down, missing Phillimore by a scant fraction of an inch. The impact splintered one edge and incidentally caused its secret drawer to spring open.

With a delighted utterance, Phillimore swooped up the burnished brass oil-lamp that lay within. He fished a handkerchief from his pocket and swiped it in long polishing strokes across the convex sides.

Great purple billows of smoke filled the room. The Princess coughed. Boris sneezed.

"*Gesundheit!*" a deep voice pronounced with exceeding distinctness and deliberation.

The smoke cleared. An enormous grinning entity squatted on the floor wheezing asthmatically and picking its teeth. Fat, dusky, jolly-looking, it had a great bare belly on which was tattooed the likeness of a brown-and-white-striped rabbit. It blinked mildly at the company and scratched its tummy, acknowledging Phillimore with a deferential bow, dismissing Boris with a "Hi, junior!" and a casual hand-wave and wink. It gave the Princess a more protracted scrutiny, but she haughtily deigned not to notice.

More for something to say than out of a need to establish credentials, Phillimore inquired, "Are you the genie of the lamp?"

Nodding, the genie pointed at the picture on his stomach. "Sure. Ain't you ever heard of the genie with the white-brown hare?" He preened proudly. "Actually I just work the lamp nights."

"What?"

"I've got the night shift."

"I don't understand," said Phillimore, surprised. "I thought genies were eternal slaves to the lamps and rings and bottles they live in . . . one genie apiece."

The genie waved a deprecating mitt. "That stuff went out with button-down togas! No more of that getting stuck in a bottle for three hundred years, then getting your cork popped by some rumbum sailor who keeps you hopping day and night digging up undressed dames. Phooey!"

"So how have things changed?"

"We formed G.A.G.S."

"*Huh?*"

"Genies, Afreets and Giaours Society. It's an international union. From now on: eight-hour days, five-day weeks, two weeks off each year. Whaddaya think, the genie game's a picnic?"

"If it's that bad," Phillimore asked, "why do you do it?"

The genie shrugged philosophically. "It's a living."

The amenities aside, the Princess attempted to get control of the genie, claiming royal privileges. But the genie showed her an iron-clad, four-point-high clause in the standard contract which all lamp-sprites carry to the effect that no other master than the "rubbee" might be served at one time.

"But stick around, Toots, and we'll work something out while I'm off-duty." He winked at her, then turned to Phillimore. "Okay, what's your pleasure? Pleasure?"

The scholar shook his head. "First of all, take care of *him*"—he indicated the wizard, who was just waking up—"before he makes a nuisance of himself."

The spirit stashed the sorcerer in a cellar in Zanzibar, then returned to hear the rest of Phillimore's instructions.

"On another world," said the scholar, "an arch-criminal named Professor Moriarty fell into a cataract, the Reichenbach Falls. I was there. So was a detective, Sherlock Holmes."

(He included all the information so the genie would be able to pinpoint the proper planet.)

"Now," Phillimore continued, "I have reason to suspect that Moriarty didn't die but instead traveled magically to another world, probably this one. Your mission is to find out whether he still lives and if he does, where he is."

The genie clopped a hand to his forehead. "Hoo-boy! Is that a toughie!"

The professor was surprised. "I thought nothing is too hard for a genie."

"Did I say I couldn't do it?" the other rejoined, somewhat stung. "I just can't give you the usual whisk-zap-your-wish-is-my-instant-command crap. This is gonna take time! First off, I have to find—"

"Never mind all that," Phillimore interrupted, afraid the explanation would take longer than the execution. Doubtfully he asked, "But you think you *can* do it?"

The genie, pride deeply wounded, said stiffly, "I don't *think* I can do it, I *know* I can; willya just gimme some time?"

"How long?"

"Maybe fifteen minutes."

"Oh, that's all right," said Phillimore, relieved that it wasn't a matter of days or weeks. "We can certainly wait that long."

"Damn decent of you," the genie grumped, dematerializing in a disgruntled huff. Thirteen-and-a-quarter minutes later, he returned, task completed, feeling a bit guilty at the surly way he'd spoken to his new master. Afraid he may have discredited the noble profession to which he belonged, he resolved to respond promptly and respectfully to any other demand that might be made of him.

Which explains what happened next.

"I found him!" the spirit eagerly informed Phillimore.

"On this world?"

"Nope. In a place you wouldn't *believe!*"

"Well, in that case," the scholar said, "I have one last task for you to carry out." He nodded in Boris' direction. "He and I must travel to that world."

"*Yessir!*" the genie exclaimed and instantly gesticulated at the pair.

"*HOLDIT!*" Phillimore yelled. "WE'RE NOT QUITE REA—"

Neither the genie nor the Princess heard the rest of the sentence. Both James Phillimore and Boris Frankenstein were gone.

Without the umbrella.

Turning end over end, Phillimore aimlessly wobbled and at the same time, purposefully sped on towards Moriarty's world. He felt like a hurtling knuckle-ball in a cosmic cricket match.

Flying via genie was decidedly worse than umbrella travel. Without the comforting reality of the leather handle to grip, he had no means of orientation; every direction was simultaneously up and down. His stomach protested. He squeezed his eyes tight to shut out some of the carnival-ride dizziness.

He heard Boris howling from some place either far above or below. "O Mighty Phillimore! Why dost thou visit this punishment upon me? Canst thou truly con-

ceive that I, who was born unwillingly, am so vile as to deserve this?" The monster moaned piteously, but the sound of his despairing voice soon dwindled and was borne away by the rushing waves of space-time, and Boris was lost in darkness and distance.

Behind his eyelids, the twinkling chaos of the shifting dimensions still danced, but gradually the penetrating glow dimmed and at length, winked out altogether. Suddenly, freefall ceased . . . his feet touched something solid . . . his body jostled against three, four, five beings . . .

A wild chorus of shrieks assailed his ears.

Phillimore opened his eyes.

Onto madness.

CHAPTER TEN

Phillimore's first thought was that a wire in his brain must have fizzled out with the result that he was nine-tenths blind and ten-tenths looney.

All he could see were lines. Lines and dots. Darting lines, gleaming lines, pulsating lines, bright dots, dots that were nearly invisible, yet more lines and dots and lines and lines and dots and

—— —— • —————— — • —————— •

Dimness. Brightness. Some kind of fog disclosed ——
——— ———— • and concealed other
— • ———— — —— and everywhere
he turned all he saw were bright ——— and dim
——— and occasionally a • or two.

Immensity of space. Fluttering. Breeze? Yes—outdoors.

He heard many screams and shouts in an unintelligible tongue, and also, from many directions at once, a strange, high ululation.

Well, he told himself, *this is it, I have gone one hundred per cent stark raving bibblebibble bonkers!*

But as a matter of fact, the scholar had lost neither his eyesight nor his marbles. Still, it was a minor wonder that the ensuing events did not serve to place him permanently in a parlor for the perpetually puzzled.

A great multitude of lines surrounded him on all sides. They produced a complicated din to which Phillimore did his best to respond by spreading out his hands in a *non-comprendez* gesture.

And he noticed he had no hands.

Also no shoulders. No legs. No feet.

His body was totally askew, it didn't make anatomic sense. He felt its thickness, its length, and with a little experimentation, realized he could move forwards, backwards, sideways . . . but *on* what, *with* what he had no idea. He could hear and he could see, though the latter faculty was reduced to perception of a uniformly thin margin of distance stretching to infinity. Within that expanse, dots and lines shimmered and scuttled everywhere while other, duller lines remained stationary. The mobile configurations appeared to alter somewhat as they hypothetically turned, and surely there was fog to aid his eyes in distinguishing shapes.

The noise that the lines made continued. It suggested a simple test to Phillimore. He waggled the place where his jaw used to be. *Yes, I think it's there* . . . Though he couldn't touch it, he was sure he had a mouth. Someplace not far from where he was able to see there seemed to be an opening. He made it gape wide, willed sound to emerge.

"HEY! WHAT IN ALL GOOD HELL IS HAPPENING?!"

He got no answer, but at least he knew he could still converse in English.

Fat lot of good that does!

Just then, the noisy conglomeration of geometric oddities parted and a much larger shining line approached through the space they quitted. The indecipherable chatter ceased, and there was a hush Phillimore could have sworn was nothing short of deferential.

The large line stopped. The teacher stared at it, instinctually certain that it was engaged reciprocally. After a brief silence, the thing rumbled. A pause, then it repeated the sound.

It's trying to talk to me!

"Look, I'm sorry," Phillimore apologized, "if you can't speak English or French or German, I'm afraid I—"

He stopped. The shining line was retreating. Sliding smoothly to one side, it rumbled a new series of sounds. Instantly, a quantity of smaller lines, short and rather shady, moved forward, closer, closer, closer to Phillimore. They hedged him in on all sides.

They stopped quite close to the professor and as they did, Phillimore noted their dimensionality, inferred their *shape*. They were not lines after all, but rather a great array of narrow triangles, probably isosceles, and they all had their deadly points aimed at him. They only appeared as lines because he was eye-level with their perimeters. If he could rise straight up and hover over them, he would be able to view them as the triangles they must certainly be from above . . .

Except that in this world, there *was* no up, no above. The only thing Phillimore could see was *edge*, and even the concept of height was a trifle confusing to him at the moment. He knew it existed, but it was difficult to picture it in this two-dimensional place.

Now Phillimore knew precisely where he was.

Flatland.

"Imagine a vast sheet of paper on which straight

Lines, Triangles, Squares, Pentagons, Hexagons, and
other figures, instead of remaining fixed in their
places, move freely about, on or in the surface, but
without the power of rising above or sinking below it,
very much like shadows—only hard and with luminous
edges—"

He remembered quite well the satirical masterpiece
by one Edwin A. Abbott, a Shakespearean scholar
who turned his avocational delight in higher mathematics into one of the first important works of specu-
lative fantasy, *Flatland:* a world of only two dimensions, length and width; where neither buildings nor
people have any perceptible height; where it is so difficult to recognize the shape (and hence, social station)
of one's neighbors that the greater portion of university
training is devoted to the science of inferring shape.

Though Phillimore saw the thin book on Moriarty's
shelf, he never considered it as a possibility. Flatland
was no picnic to live in. The angles and points of
lower-class citizens were perpetual dangers, and an
accidental trip against a square might mean impalement. What was worse, Flatland had an extremely re-
pressive social system, complete with elitist government, castes, police-state authoritarianism and state-
engineered executions of undesirables (who were
primarily those unfortunate enough to be born with
slightly irregular sides).

*Now why on all the earths would Moriarty pick this
lousy spot to come to? Surely, it has no magic, no
great instruments of power to—*

His perplexed pondering was interrupted by the
prodding of one of the isosceles triangles. Because of
their narrow angles, these Flatlanders had commen-
surately tiny brains and thus served as the country's
soldiers. Their pointed angles functioned much the

same as bayonets; there was no arguing with their insistent nudging. Clearly, they wanted Phillimore to start moving, so he did so.

Where? Why do I rate a military escort?

As they traveled, he noted the land maintained its featureless, heightless character. Every once in a while, he heard the strange ululation he'd noted before and realized it must be some woman's peace-cry. Flatlander women were straight lines, which meant that turned sideways, they presented a near-invisible dot which might skewer a careless citizen who ran upon it. Thus, by law, women in public had to keep up a constant unnerving whine. *Like a belled cat. Or a leper.*

During the journey, Phillimore considered his predicament. Translation to Flatland included adaptation of one's body to the structural logic of that world. He worried lest the return journey fail to restore him to his customary form. Then a thought kicked him: *What return journey?* Moriarty might be two feet away, and he wouldn't recognize him, and how on earth could he possibly find his umbrella when he didn't even know what shape it was presently in?

Suddenly, a great gray motionless line loomed up, stretching as far as he could see to left and right. The soldiers in front paced away and stopped, leaving an opening through which the scholar moved. He entered a dim space, bounded by distant gray lines. It was evidently indoors.

Based on his propensity to incarceration while on his cosmic adventures, Phillimore guessed he was in a Flatland prison. A large angular figure approached and gently nudged him along till he entered a place consisting solely of gray lines.

There was a clang. Phillimore turned and saw he was alone.

"Prison, sure enough," he grumbled, more to keep up his courage than in expectation of receiving a reply. He moved around the confining quarters and observed the omnipresent grayness. Dull lines. Surely the inside of a cell.

Partway along one line a series of thin openings permitted him to look into another space bordered by a more distant dull line. He induced he was staring through bars into another chamber.

"Anyone there?" he asked, wishing someone could answer in English. He'd never before realized the wonderful property of Moriarty's umbrella to eradicate language barriers for the traveler. Now that he could not communicate to anyone, the—

"Is it possible?" a voice asked, eagerly. "Have I the privilege of addressing a noble Spacelander?"

Phillimore almost dashed himself against the wall, so anxious was he to see who, in the other cell, spoke. As he peered through the bars, a bright shape that might be anything from a triangle through a polyhedron drifted into view.

"You can talk in English!" the professor exclaimed. "Are you a Flatlander or—"

"I am indeed a Flatlander," said the other, dashing Phillimore's ill-defined birthing hopes. "I doubt not it is wonderful to you that I am able to converse in the tongue of civilized Spaceland, but perhaps you are aware of the modest treatise I caused to be circulated in your glorious world?"

Yes. When Abbott first had his book published, he pseudonymously signed it as if it were written by a native Flatlander visiting, for the first time, the world of three dimensions:

FLATLAND
A Romance of Many Dimensions
With Illustrations by the Author, A SQUARE

"Indeed," said the Square, "I am that same lawyer-square who happily, sadly was permitted to spend some time in your astonishing world. Many times have I tried to convince my fellow countrymen that there is a dimension called height, but you see what contempt they hold me and my theory in!"

"Why?" Phillimore asked, a sudden chill numbing the place where he supposed a heart must be. "Where are we? In prison?"

"No," said the Square, "in a mental institution."

CHAPTER ELEVEN

Trapped!

No umbrella. No way to communicate with his captors. No way out. Phillimore flung himself against the padded lines that comprised the walls of his cell and found they were quite as efficient as any in a three-dimensional asylum. He was caught, transfixed. *Trapped!*

Gossip traveled quickly among the inmates. Soon the Square, his neighbor, was able to explain exactly why Phillimore had been brought to a ward for the insane.

"If you could speak our language," said the Square, "you would be a national hero, rather than a patient here."

"What? *How?*"

"Flatland, you see, is frequently beset by riots and insurrections that never quite come off. Our lower classes, the isosceles triangles who opt for a life of trade rather than military service, are a disgruntled lot. Together with an occasional irregular Flatlander who has somehow escaped execution—these latter are our criminal element—the dreadfully-pointed isosceles often demonstrate against the hierarchy of the polygons and circles, for you must know that the more regular sides a Flatlander possesses, the higher he stands in the social scale. (Our high priest, by common courtesy, is assumed to have at least ten thousand sides, though it would be absolutely impossible for anyone to count that many. While this ruling luminary is called a circle, only God is believed to be a perfect Circle.)

"Now nature has so admirably disposed our world's order that the less sides an individual possesses, the fewer angles he has, and the less angles, the less space for brains. By the time we descend to the common isosceles, we are dealing with a remarkably stupid lot. As for *women*—" Here the Square disdainfully sniffed and did not see fit to comment further.

"Because the isosceles are so witless," he continued, "their insurrections have always been an easy matter to put down. They simply do not have any leaders to organize their rebellions effectively. But recently, a grave thing happened here."

"Yes?" Phillimore asked, interested in the story in spite of the fact that he was sure the Square had rambled away from the subject of his own incarceration.

"A Flatlander of mysterious origin suddenly came to the fore some months ago. Though I have not seen him, I hear he presents the aspect of a nearly-perfect circle. This fact, in itself, is highly threatening to our present government. But what is worse, this stranger whom nobody seems able to identify has taken it into his head to preach civil rights for women and the isosceles class. He wants the ancient practice of painting revived. He demands passage of the Universal Colour Bill—"

"I read your book some time ago," Phillimore interrupted, "and do not clearly recall these latter things."

"Long ago in Flatland," the Square explained, "pigmentation was discovered. People began making up in all sorts of bright hues, and it suddenly became infinitely easier to recognize one another. This seemed to be a good thing at first, but soon the university arts of sight recognition and shape inference fell into disuse. Irregular figures camouflaged their abnormalities and attempted to marry into the best families! At the height of the horror, a particularly crafty irregular tried to pass the Universal Colour Bill to require everyone, even priests, to paint. The purpose was to totally demoralize our hierarchy and create a virtual state of—democracy." (Here the Square shuddered.) "It was a terrible time in our history, but eventually the rebellion was quashed and the art of chromatism lost. Today it is a crime punishable by instant puncturing to colour in any way!"

The Square huffed indignantly at the memory of the trials of yesteryear. Phillimore suddenly was struck with curiosity.

"I say, what kind of figure do *I* represent to your vision?"

"Oh, you are a hexagon," the Square stated deferentially. "It is the lowest class of our nobility. That, plus your praiseworthy action in the center of town, should have made you a national hero but for—"

"Yes, yes," Phillimore prompted impatiently, "but what *did* I do?"

"The tale circulating is that you effectively ended the new rebellion."

"What? How did I do *that?*"

"The mysterious polygon of whom I spoke was holding his penultimate demonstration for all the things inimical to our government which he organized the lower classes to obtain. There were isosceles by the thousands parading before our National Capitol, all demanding their rights—and incidentally the setting-up of this divisive polygon as our new high priest, or Chief Circle. (I doubt not this is his real reason for stirring up so much trouble.)

"In the midst of this terrifying rally, just when our state enemy seemed assured of winning, you abruptly and inexplicably descended! Evidently you landed on a number of isosceles, knocking them by accident into other of their brethren, causing puncturing and maiming in great profusion. (Indeed, you were lucky to escape accidental impalement.) Since the isosceles class is thoroughly brainless, the disturbance grew into a full-fledged brawl, abetted by the sudden, purposeful appearance of the loyal militia. Within less than five minutes, so I understand, the ranks of the opposition were totally decimated. Only their leader, the polygon, escaped alive!"

The Square paused. Phillimore had a notion he was being regarded with pity by the other. "How ironic," his neighbor murmured after a time, "how very ironic that you had bestowed upon you such an honor, and yet were unable to appreciate it."

"What honor?"

"You, a lowly polygon, were vouchsafed an audience, right there on the street, with the Chief Circle himself! But when he heard you babbling that which appeared to be nonsense, he had no choice, sad as it must have made him, but to commit you to this institution."

Just then, Phillimore heard the click of a cell-door not far away. He turned expectantly, but the Square cautioned him not to maintain any false hope of instant liberation. "That sound is but the delivery of dinner by one of the women who tend us." Again he colored the word "women" with off-handed contempt.

"Perhaps," Phillimore mused, "I could learn the Flatlander language from you. Then I could explain my situation to the Chief Circle and—"

"And you would remain here the rest of your life," the Square interrupted. "I who am a native of this land but visited your dimension and was foolish enough to tell of my discovery of *height* . . . and here I languish. You who indeed hail from Spaceland would fare no better, and perhaps worse."

"Then I could fabricate a story to get me sprung from this place! Will you teach me the tongue?"

"I should be honored. But there is ample time. The Chief Circle only visits us once a year."

Phillimore's hypothetic heart sank into his non-existent boots. A *year!* By then, Moriarty could mount a new campaign—for he had no doubt that the Professor was the mysterious polygon—or return to his native world and start up his old criminal organization.

The question was: if Moriarty came to Flatland (for what purpose Phillimore still could not imagine), why hadn't he used the umbrella ere this to escape?

The cell-door of the Square clanked open and someone entered. Phillimore smelled a pleasant food odor.

"Let me advise you," said the Square, "to stay out of reach of this domestic. Women are not generally required to utter their peace-cry indoors, but these cells are more roomy than many interior chambers and she could damage you if she were to carelessly bump against you!"

Phillimore was momentarily embarrassed that the Square would speak so disparagingly of the serving-woman in her presence, but then he remembered that she could not understand English and probably thought the other was merely indulging in lunatic ravings.

The Square's cell-door clicked shut, and after a few

seconds, Phillimore heard a key grind in his own lock. He turned and saw a portion of one gray line slide to one side, revealing another gray line further off. In the intervening space shimmered the straight line of the serving-woman. She turned sideways to pick up the dish of food and he noticed how she dwindled into a point that was almost invisible.

The woman approached with the serving-dish, and Phillimore, following his neighbor's advice, moved away to give her ample turning space. But in spite of this maneuver, she kept coming closer, closer than necessary to give him his supper.

"Here, back off," the scholar commanded, "that's close enough." But she drew nearer, so much nearer that he began to worry that the Chief Circle might have decided it would be cheaper just to finish him off . . .

"I said back off!" Then he remembered the language barrier. Hurrying over to the bars that divided the cells, he was about to call the Square to interpret to the menacing female when suddenly in his ear there sounded a surprisingly familiar, wonderfully reassuring voice.

"Shhh!" the "woman" whispered. *"Come, James, come! The game is afoot!"*

CHAPTER TWELVE

"Holmes!" Phillimore exclaimed. "Is it possible? Can it be you?"

"Shhh!" the other cautioned. "We are not yet out of danger." Turning sideways, he began rubbing against Phillimore with a steady, purposeful stroking.

"What are you doing?" the scholar wondered.

"Applying makeup," Holmes whispered. "Without hands, it's a difficult business. Women in Flatland can travel about with little notice paid them. That is why I have disguised myself thus, and propose to do the same to you if you will hold still so I can get the shading even. It's all a matter of refraction of light, and a hexagon may easily appear to be a straight line with a—"

"Yes, I know all about that," Phillimore murmured, following the detective's example and keeping his voice low. "But using makeup is a crime punishable by death."

"Dire instances require dire methods. Your timely arrival broke Moriarty's strength. Now we have but to pursue him to his lair. The Flatland aristocracy has vainly attempted to assassinate him in his homequarters, but could not locate where he secrets himself. But it was a simple matter of comprehending the rationale of architecture. Putting my theory to a test, I shadowed the Professor and ascertained his location. Unfortunately, he was well protected in his fortress, and till now, I could not move against him. *Turn around, let me do your other sides.*"

Phillimore obliged. "Then you have been here for some time?"

"I have. This was the logical place to look."

"But how did you get here sans umbrella?"

Holmes continued to apply makeup as he explained. "When I returned from South America, my brother told me of your quest . . ."

"I've been gone *that* long?"

The linear equivalent of a shrug. "Who knows what amounts of time pass during umbrella flight? At any rate, I made to examine Moriarty's bookshelf as well and reach the sole possible conclusion concerning his whereabouts. Destination decided, I quickly engineered a new umbrella, drawing on my brother's theoretical expertise."

"You have a *new* umbrella?" Phillimore exclaimed. "Where?"

"I took the precaution of strapping it to my body before employing it. Thus, though I cannot see it, I am aware by feel that it is still tied to what ought to be my arm."

A clamor from some of the cells further along caused Holmes to quicken his rubbing of makeup on Phillimore. "They are beginning to wonder where the woman is with their food . . . another few strokes and then we must dare the guards and make good your escape." More rubbing, then Holmes asked Phillimore why it took him so long to come to Flatland.

"I did not reach the same conclusions concerning Moriarty's decision at the time he pressed my umbrella's catch at Reichenbach. I assumed he would fly to a world where there was some magic tool handy for the betterment of his nefarious schemes."

"Too studied," Holmes objected. "A man in imminent danger of plunging to his death would hardly mull over the comparative advantage of one or another safety-zone. The destination would surely be a thing of chance, dependent on the random thoughts racing through his brain at that dire instant."

"And what," Phillimore asked, "do you suppose Moriarty was thinking of?"

"Elementary, my friend. It was surely something in the nature of this: 'If I should *land*, I shall be crushed *flat!*' The umbrella merely interpreted as literally as it was able."

Phillimore started to laugh, but Holmes shushed him.

"I've done you as best as the circumstances allow. Quick, James, you must emulate a needle, for that is how you shall appear to the guards . . . the din grows great, we must hurry!"

Holmes hastened through the gap in the gray line and Phillimore followed. He stayed on the detective's heels (?) as Holmes led him down one corridor and up another. There were no stairs, nothing but length, width and more length and width. Occasionally, a shining line moved past them on some errand or another, but Phillimore noted with relief that they were always afforded considerable space to pass. Women, though scorned in Flatland, were evidently much feared.

At length they reached the outdoors. An isosceles on duty at the opening grunted something and Holmes addressed him in the peculiar jargon of the country. Phillimore marveled at his companion's ability to so quickly take on the customs of so alien an environment.

Once outside, Holmes quickened their pace. "We must hurry if we are to catch Moriarty. He is holed up in a fortress out of town. The place is an abandoned weapons-house, which is why no-one thought to search it for the disruptive polygon."

"I don't understand."

"Houses in Flatland, by law, must be built with at least five sides to prevent accidents from colliding with too sharp-pointed an angle. But in the old days, weapons repositories were deliberately fashioned with many points and angles to prevent Flatlanders from approaching too close."

"I see," Phillimore said, "rather like barbed wire surrounding a U.S. Army base."

Holmes, instead of replying, suddenly let out an awful high-pitched screech. Phillimore thought he'd run on a triangle, but then realized there were polygons approaching. The scholar also produced the weird sound that was the peace cry of female Flatlanders.

They proceeded over the countryside, sometimes shrilling the unpleasant sound, sometimes hurrying on in silence. The trip seemed longer than it really was, due to the absence of distinguishing features for the eye to fix upon.

After a time, Holmes cautioned Phillimore to slow his movement.

"We are drawing near. See that confusing line in the distance?"

Phillimore said yes. The line glimmered in odd places and was shaded in others. "An irregular figure, I presume?"

"Indeed. There is a second such wall within this

first. I warn you to proceed very carefully, very slowly. Bumping against interior or exterior of either might prove fatal . . ."

They crept along, Holmes in the lead. After a time, he indicated a narrow gap in the boundary. "We slip through there." With extreme care, Holmes edged his way up to the aperture and passed through it, stopping while Phillimore did the same and joined him.

"You see," Holmes said in a low voice, "the inner wall does not permit entrance at the same point. We must work our way round till the other door is found. By no means should you go any nearer either wall than we are now."

They started forward again, and this time Phillimore rested lightly against Holmes, turning as he turned, stopping where he paused. They went at a snail's-pace, and more than once, Holmes had to carefully negotiate around some linear obstruction which Moriarty evidently placed in the path to impale anyone foolish enough to speed around the space between the two fortress-lines that were walls.

"Here, now," whispered Holmes, "here it is. The door."

"No need to whisper, my good Holmes," a dry, unpleasant voice said from within. "Come in, come in, I have been expecting you."

The line that was the detective turned to look at Phillimore. "Surely," said Holmes, "he is indulging in braggadocio. Our makeup is indistinguishable from the aspect of women."

A large line emerged from the interior of the fortress and waited some distance away. The thing chuckled nastily. "Excellent acoustics here, my dear Holmes, I have heard your whispered colloquy. However, let me assure you that my identification is no matter of guesswork. Who but my most illustrious enemy could penetrate to my hideaway and decipher my own disguise?" He moved perhaps an inch closer. "I assume the companion by your side is the good Dr. Watson?"

"Do not answer," Holmes warned Phillimore.

"Come, come, there is no reason why we cannot be open with one another," Moriarty said sweetly. "Your time is almost come, and there is some salve in discharging all one's secrets at the last."

Holmes said nothing.

"Well, well, keep your counsel if you must. The silence of kings and beggars, the silence of the grave."

"I had not known you to indulge ere this in idle threats."

"My dear Holmes, surely you know by now that nothing I promise is empty sabre-rattling!" The great line that was the evil arch-criminal suddenly called out, and out of the aperture which was the door to his inner fortress there emerged a half-dozen isosceles triangles, points directed towards Phillimore and Holmes.

"Farewell, dear nemesis," Moriarty said condolently, "I shall miss our war of wits."

The triangles began their slow, purposeful approach.

"What do we do?" Phillimore asked urgently. "Run? Fight?"

"I am afraid," said Holmes grimly, "that neither course will do us much good. Flight will certainly impale us on one of those near-invisible obstructions or else the treacherous walls will pierce us. As for combating a squad of isosceles—"

Moriarty laughed unpleasantly. "I doubt that your expertise with singlestick or baritsu will be of much aid, my soon-to-be-late friend."

"Maybe you can out-talk the Professor?" Phillimore urged. "Persuade these triangles that—"

"Save your breath," the villainous master-line stated. "These are my hand-picked guard. They are all deaf."

The points were perhaps twenty inches away, and the triangles—as cautious about the fortress walls as Holmes had been—drew steadily, slowly closer and closer.

"What about the umbrella?" Phillimore shouted. "Wouldn't you like to go back to London?"

"I shall, never fear, I shall. For a good while, I couldn't find the thing, but now I know exactly where it is. As soon as I rearouse this rebellion that you temporarily quelled, and as soon as this world pays me my due tribute, I shall move on . . . just as my soldiers are doing . . ."

Moriarty, dismissing them as lost causes, turned to reenter the fortification.

His soldiers were a mere nine inches away.

"Soon they will charge," said the detective. "There is nothing we can do but meet death stoically."

Phillimore, far from being frightened, was extremely annoyed. *All that effort outwitting Persano, escaping from Jonathan Wild, fighting the troll, and so on and on . . . and it all ends like this!? High adventure—Bah!*

The triangles stopped when they were only six inches off. They quivered for the charge, ready to dash forward and stab Moriarty's enemies . . .

One of them uttered a warlike cry. Their signal.

But before they could charge, another sound drowned out the noise of the officer-triangle.

A deafening smashing, ripping noise behind Phillimore and Holmes stopped the execution in its tracks.

The scholar whirled about to see what was happening.

The exterior wall of the fortress quivered and shook, and as they watched the line splintered into fragments that skittered forward and sideways. Something on the other side of the wall punched it again and again, enlarging the hole.

Moriarty turned to see what intruder dared his wrath.

Through the gap in the battered remnant of a wall emerged a gigantic line glowing in peculiar places, dim in others. When the isosceles triangles saw it, they screamed and began to run in three directions: left, right, backwards, anywhere but forward where the newcomer stalked.

Two of the triangles collided harmlessly, but before they could part, a third skewered both during its flight; the impaler, in trying to free its point, snapped it off and also died. The fourth and fifth isosceles tried to run around the side of the central building. Each crashed into one of the protrusions of the inner wall, thrashed, and was still.

As for the last triangle . . .

"HELP!" Moriarty screamed. "GO BACK!"

But the terrified triangle rammed directly into the Professor and turned him into a bisected line on the instant. Moriarty choked a single word of hatred at Holmes and with his dying convulsion broke his murdering triangle in two.

Silence. Holmes and Phillimore regarded their savior. It was an enormous line, but the random way in which the light played and fell on its facets suggested it must be an extremely irregular polyhedron.

And then the stillness was shattered by the grievous wail of the thing that saved them.

"*Curses!*" Boris howled. "*Scorned again!*"

CHAPTER THIRTEEN

They entered the weapons-house to seek Phillimore's original umbrella, and as they did, all three carefully circumvented the dotted line that was Moriarty's corpse. As they passed it by, Holmes pointed out the presence of makeup on one length.

"He had to make up because he was an irregular polyhedron, although the abnormality was comparatively slight. But it would have been enough to make the lower classes distrust him if the Chief Circle had found out about it."

Phillimore suddenly stopped, horrified. "I've just remembered something!"

"What?" asked Holmes.

"There is an Ür-Moriarty floating about with an umbrella, victimizing other worlds. Shouldn't he also be stopped?"

The Great Detective sighed. "I see it shall be some time ere I will be able to take up again the fairly mundane business of sleuthing in Baker Street." Again he sighed. "Yet the more I consider the fact that there may be countless worlds on which the circumstances of Victorian England are reproduced, the more probable becomes the conclusion that there shall always be a Moriarty . . ."

Phillimore concurred. Then he asked Holmes how

he proposed to find his original umbrella, the one Moriarty snatched from his grip at Reichenbach.

"Elementary. I have ascertained that Moriarty landed in this very fortress. Now he was assuredly extremely disoriented when he arrived and no doubt relinquished his hold on the umbrella and then could not find it again. In a land of lines and dots, what clue is there to the translated shape of a three-dimensional umbrella?"

"I have thought about it," said the scholar, "and I wonder whether it is possible to track it down at all! It seems unlikely."

"Not in the least," the sleuth demurred. "Moriarty himself hit upon it—probably when our disguises turned his attention anew to the art of painting."

"I don't follow."

"My dear fellow, this is a world in which color is outlawed! All we must needs do is seek the one touch of tint in this gloomy gray pile!"

It took them perhaps an hour of rummaging about to spy the still-startling trace of pastel hues that indicated the two-dimensional presence of Phillimore's incredible umbrella. He nudged it against a wall, not without affection, and managed to grasp the bright line in his mouth, his only means of holding it.

It took them another hour to figure out how to push the button.

EPILOGUE

SCENE.—*An Arcadian Landscape. A river runs around the back of the glade. A rustic bridge crosses the river.*

A troupe of Fairies enter, dancing and singing. Suddenly in their midst, two men appear. One is short and rather stocky. The other is a giant, with black ~~h~~*air, extremely white teeth and black lips. The Fairies admire the latter personage enormously, though one or two cast curious glances at the impractically-large, gaudily-dyed umbrella the smaller man totes.*

Phillimore looked about for the Fairy Queen. Spying a large woman with wings, a Disney-esque wand and a diadem that twinkled in her hair, he brought Boris meekly along to meet her.

"Welcome," she said before Phillimore could speak. "I see that you wish to find a home for this poor, injured gentleman, a place where he will be loved and not scorned, for this is what you promised him if he performed services on your behalf. I perceive that you regard our world, a world you seem to equate with one of our sisters, Iolanthe, as a gilbertandsullivan place, whatever *that* is. But you maintain that in a gilbertandsullivan world, the comely and fair are frequently villainous, while the homely are generally decent folk whose eventual rewards are great. Am I not correct?"

"Why, yes . . ." Phillimore stammered, "but—"

"Your friend is certainly welcome to stay with us," the Fairy Queen interrupted, "for we find him most attractive in a rather baroque manner—" (here Boris shyly blushed) "and I also note that having kept your word to him, you intend to travel to other worlds. Am I not correct?"

"Yes! Absolutely!" Phillimore said in mighty wonder. "But how do you know all that about me?"

The Fairy Queen's eyes sparkled as bright as her diamond tiara. "Bit of a fey quality, I fancy," she remarked.

Magnificent Fantasy From Dell

Each of these novels first appeared in the famous magazine of fantasy, *Unknown*—each is recognized as a landmark in the field—and each is illustrated by the acknowledged master of fantasy art, Edd Cartier.

Dell Bestsellers